USA TODAY BESTSELLING AUTHOR

DALE MAYER

A Psychic Visions Novel

NOW YOU SEE HER...

NOW YOU SEE HER...
Beverly Dale Mayer
Valley Publishing Ltd.

Copyright © 2015

This is a work of fiction. Names, characters, places, brands, media, and incidents are either the product of the author's imagination or are used fictitiously. Any resemblance to actual events, locales, or persons, living or dead, is entirely coincidental.

ISBN-13: 978-1-988315-70-6
Print Edition

Books in This Series:

Tuesday's Child
Hide 'n Go Seek
Maddy's Floor
Garden of Sorrow
Knock Knock…
Rare Find
Eyes to the Soul
Now You See Her
Shattered
Into the Abyss
Seeds of Malice
Eye of the Falcon
Itsy-Bitsy Spider
Unmasked
Deep Beneath
From the Ashes
Stroke of Death
Ice Maiden
Snap, Crackle…
What If…
Talking Bones
String of Tears
Inked Forever
Insanity
Soul Legacy
Coveted

About This Book

Energy. The life force of good … and evil
And sometimes evil is stronger.

Tia spent years imprisoned in a 'special' program. When she finally escaped, she ran as far away as she could. But it wouldn't leave her alone.

Only one person can help her. Stefan. But when she contacts him for help, she gets more than she bargained for. Six weeks later, she awakens from a coma to find more problems than ever – and she's still being hunted.

Dean, moonlighting as a guard at the hospital, finds himself in an impossible situation. His belief system is stretched out of control by someone whom he can't forget … and can't believe. Until he has no choice.

With everything on the line, Tia and Dean must work together to solve the problem that has somehow – in a very unique way – entwined them both.

Sign up to be notified of all Dale's releases here!
https://geni.us/DaleNews

CHAPTER 1

"OKAY TIA. IT'S now or never."

"Never." That was her vote. Besides, what was she saying? She always voted with her feet. Who needed to talk things over? It made no difference. She pushed the long strands of hair back off her face and stared out the window over the sink.

"You're at a crossroads." Simone stood up from the kitchen table and walked over to Tia. Her long arms reached out to grasp Tia's crossed arms. "You can't keep going like this."

"Sure I can," Tia muttered. "I always have."

"But you're not sixteen anymore. In fact, in the last decade you were supposed to have learned something," Simone said in exasperation.

"And I have," Tia replied, turning to face her. "But one thing that never changes is that instinct that says *go. Run. Hide.* It's kept me alive all these years."

Simone, a fine dusting of gray hair at her temples, nodded. "I understand. I'd always hoped something in your life would break and you'd be free of him." Her tone turned sad. "In a different way than my Mandy is now free."

Tia couldn't help the wince. Mandy hadn't survived childhood after being struck down with a rare cancer. "Never going to happen. Once he realized what I could do – I was done."

"But you've been safe for a long time now. How did he find you? What changed?"

Tia turned to stare out the window again, the ageless sheers hanging cheerfully off to the side. What could she say? She had no idea what had changed. She was tired of this. More tired than she ever had been. She might have to take the one step she had avoided all these years. And accept the help from the one person who cared. Who'd offered to help years ago.

She had no real reason for not accepting Stefan Kronos' help. She couldn't even formulate an answer as to why she hadn't accepted his offer – except an ingrained fear of not knowing who to trust and trusting the wrong person.

She liked to think she was capable of doing this without help. She was independent. Stiff-necked stubborn more likely. She could handle this. She'd been handling it since forever.

Until now.

Until enough years had gone by and she'd let that hard edge of awareness dull down to something much more comfortable to wear. She slept at night again. Could stop and enjoy a cup of tea without seeing bad guys behind the bushes and villains in the woods.

She'd softened. Become more accepting. She'd become complacent.

She sighed and slowly rotated her head, trying to ease the tension. What she'd done was become stupid.

And that had to stop. Before this asshole stopped her.

She knew what he wanted. Knew what he'd hoped to get from her. She couldn't let him learn her energy techniques. She didn't know if he could imitate them or not, but she didn't dare let him try. The world was so not ready for that. She stared at the thin bracelet one of her fellow inmates had given her a long time ago. She'd kept it all these years as a reminder of how being a captive had defined who she was today. That she was in charge of who she was going to be from here on in. And of a memory of someone special now lost to her.

But as she stared down the long lean years of hiding, the years that had formed her early adulthood, the loneliness, the pain, she didn't think she could go back to the person she'd been. She couldn't go back to that lifestyle. She'd let that go when she finally found herself safe for the first time.

No…she couldn't go back to that stage of her life, she wouldn't. It wasn't possible.

Neither was it required.

She reached for the phone.

Without giving the other person a chance to respond, she said, "Stefan, I need help."

THE DUSK HAD settled, giving an odd light to the various pedestrians walking down the sidewalk. But there was no mistaking the woman across the street. There she was. Finally within his grasp. Tia. He smiled. Time had been a blessing in many ways. She was stunning. Good. And she wouldn't recognize him. Too bad. She'd doted on him back then. Of course she didn't know who he really was. She'd always called the boss The Bastard. And he was. But that boss was the old bastard. Now he was the New Bastard.

He grinned. He wasn't really one of course. His family had very high connections. His birth was well documented. Maybe he deserved the name for other reasons. But his reasons had always been to benefit Tia and the others. To help them be the best they could be.

A homeless man, curled up on the newspaper in the corner, whimpered. The New Bastard turned to face the homeless man. "Leave. Now."

The homeless man's gaze widened. He opened his mouth as if to say something then snapped it shut. He nodded meekly. Grabbing up his sparse belongings, he scurried backward down the alley.

Run, little mouse, run.

The Bastard turned and stared across the street where Tia leaned so casually. As if there wasn't a care in the world. His mood darkened. Bitch. Princess. All she'd put him through. All she'd cost him. He'd been searching for her for years. But finally, she'd come home. Well, it was time for her to pay up. They'd tried all sorts of things to make her do what they wanted her to do. Tried everything they could think of.

Kept her isolated at the end. But when he'd gone back for her...somehow she'd escaped.

Now look at her. She was so defiant. Independent. Stubborn. Always had been. Too bad for her. He needed something she had. And he was going to get it.

Tonight.

He fingered the small balls in his pocket as he watched her. He'd done everything he could to make her show her true self and she'd always resisted. Well, no more.

Several people walked by staring at her, but she ignored them.

Typical of her.

Still, she was hardly someone anyone could ignore. Not the way she stood out. With her chameleon abilities, she didn't have to stand out right now. She could blend right in if she wanted to.

So she wanted to be seen.

Therefore, she was waiting for someone.

He'd have to wait. See who it was.

But energy vibrated through his fingers. Anger. Hate. He had a lot of reasons for not liking this stage of his life. Especially knowing the answer – the ability to fix all that had gone wrong – was right across the street.

Only he didn't want to wait. He wanted action. Now.

He turned his head and stared back toward the alley. And smiled.

TIA, HER LEATHER jacket tugged up high on her neck, her long hair pulled into a high ponytail, leaned against the brick wall at the city park. She hadn't been back in Portland in years, and this area was new to her. She wasn't afraid but found it hard to settle comfortably into her surroundings. She didn't fear the night or the others in the world, just the one man and the organization that pandered to his every whim. Combined they were a deadly force. One she'd like nothing to do with ever again.

As far as she could see, she was alone. A cop walked the other side of the street. A few single women scurried through the almost empty area. A couple of men strode confidently along. The profile of one caught her eye, but she couldn't get a clear glimpse of him. She kept an eye on him but he walked past. She didn't feel safe but neither did she sense imminent danger.

That spidey sense of hers was not accurate in all situations and she hadn't figured out why, but the thought that the predator might have a new tool to help knock her spidey sense out of commission had kept her senses turned on and humming in the background – for years.

Now…such a different life.

Her ribs ached, the old faded scars quivering with long submerged memories of life before her escape. She'd survived those long years, barely. And only because of Simone.

Simone hadn't been able to turn Tia away.

Thank God.

From such things great friendships were born.

She owed Simone her life. And her very sanity. She'd seen things when working on Tia that no one had ever seen. That no one would ever know or suspect were possible. And she'd kept quiet, protecting her.

Tia knew that damn asshole still wanted her, still searched for her to take her back to his lab. Rat that he was.

And she'd do a lot to avoid his cage.

A couple strolled by, holding hands, heads together wrapped up in an aura of new love. Behind them, slower and not as wrapped up, was an older couple strolling by, still holding hands after decades of marriage, still in love.

The thought made her smile. Then she remembered where she was and why. How anyone could stay innocent of the evil in the world she had no idea.

Still, like a movie on the big screen, it was a nice bit of fantasy.

The sky was eerie in the moonlight with the clouds drifting in and out. She thought she recognized a man across the street. As he stepped into the lamplight, she realized it was a stranger.

She leaned her head back and closed her eyes. She'd promised Simone she'd return to her house at ten if her meeting didn't happen.

Stefan had better show. She needed him.

The street light across the road flickered.

She tensed.

And closed her eyes. She reached out with her spidey sense to see what was disturbing the energy of the lamp.

And found…nothing.

She frowned. It could have just been a flicker in the power grid from the city center. Dirty power being an issue in many cities. But here? Not so much. At least it hadn't been a problem ten years ago. She'd left soon after and was surprised at the sprawling mess the city had become. Either it had grown or her memories had shrunk. Either way it wasn't great.

She'd become a small town girl. There, she could be who she wanted to be and ditch the personas she had to create every time she picked up and started over.

And if she told herself that often enough she might believe it, because in truth it sucked. You had to remember the lies that were the flavor of the week and over time the lies grew and had to be built upon until you started to believe some of them yourself. After all there wasn't much of a choice once you started down that path.

It was also lonely. She always had to play a part. She could never be herself. Only with Simone. But it was dangerous to stay close to her. And she'd do anything to keep her safe. She was the only person in Tia's life who cared about her.

At least until she'd ended up at Land's Edge, a small town close to the Canadian border. She'd figured that if she was found there, she might be able to slip across the border and get lost in the northern wilderness. Instead, she'd found a place to call home. At least temporarily.

It was a place of misfits. Travelers. People who'd arrived in the town and ended up staying, putting down roots. Probably thinking along the same lines she had.

Tia had parents somewhere, but when her talents had shown up they had taken her from doctor to doctor to "fix" her.

Only there'd never been anything wrong, nothing to "fix."

Her parents had taken a hard line and their actions at that point forever divided her from them. Her baby brother had arrived soon after. Her parents, wanting the taint to stay contained with her, isolated her from him while they tried to deal with Tia's problems.

Of course the problem never was resolved so she never got a chance to get to know her little brother. A decade younger than her, she wouldn't be surprised if her parents had erased her existence from his memory. An easy thing to do in one so young. Especially after they put her in that program.

She shifted restlessly as the evening cooled down. The bricks were uncomfortable on her back. She deliberately removed some of the energy from her shoulder blades, minimizing their ability to scream in pain.

The lights flickered again.

Shit.

She tensed and slid a little further down the wall. Deeper into the shadows.

He'd found her.

No, she argued silently. He couldn't have. No one knew. Just Stefan, and he'd never tell. Not the Stefan she'd heard so much about. He had almost a cult-like following. People loved him.

But that didn't mean he didn't accidentally tell someone.

Maybe his phone line was bugged.

Maybe his own security had been breached.

All things were possible.

But not likely.

She closed her eyes as pain suddenly slammed into her heart. There was only one other person who'd known where she was coming and when.

Simone.

Shit. Shit. *Shit.*

Had something happened to her? She slid her cell phone out of her pocket, and shielding the light from the screen, she checked for messages.

There was one from Simone. *Someone broke in tonight. Run.*

The hair on her skin rose up straight and her breath caught up in her chest.

Her instinct said to pick up her feet and go. And keep running. She took a deep breath and fought against the urge. She'd been at this point too many times in her life. No more. When would this ever stop?

She texted Simone. *Protect yourself.*

The danger, whatever it was and whatever form it was taking, approached from the left. She slipped her phone into her pocket, closed her eyes and went still. Very still.

As in sinking her bony frame into the hard bricks. As in letting the sensation of her feet sinking into cracked cement become real. Becoming one with her surroundings. Being one with the universe. Old energy at her feet. Newer energy at her back. Fresh energy in front of her from those who passed by in the last day. This was an old area. She frowned, hating the fear that spiked. Had she been set up?

Old energy was one thing. Ancient energy was something else altogether. She couldn't do ancient. Yet inside she knew she should be able to. Energy was energy, supposedly. It could be used for good and bad. That rule at least applied to most energy.

As she stood still sinking in sensation, her foot trembled. She shuddered.

No, this couldn't be happening. It wasn't supposed to be like this.

It couldn't be.

She tried to lift her foot, tried to step away, but tentacles, faint tendrils of energy lifting and sliding up over her shoe stopped her. She couldn't move it.

She hadn't had time to react. But knew inside it didn't matter. This force of the ancient earth had already taken place. She'd felt it before, once.

She'd escaped that energy – once.

The energy moved up her ankle.

She was caught.

Damn right you're caught, bitch.

She shuddered as panic overwhelmed her. This shouldn't be happening. She couldn't be imprisoned like this. She wouldn't be. Her life couldn't happen in this way. Not again.

She needed help.

She'd never be a lab rat again.

Never be a test subject for them to work on.

She'd die first.

And if that happened now, at this moment, fine. She had no life worth missing. No friends to love. Nobody to miss her if she were gone. Only Simone. And if this asshole had hurt Simone…

Death was the best answer.

But instinct just didn't give way to passive nothing. Her will to live didn't just roll over and wait for death.

Her body still fought for survival, still fought to survive this horrible scenario.

She couldn't go out this way.

How completely undignified.

How completely ironic that she who dealt in energy was going to die by an older and more skilled energy.

A cosmic joke.

Go.

A new voice slammed into her brain, making her groan out loud. She had no idea where it came from or who it was.

Still, she tried to fight the restraints on her feet. She struggled, hearing a horrible laughter in front of her. She didn't know who was laughing.

Now. I said go.

Damn it, I can't, she screamed at the intruder in her head. *I'm caught.* But they obviously didn't understand what was going on. She couldn't "go" anywhere. *Who are you?*

Stefan. And you are not caught. You can't be caught.

I am a prisoner. My feet are stuck. She trembled with panic as the binds holding her fast to the ground climbed higher and higher up her legs. Her feet were cold and numb, but the leading edge of that horrible energy burned hot, scalding her with the heat of its moment. *I'm chained to the earth, I can't get free.*

The volume of the voice rose to the point it pounded at a pitch she couldn't stand.

Go, I said, he roared. *Now!*

She screamed back. *I can't.*

Of course she can't, she's mine now. I don't know who the hell you are, but get lost.

Tia froze, the bile rising up her throat, and she knew she was done. This was it. There was only a small ball of regret. For the things she hadn't done. For the pet she hadn't been able to have. The friends she'd never know. The family she could never have.

Do you want a future? Stefan asked. *Or do you want to give up and die?*

Damn it, she cried out. *I don't have a choice, can't you see that?*

I see an exquisitely powerful woman who has no idea what she can do and right now, if she doesn't do something, she's going to die. Or worse. Stefan's voice hardened. *She's going to wish she were dead.*

She closed her eyes again at his words, her body buffeted by a weird sensation. That creeping feeling of having been caught in a spider's web. That horrible sensation of being spun into a cocoon saved for a better day.

Only there were two people here.

Who was the spider and who was her rescuer?

Or were they both out to get her?

She couldn't tell friend from foe.

Of course not, you don't know me, Stefan said in her head. *But what are you going to do about it. Will you believe me when the vehicle pulls up and they throw you, now fully paralyzed into it? Or will you have to wake in a padded room, tied down to a metal bedpost to realize what's happened?*

She groaned, her body trembling in fear, that horrible burning edge of paralysis climbing higher and higher. *I can't live that way again.* She pulled at her legs desperately to lift them, desperate to get away.

That's your future if you don't move, Stefan urged. *Now.*

I'm trying, she cried out. *I can't. The energy is too strong. Too old. Don't you get it? I'm not stuck here by any normal energy, this is ancient energy. I can't…move.*

Stefan gave a heavy sigh. *Die then.*

There was a horrible sound, a burning in her gut, then a horrible flash of heat as her spine turned to burning ash.

What's happening she screamed. She twisted and twisted but couldn't escape from the pain. She was going to die. *I'm so sorry*, she sobbed. *I don't know what I've done to deserve this but if there is anything – anything I can do to get away then help me. Please.*

Damn it. Stefan's voice whispered through her.

She almost laughed then cried. Stefan hadn't left her.

Sure he has. You're all alone. You've always been all alone. That hated evilness twisted through her mind, its poisonous tone dominating her thoughts.

"Miss, are you okay?" A strange voice penetrated through the mess in her head, his voice dark mysterious. "Can I help you?"

She groaned. No, please not an innocent bystander. He wouldn't understand. "No," she whispered. "Run or you'll get hurt too."

"What?"

In the background there was more noise. The stranger spoke to someone. Dimly she understood he was calling for an ambulance. Oh Lord, he was going to get hurt. She couldn't have another death on her conscience.

But overriding the worry of the stranger wove the hated voice of her nightmares. Too Late. *You were promised to me years ago. It might have taken this long to corner you, but I'm not going to lose out on my best test subject. I've waited a long time to have you come back to me.* He laughed. *But don't worry, I'll make sure you live a long and healthy life.*

"No," she cried out loud. "I'd rather die."

Yes. Stefan spoke up again. *That's exactly right, finally. Do it. Die.*

"Whoa," the stranger crouched beside her called out. "Take it easy. Help is coming."

The help was too late for her. It had always been too late for her.

And it's too late for him. This innocent stranger you've sucked into this mess. I'm going to kill him too.

She couldn't let that happen. She reached out to save the man trying to help her. He needed to disconnect from her. From this. Or he'd be lost.

Only she couldn't feel him. Or see him, but she was connected…somehow. She reached out a hand and drove a bolt of energy at him, trying to cut him loose. To push him away from her. To remove his hand on her wrist. Then it was too late. Too late to wonder…to worry. She finally gave up on it and gave into the paralysis, the pain, the torment and she relaxed her grip on her life.

And passed peacefully. Screams from her tormentor echoed *No* in her head as she slowly, one tiny fragment at a time – died.

Free from him at last.

CHAPTER 2

T IA OPENED HER eyes. White blinding light hit her, forcing her to slam them back closed again. She whimpered in pain. What happened? Her memories were dim, fuzzy. She couldn't remember anything.

She lay quiet while the back of her eyeballs adjusted to the aftershock of so much white.

She'd never seen anything like it.

Then it hit her. Please no. But she had to consider it. She'd said she'd never be taken alive. And the pain, the panic rippled through her as memories – as faded and dim as roses past their prime, but still there – rolled ever onward.

She'd been found out. Caught.

Maybe even betrayed. And she'd let go. Of the struggle. Of everything she'd ever known. Of life.

Then what the hell was she doing here? And where was here?

Unless she truly was…dead…and this is what came after?

Shit. *Okay, breathe girl, breathe.*

She was dead. There. Okay, she'd said it. So what? Apparently she could still think – or rather panic. Her breath was coming out in tiny puffs, her chest rising and falling in tiny increments. As if she was unable to do more. But her blood pulsed deep inside, clouding her hearing so there was only that steady *boom boom* going on inside.

That wouldn't happen if she was dead.

Right?

She splayed out her fingers. She could move them and her arms. Slowly, carefully, she took stock of her body, feet, legs. They were all functioning. The sheet on top of her was normal cotton. Not the silkiest on her skin, but not the worst she'd ever experienced.

Her right wrist felt odd. Bare.

Her bracelet was gone. She frowned, not bothered about the loss. Why was that?

And where the hell was she? Instinctively she smoothed her hand over her belly. She had on clothing of some kind. She always slept in her undies. This was so not her underwear.

Taking a deep breath she opened her eyes to slits, enough to try and see without being blinded.

White everywhere.

The walls and ceiling. The light fixture and lamp. Her sheet. Her bed. Carefully sitting up in case of a headache from the movement, she tried to search out anything in the room that would explain where she was.

Then she glanced down at her left wrist and the plastic band encircling it, a white hospital band.

Crap. She turned to look again around the room. It was the oddest hospital room she'd ever seen. She pinched the name tag and turned it.

Jane Doe.

All senses alert, she slipped out of bed, gasping as her bare toes hit the cool floor. A draft slipped down her bare back, and she shuddered. Yep, a hospital gown with the damn ties at her neck. Gross.

Still, it confirmed where she might be.

She checked out the machines beside her. As she wasn't connected, she wasn't bothered. But there was redness on her wrist and a bandage to say she might have been hooked up at one time.

The small room had a door on the left and a door on the right. She moved to the door with a window and snuck up on it from the side. She peered out. There was a type of grid work in the glass but not bars. She studied them then shrugged. If she had to she could break it, but the hole wasn't big enough for her to squeeze through – even as skinny as she was.

And damn if she didn't feel as gaunt as a prisoner from a war camp. How long had she been here?

Outside the window was another white wall. Everywhere she looked were white walls.

Bending, she slipped under the glass to the other side and checked out that view. A hallway. And a man standing outside waiting. He had no white coat of a doctor and didn't appear to be wearing a uniform of any kind. So not likely staff.

A cop? A guard? An observer? Waiting for someone. Waiting to see someone?

The possibilities ripped through her mind as she considered the threat factor.

He wasn't looking her way, didn't appear to care if she was there or not.

She frowned.

For the moment, she'd lower the danger factor his presence would normally garner. As there was no one else, no signs or exits showing outside her door, she turned her attention to the rest of the room. The second door was a washroom. She used the facilities and washed her hands, keeping the door open so she could hear if anyone came in. Done, she walked to the window, half hidden by curtains, and stared out. Light evening with darkness quickly falling. In the half light she could see beautiful lawns and gardens below. Dozens of lights shone around the area, but more as soft atmospheric lighting than keeping the area safe from predators type of lighting.

Neither could she see much in the distance. A city skyline but not one she recognized.

What kind of hospital was this?

A private hospital? Surely a government run one didn't have this kind of money. She could barely see the corner of a parking lot off to the side. Yet a bright light shone on a Jaguar and what looked like the latest in Porsches parked close to the building. She frowned.

That didn't make sense in her world.

Sure doctors made good money, but this kind of money?

She turned to stare at the rest of the room. There had to be something here to help identify her surroundings.

Moving swiftly, she opened the few cupboards, delighted to see her clothing hanging inside the first one. The rest of the room appeared to be empty.

Voices sounded outside her door. Making a fast decision, she ran back to her bed and slipped under the covers. Giving into instinct, she rolled over and pretended to be asleep while keeping her eyes open barely enough to see.

A woman in a bright fuchsia pink uniform walked in.

The pink was almost as hard to handle as all the white.

The sound of the woman's footsteps was quiet. No clipping, just a slight squeak of a rubber tread.

She waited, pretending to be asleep, but her nostrils

flared at the smell. It wasn't perfume. But…

"I'm sorry you're still asleep. These are beautiful. I'll just put them on the side here. You'll see them when you wake up."

The woman's cheerful voice kept up a running stream of chit chat as if the sound of her voice would make Tia rest easier.

It was comforting.

Until she stopped talking.

The squeak came closer and closer. She tensed. She didn't know what the woman was looking for or planning to do, but Tia wasn't having any drugs or tests of any kind.

After a moment she heard the door open.

"She's still asleep. Keep an eye on her but there doesn't appear to be any change."

In the background she heard a deep rumbling voice. "Will do."

So that was a guard.

That's all the confirmation she needed. A guard had to guard something. That meant she was a prisoner. She was out of here.

DEAN WALKER LEANED back against the hallway wall. Why did the extra shifts he'd picked up have to be at the hospital? Didn't anyone understand – people died here.

Too many of them.

Besides, this place was a little too close to home. He'd been seeing a shrink himself for the last month. Dr. John Loring was on the departmental payroll and had been keeping an eye on Dean since he'd started to slide so badly.

He shook his head. He'd been a cop for a decade, and

now that he had his little boy to think of, extra money was required, especially with his current health issue. He squashed that thought and the insidious fear inside waiting to strike at his hard won control. But nighttime? At a hospital? Good thing Grandma had Jeremy at her house for a sleepover. Then again, Jeremy loved his grandmother almost as much as he loved his dad.

Thank heavens.

A few staff members walked down the hallway. One talking to another and the third muttering over something on his tablet.

Nothing major and nothing unusual.

Not here on the psych ward. Not that it was officially called that – except among the staff – and the cops. He hated that even worse. It was one thing to have a thing about hospitals where people died, but on this side of the building the patients were bat-shit crazy.

Especially the beautiful woman he was here to protect. At least according to her team of doctors. Sure they had fancy names for her condition, but that was the bottom line.

She wasn't big enough to fight anyone off should it come to that and appeared to be sick enough that she might not survive whatever happened to her to begin with. She was thin, long and lean. Her features waxy, lax.

He hated to think she was dying, but he hadn't seen any sign of life since he'd been on his shift tonight.

And why was he here again? Right, because Stefan Kronos had asked. And was apparently footing the bill.

So far the woman hadn't even had a visitor. Did no one care?

Then again, the couple of times he'd looked in on her, she'd been sleeping, or maybe unconscious might be the better term. It could be that she had no family or no one knew she was here, or maybe they were waiting for her to wake up before they came to visit.

He crossed his arms over his chest. It was past one in the morning. He was here for another hour then would be replaced by Greg – another cop he knew. Sad that so many of them needed the extra money these days. But the facts were the facts and bills had to be paid – one way or another. He studied the pure white hallway, wondering at the color choice. He understood it was light and made the small rooms look bigger, but surely something other than institutional white was more cheerful.

At a quarter past he walked into her room and took a look to make sure all was well, as he did every quarter hour. She slept soundly.

Good. He wasn't sure what he'd do if she woke up and started doing something weird. Although if she did wake up, the machines she was hooked up to would likely go nuts. How appropriate. He looked closer and realized somewhere along the line the machines had been turned off. And she'd been disconnected.

So maybe she was doing better. Good for her.

Or maybe that was bad. He wasn't sure.

This place was enough to give him the creeps.

He turned to leave when the hair on the back of his head rose. Instinctively, he spun around, his hand to the gun holstered at his side. "Who's there?"

Silence. Taking a deep breath he checked the room to make sure nothing had changed. It was small. His gaze slipped past the bed, then hit the brakes and jammed into reverse.

The bed was empty.

What the hell?

He spun around in a panic. Where was she? She had just been there. He raced to the bathroom, the door was ajar but he pushed it wide, not taking his gaze off the bedroom. He glanced inside the bathroom. It was empty. He could see the shower and the door flattened to the wall. She wasn't in either hiding spot.

With narrowed eyes and his hand already pulling out his cell phone, he did a quick sweep of the room, under the bed, opening all closets.

But the room was empty.

She'd disappeared.

Where the hell had she gone? And how?

THE BASTARD WALKED into the hospital and smiled at the night admissions clerk. Harried from too much work and long days, the woman barely gave him a glance.

Perfect. He'd been counting on that. Now to find out where the bitch was staying. And who was paying the horrific bill. That's who he wanted.

Someone was backing her. Someone was protecting her. Without that assistance he'd have caught his prey a long time ago.

The elevator was up ahead. What he needed was a distraction to get into the computer system and find out what bed she was in.

As he walked toward the elevator, it opened in front of him and an obese male, his loose shirttails flapping in the wind, raced out to the front counter and snapped at the poor woman at the desk, "This isn't acceptable. She needs better food here. She –"

He didn't bother to listen to the rest. He probably wouldn't get a better chance. He opened the door leading into the offices and stopped at the first computer that was on. Bringing up the registration, he typed in her name.

Nothing.

He frowned. Why? If not her name, then what name? He tried several variations and still came up blank. He heard loud voices coming toward him. There was no time. He'd just have to walk through the damn hospital and find her himself.

In order to do that, he'd have to change into something slightly less…obvious.

CHAPTER 3

T IA STUDIED THE man in front of her. He'd gone from relaxed guard to cop instantly. Shit. A guard she could get past – no problem. Most were lazy shifty eyed guys looking for an easy buck.

This guy? Hell no. He'd gone from slightly stiff and unhappy, but aware, to cop mode as soon as he'd realized she'd disappeared. Was he a damn cop?

His glance had gone over her, intent, assessing, but not seeing her. When she realized that, she'd relaxed slightly. He couldn't see energy. Perfect. Now to make sure no one else around her could either.

"Stefan, she's gone." Cold and abrupt. The guard made no excuses. "I turned around and she'd disappeared."

Crap. He was working with Stefan. And who knew where Stefan stood? She didn't know him, only what she'd heard, and considering the last memory she could access, she didn't trust him. She sidled up to the door and peered around it. It was closed and she could hardly open it in front of him. But there was no way she was going to stay here and wait for Stefan to show up.

Stefan would be able to see her.

"No. I saw her then turned around and the bed was empty." He shook his head, listening to something Stefan said. "The door hasn't opened since I entered and it's closed now."

Double shit.

Still holding the phone to his ear, he spun around. "No, she's not hiding in the room," he said in exasperation. "I've done this a time or two. When I say the room is empty and she's gone – I mean the damn room is empty and she is gone!"

Tia snickered. And damn if he didn't spin around and stare right at her. *Oh shit.* She froze and gazed back at him, terrified to breathe in case he heard it. He still held the phone in his hand as he studied the area where she stood.

But there was no awareness in his eyes. Nothing to say he understood she was there.

"No. I'll be here." He nodded a couple of times, his face hard and cold. "Absolutely."

He closed his phone and put it away then walked to the doorway, crossed his arms in front of his chest and stood in front of the closed door.

Blocking her exit.

She slid back around the corner of the wall and took a deep breath. What was she going to do now? Damn it, Stefan. What was he up to?

Was she a prisoner?

If so, why?

She slid back over to the bed and stood undecided. She had to do this at the right moment – or else.

Only the guard never closed his damn eyes.

Hard footsteps walked down the hallway toward them. She groaned. His gaze swiveled in her direction. She glared at him. How could he hear her? That was something she hadn't expected. No one did that. Why did he have super spidey hearing? Like how freaking inconvenient for her.

The guard turned to look out the small window in the door. Perfect. She slid under the covers and curled up in a ball, sleeping.

Or at least pretending to sleep.

The door opened.

"Stefan," the guard said, relief pouring through his voice. "Am I glad to see you."

"I was in the hospital already, so good timing. Now let's see what we have here, Dean."

"Right." The cop's voice turned businesslike. "I haven't left the door like you asked. I was outside. Came in, did my check, and before I was done, she was gone. I swear the door was closed. But somehow she's gone missing. See, the bedding –"

He stopped. Then exploded. "What the hell?" She couldn't see him from her position but mentally she could picture him standing and pointing in her direction. At least now she knew his name. Dean.

"I swear she wasn't there a few minutes ago. Until you came up the hallway this bed was empty." He groaned. "Honest. I feel like I'm losing my mind."

She held her laughter back in. Served him right.

"That's all right, I feel that way a lot." Stefan's voice was threaded with humor. "And I believe you."

DEAN'S DISBELIEVING GAZE went from the full bed with a sleeping woman to the man at his side. He needed to see Dr. Loring again. Maybe the psychologist would believe him now. Or he'd have Dean committed. "How can you possibly believe me? *I* don't believe me?"

Stefan's laughter boomed freely around the room. "I can

see things a little differently."

"Right. And what the hell is there to see now that there wasn't a little while ago."

"Her." Stefan walked to the bed while Dean watched. "Tia, enough pretending. You're going to give Dean nightmares."

Dean watched in shock as Tia sat up straight in the bed, her expression aggressive, her legs already swinging over the side ready to bolt.

"What? She wasn't sleeping? She wasn't out of this bed?"

"Oh, she was," Stefan said quietly. "She was planning to run, weren't you, Tia?"

"I want to leave – now!" The slender woman in the bed glared at him. "What happened and why am I here? And where is here?"

The questions and words slid out so fast Dean had trouble understanding what she was saying.

"Where were you when I was in here earlier?" he asked.

"You never left so there was no earlier," she snapped, still glaring up at Stefan. "And you haven't answered *my* questions."

Stefan sat down on the side of the bed and reached for her hand. "You're in a hospital. In the psych ward for examinations."

Her gaze widened in shock. She searched the room frantically as if looking for a way out.

And that's when Dean noticed she was fully dressed.

"When the hell did you get clothes on and from where?" he growled. Damn he'd been played the fool by this slip of a girl, and it was pissing him off. How the hell had she done that?

"Easy." Stefan restrained Tia. "You need to stay here for

a little bit."

"Hell no." She twisted out of his grasp and rolled to the opposite side of the bed and bolted off before either man could get to her.

Dean grinned. He liked the spitfire for her spirit but she'd made a fool of him once. Like hell she was going to do it again. He stepped in front of her and reached out to grab her.

Only she wasn't there.

She'd disappeared right in front of his eyes. As in here one moment and gone the next. Like, what the hell?

CHAPTER 4

TIA STEPPED SIDEWAYS out of Dean's grasp and slid toward the door. She was almost there. Almost free. Once out in the hallway she could make a run for it. Get away. She'd done it before. She could do it again.

The door slammed shut just as she reached out, and it clicked locked.

Shit. She yanked on the handle and tried to turn the lock. It wouldn't budge. Returning her energy back to normal, she spun around and glared at Stefan. "Not fair."

But he sat on the bed where he'd been and raised an eyebrow, his gaze only slightly amused. "If you're going to play with energy, then I will too."

She stomped past the guard and threw herself onto the bed, showing herself again. She couldn't afford to waste energy. "I don't have to do whatever you want me to do."

"What? Stay alive?" Now there was real amusement in his tone. "All I want to do is help you. I thought we understood that already."

"That was before you set me up."

"How did I do that?" he asked curiously. "I planned to meet you as arranged, and when I got there you were under attack. I thought I helped then."

She stared at him. "You didn't send the assassin?"

"No." His eyebrows shot up and his gaze sharpened.

"Were you targeted? As in this wasn't a random attack?"

"There was nothing random about that man. He, or one of his cohorts, has been after me for years. A decade by now. I figured you'd betrayed me."

"Did you consider your attacker might have been tracking your phone?" Dean asked. "Your money and movements."

She turned to stare at the man she'd outfoxed twice. "No money and no phone until recently."

She felt his startled response but was already turning back to Stefan, her gaze locking on his, wishing she could read him. She'd never seen him before, but he was a legend. She knew others had insight into his character, but it wasn't the same as knowing for sure herself.

"I didn't betray you," Stefan said quietly. "I wouldn't."

And damn if his energy didn't match his words. Strong, clean, unwavering in a beautiful white. He was sincere. Her shoulders slumped. "If not you, who?"

He reached over and picked up her hand. "Anyone know where you were going to be?"

"Simone. She helped me set up the meet. But she wouldn't have betrayed me. She couldn't. But…" she turned a horrified gasp to Stefan, "someone might have coerced her. She told me there'd been an intruder and to run." Her lower lip trembled. "The only way that information would have left Simone's lips is if she couldn't hold out any longer. That would mean she's dead."

"Call her." Stefan held out her cell phone. "Find out if she's okay."

Hating to use her phone again if it was bugged, she said, "Let me use your phone, just in case."

He held it out. She snatched it up and quickly dialed.

After several rings she realized there wasn't going to be a response. "No answer." She stared at the phone then hopped off the bed on the side away from Stefan, only to find him still holding her hand. She tried to tug it free. "I have to go. See if she's okay."

"You can't," Stefan said.

"You don't understand. Simone is all I have in this world. If that bastard got a hold of her, there's no knowing what he'd do."

"I'll have someone check on her," he said calmly. "You will stay here where you are safe."

"What? Are you nuts?" She couldn't believe what she was hearing. "How can I be safe here?"

"Because I've got the room under surveillance," he said. "Woven in energy strands. You will be safe here."

"Your watchdog got in, so why couldn't this other guy? He works energy too," she said scornfully. "Or did you think just anyone could take me down?"

"Not at all. But he has his weakness too."

Stefan stood up. "Rest. Sleep. Recharge. I'll call you on your cell phone when I have news about Simone."

"Take me with you, damn it."

"No." He walked through the doorway and she raced after him.

Until she reached the opened doorway and hit some kind of force field. There were shocks and little blasts of light and she bounced back.

"Shit," she cried out. "That hurt."

Stefan already several steps away turned to smile at her. "That's okay. Now that you know, you won't do it again."

He motioned to Dean to walk through. "I need to speak with you."

DEAN HADN'T SEEN anything like that invisible wall the woman had slammed into, but then he hadn't ever seen a woman go invisible. And just for thinking this, he needed another mental health check-up himself.

He still wasn't sure what he'd seen, but he knew the man waiting for him had the answers. At least he hoped he did.

Taking a deep breath, reminding himself he trusted the man who'd saved his son, he walked through the doorway. He felt nothing. Frowning, he turned back to see Tia standing on the other side glaring at him as if he were to blame. She rubbed her arms for a long moment before her shoulders took a downward slide and she turned back to her bed.

He hated to see her spirit take a beating like that. She'd been a spitfire up to now. Except someone she cared about was in trouble, she was a prisoner and someone apparently had the upper hand in this business. He'd bet on Stefan any day. In fact, he already had.

"Stefan, what the hell is going on?"

"Tia is special," Stefan said. "As you could see."

"Did she really disappear?" he asked incredulously. "I couldn't believe what I was seeing."

"She doesn't disappear as much as she plays with energy and can make it look like she's not actually there. But, in fact, she is."

"So when I thought she'd escaped on me, she was actually still in the room?" It was the only answer that made any sense and even that explanation didn't hold up for long.

"More or less. I don't know all she can do. Not sure she does either. Often with these weird energy abilities, the person doesn't know until they are actually in a situation where they are forced to push the limits of their abilities and then they find out something new about themselves."

Dean nodded as if he understood. Like hell he did. "So now what?"

"When are you off tonight?"

Dean glanced at his watch. "As soon as my replacement shows up."

"Are you heading home then or would you be interested in checking out Simone's situation for me?"

"For you, I will. For her, no." He nodded at the woman now sitting cross-legged on her bed glaring at the two of them.

"Don't feel bad at having been fooled by her. She's developed her abilities out of a need to protect herself. She's been hunted for a long time. Survival is something we all understand."

Oh crap. He studied Tia. "Someone is really after her?"

"Potentially, more than one someone. That's why I need to know if Simone is safe." Stefan's voice dropped. "Or if she's involved."

Dean turned to him in surprise. "I wondered at that possibility. I'm surprised it didn't occur to her."

"She'll avoid thinking it. She's alone in the world. She's got no support system, and she's been on the run for a long time. She's survived and for that, she's done amazingly well."

Dean hated to hear she'd had such a tough life. Everyone deserved to have someone.

"I'll go," he said abruptly. "At least we can make sure this Simone is okay. Finding out if she's involved will likely take much longer."

"Maybe." Stefan turned as if to leave. "First things first."

"And you have her address, I presume?"

"Yep, managed to read Tia's mind when she was worrying about how to find out if Simone was safe as she dialed the phone." Stefan reached into his pocket and pulled out a small notepad. He quickly jotted the address down. "Here."

Dean took the paper and read the address. He knew the area. Not a slum but definitely in the lower income part of town. "She might have sold Tia out."

"Yes," Stefan said. "She might have."

CHAPTER 5

SHE WASN'T GOING to stay. No way. Stefan might be a little better on the energy stuff than she was – that doorway thing he did was freaking awesome. She needed to learn that trick. The easiest way was to learn how to diffuse it. Now that she had no cop standing guard, maybe she could try. She'd watched the cop and Stefan walk through his energy field. Could hear their muted voices matching the retreating footsteps.

He hadn't let her out but had let others in *and* out.

Like, what the hell? She was the one who needed to be safe. Not to be *kept* safe.

Of course that was a fine distinction and maybe only one in the eyes of the beholder. But how did that difference matter to energy? She studied the doorway, wishing she could see the colors better. Color edged the wood and hinges, but was fuzzy. It wasn't clear enough to see what Stefan had done.

It was effective though.

A nurse came to the door. "How are we feeling this morning?"

Tia glared at her. What the hell was with the *we*? Was the nurse locked up in a mental ward? No. Only Tia was. So what the hell kind of answer did she expect?

Then she brightened. There was food here, hospital

food. It likely sucked big time, but it was food and she'd be on the run soon enough. She needed sustenance.

She smiled at the woman, noting the relief on her face that Tia might actually be reasonable, and said, "I'm hungry. Could I get something to eat please?"

"Oh dear. It's hours until breakfast." The nurse looked doubtful. "The doctor says you're only allowed clear liquids on first awakening."

"Exactly," Tia said in a plaintive voice. "And I'm hungry now. Toast? Jam? Juice? A muffin?" she appealed to the nurse. She couldn't remember when she'd eaten last. "Surely there's something I could have."

On cue her stomach rumbled loudly enough for the woman to hear.

"Oh goodness. You are hungry."

"I don't think I've eaten in a long time," Tia added thoughtfully. And that was no lie.

"I'll contact the doctor and see what he suggests." The nurse bustled off.

Tia didn't remember if there'd been food at Simone's to eat or not. Seemed like she'd been running for days.

After eating she needed to see what was going on at this hospital. There was a guard changing soon or had it already happened? If it was coming up she might get out then. Stefan didn't know all her tricks.

She hoped.

She walked to the window and looked out to see if there were balconies or decks outside. Something she could access from where she stood. Nothing. She checked out the bathroom – same thing.

By her bed, she grabbed up her phone and checked the GPS. She had no idea where she was, but damn she needed to find out.

She paced her room as her phone and her mind tried to sort out the mess. She had to find Simone and fast. Make sure her friend was okay. To do that she had to get the hell out of here.

Just when she figured out she was still in the Portland area, she heard a commotion outside. She closed the bathroom door to make it look like she was there. Then she raced to the wall behind the door and waited for the nurse to enter pushing the cart ahead of her. Perfect.

Here was her chance. She slipped into her camouflage mode, allowing her to blend into her surroundings, and slipped outside. There was a shock from Stefan's energy guard, but she'd taken advantage of the metal from the cart disrupting the energy.

The hallway was empty.

She had no idea why, but she wasn't going to waste the opportunity. The elevators were straight ahead, the stairs to the left. No one needed to tell her twice.

She was gone.

DEAN WALKED OUT to the parking lot and stared up at the early morning sky. He rolled his shoulders and gently massaged his neck. He shouldn't be knotted up, but the things he'd seen tonight…well, the two halves of his brain weren't agreeing on just what he had seen, resulting in massive stress to his neck.

He yawned. Greg had shown up on time and after giving him a quick rundown of the evening, leaving out the oddities, Dean had warned him to only open the door for the nurse and then close it immediately behind her as she came and went. Given the hour there should only be one more check at rounds. But he needed to be alert as the hospital was getting busier.

Who knew how they'd keep track of Tia for the rest of the day?

Thankfully that wasn't his problem.

His old truck was parked at the far end of the lot. The few minutes of fresh air were invigorating. He needed that considering he still had a job to do. Stefan's request, given the odd situation, was reasonable. He wouldn't want to call the cops and try to explain what or why either. At least not at this point. He knew Stefan worked alongside the cops all over the world. So some must be used to him and his unusual requests.

Dean had seen Stefan do a hell of a lot of woo woo things that scared the crap out of him. Then he'd had enough weird things happen this last month that he had to wonder.

That didn't mean he believed any of it. But there was no doubt Stefan had made magic happen with Dean's boy. And for that, he'd do the trip to Simone's without a problem. And anything else Stefan asked of him.

As he pulled out onto the main road, Dean looked down at his phone for instructions on where to go. It was a ten minute drive. Fine.

If he hadn't stopped to visit with one of the nurses downstairs for a little while – the wife of a buddy of his – he'd have been there and back, and likely home by now.

Instead…

Oh well.

He turned on the radio and listened as country music blared through the inside of the cab. The drive was uneventful and the traffic was light. He drove into the complex and found number 221 without much trouble. It looked to be a trailer park. He parked out front and turned off the engine.

He studied the darkened trailer. There were no lights. No sign of anyone awake. In fact, there was no sign anyone lived there.

Ever. The trees out front needed pruning in a big way. The lawn hadn't been mowed since forever. Frowning, he opened his door and hopped out. Holding his cell phone up as a light, he walked to the front door, looking for a number. Yes, there was the correct number on the right side of the front door.

So it was the right house.

Now where was Simone? No garage and no outbuildings in the front of the trailer. No vehicle either. He knocked on the door. No answer. No sounds shuffling toward him. Then again, it was in the wee hours of the morning. No one should be answering a random knock on the door.

He knocked again, louder. "Simone, are you in there? Tia asked me to check on you."

He glanced back at his truck, realizing he'd left the door slightly open. As he had the keys in his pocket, he shrugged and pounded hard again.

This time the door opened slowly in front as if the last pound had unlocked the catch.

He unhooked his holster and kept his hand on the handle. Glancing behind him to make sure he was alone, he pushed the front door open.

"Hello? Is anyone home? This is the police."

No answer. He stepped inside, the door wide open, and moved forward several feet.

And damn if he didn't hear someone breathing. Shit. He

spun around, his gun in his hand. "Who's there," he snapped.

But there was no one there. He spun around again, feeling the hairs on the back of his neck rising. More woo woo stuff.

Get a hold of yourself, Dean. There's nothing here. It was just a normal derelict house. Bad area of town. Nothing he hadn't seen before.

He looked for a light switch but there didn't appear to be one close. He stepped into the living room and held up his phone, the small light giving off barely enough light to see. He could make out wallpaper on the walls – from the eighties if the fuzzy texture was anything to go by. An old couch sat on one side and a busted coffee table on the other. He carried on into the kitchen. Old dishes sat discarded on the counter, a layer of dust on every surface. He bent slightly so he could see if there were spots where the dust had been disturbed.

And found none.

He opened the fridge. It had power and the light worked.

There was food inside. Not much and nothing that looked recent. A can of pop in the door. A bottle of hot sauce on the shelf.

Interesting.

He moved through the rest of the house and found two small bedrooms. One was empty with a mattress on the floor. The other held a large bed with bedding tossed on the top. There was an old dresser on the side, its drawers empty and open.

He walked to the closet. There were only a few items hanging. Someone either had lived here only temporarily, had left in a hurry or…this place had been deserted for a long time. How did that fit with Simone and Tia?

Pulling out his phone, he walked through to the backyard and glanced around. A couple of old buckets had been tossed against the back. Weeds were knee high and dry, dead looking. A shed sagged in the back corner of the lot. The door sat ajar, swinging drunkenly in the night. The weeds leading up to it were undisturbed.

"Stefan, it's the wrong place. This is a deserted mobile home in a rundown trailer park. No one has been here in a long time. It's in pretty rough shape."

"Okay, take note of anything inconsistent and call it a night. I'll see if I can run this Simone down to a current address. With her phone number I shouldn't have any trouble."

"Do it now and I'll go take a look. I'm not sure what this address meant to Tia, but it's not the home of her friend."

"I'll find out. Thanks for checking."

"Not a problem. Get the other address for me, and I'll swing by on my way home."

"I'll have it for you in a few minutes." There was an odd silence as Stefan clicked several keys. "Simone Depres. 894 Southwind Drive."

"Got it. That's not too far from my place." He turned and walked out of the dismal backyard, past the horrible trailer and back to his truck.

"I'll go now and give you a call in a few minutes."

FINALLY, HIS THIRD attempt to get to the right room. How could such a place be so difficult? The Bastard walked the hallway heading toward the room Tia slept.

Someone was playing games. And that pissed him right off. This was taking time he didn't have. He'd had to befriend one of the guards, and now he knew she was up top. Dressing in medical whites helped loosen a lot of tongues. Good thing. He was out of patience. Tonight he'd take that bitch out of here – one way or the other.

His steps slowed as he climbed the stairs to the right floor. He opened the doors and strode through, and almost stopped. Several people, busy talking, raced a stretcher down the hallway toward the elevator.

That had better not be her. He waited until they disappeared around the corner before he carried on. The guard was standing at the elevator, helping the team get into the elevator fast.

Perfect. He walked over to her room and glanced inside the door. The bed was empty. With a quick look behind him, he slipped inside.

And roared silently in rage.

She was gone.

Again.

CHAPTER 6

TIA STOOD IN shock in front of her old home. Only it had never looked like this. She hadn't been here in over a decade. Why the hell would he have come here? And why now? If he was looking for Simone, why here?

Her own system shuddered at seeing a place so far back in her memory. How did this connect? Did she even know this address herself? How had Stefan?

She walked to the front door and hesitated. Her footsteps dragged with the pain of the memories. Yet the image of the place, so rundown and ready to be flattened, didn't match those in her mind of happier times. The images wouldn't superimpose.

The hollowness of the house almost matched the hollowness of her experience while living there. Sad. And damn if tears didn't burn at the corner of her eyes.

Resolutely she turned and walked back to the truck. With the door still open, she crawled inside and sat curled up in a corner, staring at a trip down memory lane she'd never wanted to take.

Her fault. She'd followed Dean out to the parking lot and crawled into the open truck box in order to escape the hospital. She'd thought they'd be going to Simone's place.

Only to end up here.

After hearing Dean's phone call, she waited for him to

get in. Now they could go to Simone's. If they'd asked her, she'd have given them the address. She paused. Well, maybe not.

The truck pulled out on the main road and took a left. Her mind was confused, still reeling. How could Stefan have known about the dilapidated house?

And what else did he know?

Dean reached over and turned on the radio. She watched him drive. Maybe it wasn't fair to be able to hide in plain sight – so he couldn't see her – yet be able to observe him, but she wasn't feeling terribly charitable toward him as it was.

His phone rang. He picked it up, glanced at the number and winced.

"Shit." He pulled up and parked at the shoulder of the highway. "Hi, Mom. How's Jeremy doing?"

Tia leaned forward. His mother? Really? At this hour.

"I know his nightmares have been getting better, but they can still be rough." He listened. "I'm running a bit late...are you sure? I can crash at home then run by in the morning if that's better for you?"

He grinned at something she said. "Thanks, Mom, I'll see you tomorrow."

After a moment he closed his phone and tossed it down on the bench beside him. "Shit," he said under his breath. "I hope he stops having these damn things soon."

Nightmares? Did Dean have a son? If so why was he working evenings? He needed to be home with his boy. Sounded like his mother was babysitting, and that couldn't be an ideal situation. Where was the boy's mother?

And why did she care?

She shouldn't. She didn't. She wouldn't. She couldn't.

She had no ties. Deliberately. She couldn't afford to care about anyone. It would put them in danger. She couldn't have anyone hurt because of her.

If something had happened to Simone she'd never forgive herself. Simone had to be safe. She couldn't bear it if she was hurt from this.

She should have told her to offer the information if anyone came after her, it wasn't worth getting hurt over.

But she hadn't had that talk with Simone. At least not seriously. Simone had often said, "You know I've got your back, right?"

There'd never been any doubt about that.

With the sky starting to dump a light rain on the windshield, she hated the tension coiling up on the inside. That inability to swallow from the fear clogging her throat.

Simone had to be okay.

Dean pulled into Simone's place and parked in the driveway. She searched the dark night sky for some sign there'd been trouble in the few hours she'd been gone. She couldn't see anything. There were no lights on. Then again, why would there be? Simone should be asleep.

There were no strange vehicles parked outside the house either. In fact, Simone's vehicle wasn't even there. Maybe she had bolted. That was better than many options.

Dean hopped out and slammed the door closed. Crap. She couldn't get out in time. She'd have to wait for him to enter the house before she exited the truck. She watched as he walked up to the front door and knocked. She almost smiled. Simone was no one's fool. She'd never open the door to a stranger.

He rang the doorbell.

No answer.

Of course not. It was the middle of the night.

Then he reached for the doorknob and turned the handle. And pushed the unlocked door open.

Tia stiffened in disbelief. That couldn't be. Simone was paranoid about locking her doors. She'd never have gone to bed without locking up and setting the security system. It had been a joke between them for years.

For Dean to have done that meant something bad had happened. She bit back a cry. Her hand on the door handle, she mentally urged him to go inside so she could get out.

"Hello, Simone Depres? Are you here? I'm with the police. We've gotten a call suggesting you might be in trouble."

No answer.

So he was a cop. Damn. She shoved that deep inside to consider later. Simone was more important at this point.

No lights on anywhere. She stared at the other windows, the upper left one in particular. That was Simone's bedroom. No light. No shadows. Tia returned her gaze to the front door to realize Dean had walked inside. She opened her door and slid out then closed the door softly before racing to the front door and her friend.

DEAN STOOD IN the front hallway of the brick two-story building. There were many houses in the neighborhood just like this one, which had been a popular design in the nineties. There appeared to be a half dozen on this block alone.

There was no one home from what he could see. Or she was sleeping soundly. He hated to walk through her house. "Hello? Simone? Are you home? Tia sent me."

He said that last bit slightly louder, hoping Tia's name

would make a difference. The open kitchen was on the left. The living room in front had double French doors leading to a small backyard. He stood at the side and peered out into the backyard, a small grassy space with a couple of chairs. No sign of anyone. The furniture was in decent shape but not designer. The house was middle class and in good condition. She'd looked after the place.

The stairs were on the right of the living room. No sign of a door to a basement. Good. He didn't like basements. At the stairs he stopped and called up, "Simone? I'm with the police. Tia sent us. She's worried about you."

Still no answer. With a last look around, he walked up the stairs. "Simone, it's just me. My name is Dean. I'm a detective with the Portland Police Department. I'm coming up."

There were three doors at the top of the stairs. One a bathroom and one a spare bedroom. The master bedroom door was open. He pushed it wider and stepped in.

The room showed someone having packed in a hurry. There was a suitcase open on the floor, a few items tossed inside, but there was a depression on the bed where another one might have sat. He stood in the doorway and studied the layout. The bed was empty. There were a few items on the floor. The closet was open. There was a gap in the hangers, with clothes on either side, indicating a large group had been removed. The dresser on the side wall had a drawer open and most of the clothing out. He couldn't tell if the other drawers were full or not.

There was a pair of sandals on the floor. And several likely missing from below the hangers as another gap in the long line of shoes said there'd been some there but no longer.

He didn't know if she'd run ahead of someone or if

she'd just panicked and booked it. If she knew Tia and understood her situation, she had street smarts. Had she the instincts to hide the same way? If so, then they'd be lucky to find her.

He walked into the bedroom and studied the open drawers. Some clothes remained, tossed into disarray. There was a night table sitting beside the bed. Using a tissue from the box on top, he pulled the drawer open to see a few personal items inside but nothing important. He glanced over the bed and realized there was a second door. He walked around the bed and pushed the door open. A small en suite with a bathtub and shower. He turned on the light. And stared. The toiletries presumably from the counter had been tossed to the floor. A pair of sandals sat on the small mat and…

A body lay crumpled, fully dressed in the bathtub.

A man.

A very dead man.

CHAPTER 7

TIA RACED THROUGH Simone's house, following on
Dean's heels. This didn't make any sense. She made it
to the bedroom as he stepped into the bathroom. Her heart
stuttered to a stop when she heard him say, "Shit."

She glanced around the light disarray in the bedroom.
Simone was meticulously clean. She'd never have let her
bedroom look like this. And…her suitcase was gone.

She brightened. Good. Simone had managed to clear
out.

Dean came out of the bathroom, his phone against his
ear.

"Stefan. She's gone. There's a dead man here."

What?

Tia snuck around him and raced to the bathroom to see
the folded body of a man. "Oh God," she whispered. "It's
Brennan."

And heard a sound behind her.

She spun around.

Dean glared at her.

As in he glared at *her*.

As in he could see her.

Shit.

She caught her breath and waited, her eyes darting to the
entrance where he spread his legs in a square stance, effec-

tively filling the doorway. He wasn't going to let her out. Did he know she was there or was he only guessing? He'd had wonderful hearing in the hospital. And she'd just spoken out loud.

But he didn't know for sure.

She slowed her breathing down.

"You might as well show yourself. I'm not letting you out of here."

The nerve of him. What did he know? This was her friend's house he was searching. Did he have any answers – no. He couldn't stay here all day. She'd just wait him out.

"Stefan, your little tricky friend is here too." Dean grinned. "At least I think it's her. I can hear her, not see her. She's in the bathroom with the dead man."

There was silence while she considered her options. She felt like a school kid caught out on a prank.

"No, I've called in the police. The place will need to be gone over. So far I'm not sure where Simone is, but it looks like she left in a hurry. The question now is did she kill this man before leaving?"

"No, she wouldn't," Tia muttered. "They'd been together for years."

"Ah, she speaks," mocked Dean. "Did you hear that Stefan? Tia says the man was Simone's partner."

Dean listened for a few more minutes. "You can make that decision. I'm not. She's here and she's your problem. Finding a dead man shoots my chance to get some sleep tonight. I'll call you tomorrow if we find anything."

He closed his phone and tucked it into his pocket. "Why waste energy trying to hide? I know you're here. You obviously came in my truck so stop being a child and show yourself."

"I'm not a child." She dropped her energy guard and showed herself. "It's been a long time since I was a child – if I ever was."

And something in her voice must have gotten through to him for he stared at her hard for a moment then gave a clipped nod. "Then stop disappearing and running away."

"I'm being hunted," she said sarcastically. "Maybe that doesn't mean anything to you, but I'd kinda like to stay alive, thanks."

"I got that. But if you're going to hide from those trying to help you, how far do you think you're going to get?"

She hated the truth of his words, but trust wasn't something she did easily. "What do you think happened here?" She motioned to the bathroom, deliberately not mentioning the body at her feet. She had no trouble recognizing Brennan. Simone had talked about him for years, even sending Tia photos, but Tia hadn't actually met the man as he hadn't been home last night – deliberate choice on their part. The less people who knew she was here the better.

Not that her attempt to keep him out of this mess had done anything for him.

"She either was attacked by him or someone else came in and killed him but she got away. Or she killed him then left."

But Tia was already shaking her head. "She wouldn't have killed him. They had arguments like any relationship, but she'd never kill anyone. She was a nurse. She lived to help people."

"Let's say I believe you for the moment, what do you think happened here?"

"I think I made a mistake and somehow someone followed me to her place and went after her. She might have had a warning considering she packed a few things. Simone is very street smart." She'd have disappeared by now. Chances were good Tia wouldn't ever see her friend again. As long as Simone was free and clear, Tia would be happy for her.

Her heart tripped over the thought of Simone not being free. Could she have been taken? She was a beautiful woman and she was Tia's friend. She didn't know if the asshole would do anything to Simone or if he'd keep her as part of his living collection. If so, maybe then Tia could get to her and save her before it got too bad. As long as she was still alive, she could heal. But Tia had to find her and save her. If she hadn't been taken then there was no finding her. She had street smarts. *She'll find you – if she cares to.*

She walked out of the bathroom and collapsed down on the side of Simone's bed. "I suppose the cops will be all over the place now."

"In a few minutes, yes."

"And you have to stay here?"

"Not for the whole mess of things about to happen, but I will have to for at least an hour or so."

She nodded. It was just setting in. Simone had lost Brennan and she had lost Simone. She stared dry-eyed at her present life and didn't like the look of it. The future was even more depressing. Shit.

"You can go into my truck and wait. Don't let them see you. Oh wait, damn it. What about your fingertips. Do you leave prints?"

She nodded absently. "I do but I haven't touched anything." She straightened. "Oh, but I did earlier."

He nodded, his tone serious as he said, "We might need to take your prints to compare to the ones here."

A broken laugh escaped her. "No, you won't need to. You'll run the prints and mine will come up."

"Come up for what?" He walked to stand in front of her, effectively caging her in case she tried to bolt.

Only she had no plans to bolt. She was just realizing what kind of trouble she was in. Stefan might not be able to save her this time.

"Just how much trouble are you in?"

"Prison type of trouble," she said shortly. "Maybe."

"What did you do?"

"I escaped a place where I was supposed to stay. Only I was a prisoner. When I had an opportunity, I ran and never looked back," she said softly. "With my prints all over the place, they might think I did it."

"Did what?"

"Killed the doctor," she whispered. "But I didn't kill anyone. I'm not even sure he's dead. If he is, then I think whoever did kill him is after me…and if he's not dead…then he's the one chasing me."

THIS WAS WHY he didn't like cases involving psych wards. Sure, a dead man was chasing her.

He stared down at the bent head, her body solid enough to make anyone believe she was there. And she was – at least right now. Where she'd be in a few minutes was a different story.

He groaned. The problem was – there really was a dead man in the bathroom, and if her friend was in trouble then in theory her story might check out. He trusted Stefan. He didn't trust someone he couldn't see from one moment to the next.

That she could do that blew him away and that she'd taken him for a ride – literally – twice now, just pissed him off.

But…what if she was telling the truth? What if someone was after her and the world thought this man was supposed to be dead?

She'd have a hard time convincing anyone otherwise.

"Tell me the whole story."

Just then sirens hit the air. She gave a broken laugh. "No time. Story of my life."

He reached down and grabbed her arm. "Stop it. This is no time for games. Did you or did you not kill someone?"

She glared at him. "I did not."

He gazed intently into her eyes and saw nothing but painful truths.

Then she ruined it by saying, "But I wanted to. And I will if I ever get the chance."

He gave her a little shake. "Stop it." He wanted to give her a much harder shake, and maybe rattle her cage enough to get some sense inside. "You can't go around saying things like that."

She stood up. "And I can't keep living on the run. I thought I was fine all this time. I thought I was safe to come out of hiding and contact Stefan for a way to get out of this mess permanently, but he, whoever he is, found me. He found Simone."

The police cars pulled up to the front of the house.

"You'd better go," she said. "You have to meet them at the door or else they'll assume you got into trouble here yourself."

She was right, but that didn't mean he wanted to end this conversation. "Go wait in my truck. I'll finish up as fast as I can."

She nodded, but it was a little too fast. A little too easy.

He glared at her. "Don't let anyone see you and don't leave my truck. If you want help to get out of this nightmare, you'll do what you're told for once."

She glared right back. And disappeared before his eyes. He glanced down at the arm he held in his hand. It felt solid. Like an arm, skin, flesh. But all he could see was the bedding behind her. She shifted slightly and it was as if someone on the bedding moved, but he couldn't really see who. Now that he knew what he was looking for, he could make out a slight outline of a person.

"That is crazy. How did you do that?" Then he heard the voices downstairs. "Never mind, we'll talk later."

He let go of her arm, knowing that the chances of her sticking around weren't good, but he had to deal with what he could see at this point, and that was the dead man in the bathroom.

Taking the stairs two at a time, he went down and opened the front door for his coworkers.

CHAPTER 8

S HE HAD NO intention of hiding away in the truck. Not right now. She waited in the bedroom for the men to arrive, and arrive they did. Cops in uniform. Men in suits. Guys in some weird coveralls. The whole town looked to have shown up. Maybe she should have left after all. It would be hard to find a place to stand and not be in the way. She might seem invisible but she was solid. If they ran into her, they'd realize that soon enough. There was no deck here or balcony doors for her to escape. Torn between wanting to be here to see if they found anything and wanting to escape to keep her cover, she realized several of the men were leaving to grab more equipment from the vehicles. She skittered down the stairs behind them.

Outside, she stood undecided, trying to figure out her next move. She didn't have much cash on her, the night was quickly turning to morning and she needed rest. While she was worried about her friend, getting answers quickly wasn't likely to happen.

There was a cool dampness to the early morning air. She'd spent many such nights just walking. Not sure of her next step. She recognized the atmosphere tonight. It held the inner confusion she'd felt many times before.

Dean's truck was in the driveway, but there were so many people around she could hardly open a door without it being noticed. Still, he had no canopy, making it easy for her to hop into the back and lie down on the hard box. She sighed and closed her eyes. She wouldn't be able to sleep, but she desperately needed to think.

The conversations rolled around and through her consciousness as she lay there and waited. She sat and watched as more vehicles arrived. The ambulance driver unloaded a gurney and took it inside and upstairs. A few minutes later, Dean walked toward her. She didn't know if he'd seen her or not.

He opened his driver's side door. Then stopped. He turned toward her and said in a low voice, "It's more comfortable inside. Hop in."

Damn it. How was it he could see her now? He hadn't been able to before? She jumped down out of the box and slipped into the front cab. She'd have sworn up to five minutes ago she'd be leaving without him. The last thing she needed was to hook up with a cop.

Well, maybe not the last thing as walking away from Simone's house hadn't appealed either. And it wasn't like Dean was easy to ignore. Brown wavy hair that was short but just impudent enough to have a curl cover his forehead. Square jaw and those eyes. They meant business. The thing about him that almost reassured her was that hard determined attitude. As if he was someone to be counted on. Someone she could lean on – just for a moment. Someone who wouldn't let others down.

Okay, she liked to read fiction, and it sounded like she was writing a story right now. Still, it was her story, so she could do what she wanted. Casting him as the hero worked, but herself, yeah she was the furthest thing from a heroine as possible.

"You okay?" he asked.

She studied his profile. Yeah, square cheek bones, square jaw. Lean features. Brilliant eyes. She sighed. Definitely dependable take charge kind of person. So damn appealing. But not for her. Never for her. That wasn't something she could afford in her life.

Especially not now.

"I'm fine," she said shortly.

"You don't sound it."

She snorted. "Duh. My best friend is missing and her partner is dead. What am I supposed to think?"

"I don't know. He's been shot."

She gasped. "What? I didn't see any blood or bullet holes."

"Small caliber, and the way he was folded over stopped the bleeding from spreading. As soon as they straightened him out and got him on the gurney there was enough blood to see the hole."

"In the heart?" she questioned.

He nodded. "In the heart. That makes it up front and personal."

"Shit." At his sharp look, she snapped, "They are going to look at her as the killer and at no one else now. In the heart, small caliber, bathroom and her missing. Someone who knew him well, had access and opportunity. Simone just became the prime suspect."

"She did. However, they are printing the house so you are likely to come up as a suspect pretty quick if what you say is true."

"Of course I will," she muttered, staring out the window. She'd given up on her camouflage a long time ago, as long as there was no chance of others seeing her, but now she wanted to go back to being invisible so he couldn't see her – couldn't read her.

She was used to hiding. Keeping her thoughts, feelings, actions secret. Not this pain of stripping down each of her outer layers. And that seemed to be what he was doing to her.

And what was really confusing was she was letting him.

"I want you to stay with me."

At his words she swiveled in the front seat to stare at him. "What? Why?"

"You need a place to crash, I have one. You need help and I can help."

"And again, I have to ask, why?" His words had hit her like a blow to the side of her head. He was a stranger, and yet he was offering to help her. She didn't get it.

"You need help."

"Maybe I do. But I can handle my own affairs."

"Prickly aren't you?" But he said it with laughter in his voice.

"Why were you at the hospital?" She knew but wondered if he'd offer something she didn't know.

"Trying to keep you safe."

"What?" Everything he was saying was throwing her off sideways. "Safe?" Her voice rose in confusion. "I thought you were guarding me?"

"Sure, as in bodyguard. You weren't a prisoner," he said. "Stefan was trying to make sure no one made an attempt to get at you while you were unconscious."

"Oh," she said in a small voice, sinking back down on her seat. "I woke up, realized something was wrong if I was being guarded and was afraid I was a prisoner again. I just wanted to get the hell out of there."

"It wasn't like that." He turned a corner. "Stefan asked me to keep an eye on you."

"Stefan?" Okay now she was really confused. "He was there when I was attacked too. There were several people. I didn't know who they were. It was all so confusing while I was fighting for my life, and when I woke up, I seemed to be confused still. I didn't know who was who or who was on whose side."

"And neither did you give anyone a chance to explain." He waited a moment then asked, "Are you always this combative?"

Still lost in her thought, she didn't catch his question at first, then it filtered through. "No," she said shortly. "It comes from running from bad guys all my life."

"All your life?" He slid a sideways glance her way as he approached a right hand corner. He returned his gaze to the road and made the turn. "We're almost at my place."

"And if I don't want to stay?"

"Then don't." He shrugged. "You're not a prisoner. Leave if you want. But you'd be safer with me."

HE HOPED SHE'D stay with him but had to wonder at himself. He'd never been into prickly pear cactus women before. In fact, he wasn't into any cacti, and she definitely qualified as one. He understood she was in trouble and hadn't had an easy time of it, but he was trying to help her. So was Stefan but she didn't seem to believe that either.

Stefan's loyalty to people was never in question. He helped so many people in so many ways it made Dean angry to think that this girl doubted him.

He also had to wonder what the hell he was doing bringing her home. If he did, he couldn't in any way bring his son home. Not if she was bringing danger with her.

She was being chased. If they found her they'd find him and, as he'd already seen, they didn't care who got hurt in the process.

Still, his mother had been asking for Jeremy to stay for a weekend since she'd moved West. She had plans for the two of them. He knew his boy would love the holiday too. It all depended on Tia and what decision she made.

"It's dangerous to involve anyone else," she said. "Look what happened to Simone and her partner."

He slid a look her way. "We don't know what happened there."

"No, but Brennan is dead. That we do know." She glared out the windshield.

"Yes, but how long since you'd seen her?" He turned the corner, grateful the highway was as empty as it was. The side streets were completely clear, making the drive nice and easy.

She snorted. "You don't listen much, do you? I said I spoke with her earlier last night. Before the attack." She glared at him. "Why are you asking?"

He nodded as if he understood, but in truth there was no understanding this.

"I just wondered if something might have happened with their relationship, or if they had plans to go somewhere anyway. Maybe Simone left him before he was attacked."

The cab of the truck went quiet. "No, that doesn't make any sense. He was supposed to be out of town yesterday."

"Yesterday?"

"Yes. When I saw Simone, I asked when he would be back."

"Interesting, and as for yesterday, last night… You do

realize you've been unconscious for weeks, right?"

After a strangled sound and a horrified look at Dean, Tia collapsed into the far corner of the bench seat in shock.

"I guess not, huh?" He pulled the truck onto another smaller street. "Almost home. You have to make a decision soon." He cast another glance her way. "Except from the looks of you, there won't be any decision making any time soon."

Silence.

His driveway was up ahead. He pulled up to his small two bedroom home that had been nice and big for him and his son and would now have its first overnight visitor.

There was something wrong about this mess. He should call Stefan and have him swing by. Maybe she did belong back in the mental ward.

Figures.

Most interesting female around and she was missing her marbles.

He pulled up to the front of the house and said, "In truth, it's been six weeks since you were found collapsed on the street."

CHAPTER 9

TIA WATCHED AS Dean parked the truck outside a brick bungalow then got out and walked around to her side. He opened her door and helped her out as if she were a child. She wasn't, but she was in shock. How could she have missed out on six weeks of her life? And how had the hospital let her go like they had? Didn't six weeks in a coma mean needing time to adjust to the world when she came back to awareness? As in physical therapy etc. Then again, she hadn't given them an option. Yet, she'd jumped right out of bed as if it had been only overnight.

Why had no one said anything?

They'd all reacted as if her behavior had been normal.

And what about Simone? Her poor friend. She must have been waiting forever for Tia to return or at least to contact her. She must have assumed Tia had been captured or killed.

Six weeks was a long time to be out of contact with those you loved.

Dean opened the door and walked in. Still struggling with his news, Tia followed behind him blindly.

"Given the hour, I'm going to crash."

She stared at him then let her gaze look around the small living room. She was desperate for sleep too. But where?

"You can sleep in my son's bed."

At his words she stiffened. He had a child. She could put them in danger. "It's too dangerous to be here."

"My son is staying at his grandma's overnight. His bed is empty." Dean crossed the living room to a set of stairs on the other side and walked straight up. He didn't seem to care if she followed or not.

She hurried behind him. The living room was clean and masculine with large oversized furniture and a huge TV. A bay window and hardwood floors classed it up slightly. The stairs led to a small upstairs. Dean pointed to a room on his left. "This is where you sleep." He pushed the door open wider. A superman comforter sprawled across the bed in a room already stuffed with evidence of a lively mind. From rocks to bats and a collection of balls to stuffed bears and a small easel full of paints.

She felt right at home.

"Thank you."

"No problem. Sleep. It's already another day but a rest will make this look better."

She doubted it, but she was willing to try it his way. Whatever energy she'd woken up with was gone. Just the thought of having slept for six weeks should have made sleep the last thing on her mind. Instead, her body, as if realizing how much unexpected movement had completely taxed her system, was ready to collapse.

There was a bathroom on the left. She waited until Dean entered the room at the end of the short hallway before slipping across to use the facilities. In the bathroom mirror, the face that stared back at her had zero color, and her eyes had grown to twice the size. Even she could see the fear lurking deep inside. With her hair long and desperately in need of a cut, she looked horrible.

She washed up quickly and walked across the hallway to lie down on the boy's bed. Such an odd feeling to go from the hospital to here in just a few hours. She groaned softly. What had she done? Was her physical body okay? Did she need help or had she just slept long enough and it was the right time to wake up?

The thoughts spinning inside her head made no sense. Why had she been unconscious for so long? Her attack was still so clear in her mind, she was sure it had happened just yesterday.

She'd been sleeping on the bus the previous night before finding Simone.

That reminded her of something else. Where was her bag with the rest of her belongings?

She had them with her when she was attacked. She dimly remembered something about it.

Then she realized the cops would have found them. And that was likely to identify her as being in the hospital and then as having escaped. If they could pin that time frame together nicely, they'd likely say she'd returned to her friend's house, got into an altercation with the boyfriend, killed him and ran.

After all, as far as they were concerned she was an escapee from a mental hospital.

Man, she could get into trouble even while sleeping.

She never thought she'd say it, but she should have stayed at the hospital under Stefan's watch.

At least then she wouldn't be suspected of murder – again.

With that last horrible thought ringing through her mind, she fell asleep.

"STEFAN, I KNOW. I shouldn't have brought her here, but I've been up for twenty-four hours and need sleep. I couldn't leave her running around like a loose cannon getting into any vehicle she wanted and travelling who knows where. Look, Jeremy isn't here right now. As soon as I'm awake I'll take her back to the hospital."

Stefan said, "It's too late for that. She's out and there won't be any closing that box again. Damn."

"What's going on? I don't know much about her mental state, but she's not crazy. The stuff she can do – yeah, that's crazy. I hadn't expected her to not know how long she'd been in a coma either. She took it relatively well, considering."

"Did she?" Stefan laughed. "I doubt it. The news probably hasn't sunk in yet."

"I'm hoping the time of death for our male at Simone's place shows as being earlier than Tia's escape. I'd hate to think that the police would jump onto her as a possible suspect."

"Let's hope not. If they find her prints they'll be all over her anyway."

"And why is that? She gave me a garbled explanation, but I never really understood it."

"She's good at that."

Dean frowned. He hadn't expected Stefan to know Tia that well, but why wouldn't he? She'd been his responsibility at the hospital. "So what do you want me to do with her?"

"Sleep and I'll think about it."

For the first time Dean could hear the fatigue in his friend's voice. "You need to rest too."

"Sure, and maybe now that you are home with her I can. The hospital sent out the alarm an hour ago. I'll call them to let them know she's safe. We'll need to collect the rest of her personal belongings as well, and then try to catch some shut-eye. We'll talk tomorrow."

After hanging up Dean headed for a shower. Lord he was tired. He just wanted to crash. But there was nothing like the smell of death to clog your throat and fill your nostrils. It was also damn hard to get rid of.

He finished his shower quickly. Afterward, dressed in clean boxers, he pulled the blanket back off the bed and was about to climb in when he heard something. A whimper? He frowned. Damn it. His son had nightmares all the time. They caused him no end of pain. Groaning, he walked the short hallway to check on his guest.

And froze.

What the hell? She lay on the bed, dressed in panties and a t-shirt, except the lower half of her body was missing.

She moaned again, flipped over and this time one leg appeared but the other was still missing.

Fascinated, he watched for a moment longer, wondering if she felt anything. If the energy of the missing pieces could send signals to her brain. And why was this happening when she was asleep? The nightmare?

He hated to stand there and watch but knew she had to be the only female in the world who could possibly do what she was doing.

Suddenly she cried out, her arms throwing up defensively in front of herself. And damn if her arms didn't go invisible. He could still see her shoulders.

Did she know this happened when asleep? Should he take a picture? Show her? He didn't know what to do. He took one step back out into the hallway, his gaze glued to the tormented woman in front of him. This wasn't good. He hated to see women in distress. This one was a prickly version, but her distress seemed even more than most.

That she suffered from major nightmares was obvious, but if they were based on issues from her life, well her life had been worse than he thought.

A sudden backfire from a truck outside on the street had him spinning around. Realizing what it was, he turned back for a final look at his guest and realized – she was gone. The bed was empty.

The covers straightened and clean – as if she'd never slept there at all.

He glanced around the room but couldn't see any sign of her. Earlier if he looked sideways there was an odd shimmer he'd quickly come to associate as being her.

But he couldn't see that same weird lighting effect now. He walked through her room looking.

"Tia? Are you here?"

But there was no answer.

CHAPTER 10

TIA LEANED AGAINST the wall, the shock waves still rippling down her body. She closed her eyes and tried to focus on her breathing. Dean was still in the bedroom while she'd booked it out to the hallway.

The combination of that nightmare – the same damn nightmare she'd had since puberty – the shocking sound of the truck backfiring and waking up to find an almost nude male standing at the doorway watching her, sent her body into overdrive.

Her heart still didn't want to cooperate. She could feel her throat rasping as she tried hard to swallow. A cool breeze brushed down the hallway as Dean came out and stood, hands on his hips just feet beside her. She eyed him carefully. Could he see her this time? Then he cocked his head, looked directly at her and said, "Are you okay?"

Damn.

After a long moment she said, "I think so."

"I'm sorry, I didn't mean to scare you."

"Sure. I'm used to waking up to men watching me sleep," she snapped.

"I wasn't. Not really. The reason I came in the first place was that you were crying out. I presume you have nightmares."

"Such a mild word. As if what I have falls into that category." She snorted. "But yes, as far as what you and the rest of the world would say, I have nightmares."

"My son does too." He gave her a small apologetic smile. "I couldn't *not* check on you. But I didn't mean…" he swept his arm toward the hallway, "to scare you so badly."

"It doesn't matter." She sighed. "I live in running mode."

"I see that." He watched her, his gaze serious, steady. "You've hardly had any rest. Please go back, and I promise I won't check on you if you cry out again."

A broken laugh escaped. "Thanks for checking in the first place and sorry for overreacting."

"Well your instincts are sound – a little overwrought maybe, but sound." He smiled at her. "You're safe here."

"For the moment." She walked back into the bedroom and added, "Until he finds me."

She lay back down on the bed and curled up in a tiny ball. She listened to him walk down the hallway and close his bedroom door behind him. She hated this. The nightmare had set her off again, and now her mind refused to rest. God, this one had been bad. She'd be recovering for hours.

And she was so cold. She could crawl under the covers, but for some reason that felt like she'd be intruding.

She punched the pillow and rolled over – again.

It had to be almost morning. Maybe she should just leave.

But go where? Simone's was out. Plus, six weeks ago she'd hoped for Stefan's help. Now what? Six weeks? No wonder her body felt odd, out of control. As if not quite there sometimes. Uncoordinated. She groaned and flipped onto her back.

Her eyes had a gritty feel to them. She stared up at the

ceiling and realized little plastic stars dotted the paint. For some reason that made her smile.

Just when she couldn't stand it anymore, she heard Dean's bedroom door open and Dean striding down the hallway toward her.

She sat up as he opened the door and walked in. "What's wrong?"

"You," he said in exasperation. "I can't sleep with you thinking so loud."

Before she knew what was happening, he'd bent down, scooped her up and strode with her in his arms back to his room. The room was lit with the early dawn sky. The bed had covers pulled back on one side only. A huge bed. A king size bed.

He shifted his grip, reached down and pulled back the covers on the side closest to them, then dropped her gently on the sheet below. She gasped in shock. But he tossed the covers over her head and snapped, "Now you're safe. Sleep."

Within minutes he'd settled into his side of the bed and fallen asleep.

Once she realized what he was doing, she'd frozen on the spot, her mind trying to figure out how long it would take her to get through the door. As he got in, the mattress lurched beneath her and she'd been waiting…for what she didn't know…ever since. He looked to be in great physical shape but she was fast too. Nothing like years on the run to keep her honed and healthy.

In disbelief she heard the deep rattling snore. He'd actually fallen asleep.

What the hell? Why had he done that? He had freaking unbelievable hearing. Could he hear her tossing and turning? As if sleeping in a stranger's bed was any better than sleeping on top of a child's bed alone.

For some reason that made her grin.

She rolled over shoved the covers down to her shoulders. She gave another thought to assessing the danger and realizing she didn't feel any…that life was calm and quiet and that he was right, somehow she felt…safe…and quickly fell asleep.

HE DESERVED A medal for this.

Now that she'd finally relaxed enough to let go and sleep, her body had a mind of its own. And had wrapped itself around Dean. Like from head to toe. He'd fallen asleep instantly, which surprised him given he didn't trust her. Who knew who she was, and given the weird shit he'd seen…what she was?

He'd woken up a few minutes before as in he'd woken up in all ways. His body hummed with happiness and hopefulness.

It wasn't going to happen, and if she woke up and saw him in this condition she'd book it right out of his house.

Although he couldn't move without disturbing her, he needed to shower and shave. Only, she slept like she hadn't slept in forever. Only he knew she'd been asleep for weeks. That it was exhausting to heal, and she'd been through more than anyone should since waking up.

What was the deal here?

His mind flipped and turned and went over all the stuff he'd learned since she'd woken up. None of it added up. That it was woo woo stuff just added to the gaps in his knowledge. He'd already checked the Internet on his phone, but there was no mention of anyone with invisible body parts. Lots of people talking about phantom pain but that wasn't the same thing.

If she was for real and some geneticist found out then sure he could see people wanting her DNA, but really, that was as easy as a swab in her mouth, wasn't it? Not kidnapping her. He didn't know much about cutting edge research but he doubted the average company could get away with it. Then again, there was nothing average about this scenario.

Or her.

She moaned, and her hand slid across his chest and around his waist. He shuddered. He'd worn his boxers to bed and she'd slept in only slightly more. Oh good Lord. Her arm pulled up against his chest, stroking across his belly.

He shuddered.

He deserved two medals for this.

Trying to shift so as not to wake her, he rolled sideways. She flipped onto her back, her arms and legs spread. In his mind he could see her breasts gently rolling with the movement. He didn't dare look. She was too damn attractive.

Longish hair, smooth clear skin and in the morning, she was soft and gentle.

Unlike the abrasive personality he'd met so far. He glanced at the time and realized it was ten o'clock. He'd not had enough sleep to make up for the lost night but enough he could function for the day. Now if only he knew what the day would bring.

He slipped out from under the covers and headed for the washroom. His cell phone buzzed as he passed his charger. He snatched it up and carried on into the washroom.

Stefan. Good.

He read the short message. Stefan hadn't found a missing person's report on either the deceased male or Simone. Figured. She'd likely killed him and booked it.

He stepped into the shower. The water hit his sore back, making him lean over and let the heat pound away at the muscles.

He didn't know what to do with Tia next. She was supposed to have been meeting Stefan when she was attacked. Maybe he could convince her to continue with that plan this morning. He couldn't have let her walk out to the streets last night. She'd been ready to but he'd seen the hesitancy, maybe the fear. She might have been on the streets for years, but she'd lost that edge somewhere in between. In that time she'd gotten lax. And when forced back into the old situation, weak. That's how her attackers had gotten to her. She might not have been able to fight off or avoid the confrontation when she'd been street smart, but now there was a layer of *I don't want to live like this anymore* surrounding her.

He didn't blame her. He wouldn't want to either.

He finished his shower and managed to run his electric razor over his heavy stubble. Feeling better, he wrapped the towel around his waist and walked into his bedroom.

And damn if his bed wasn't empty.

His heart pounding, he stopped in place. Had she been taken or just woken up in a weird place and been frightened?

The door to his bedroom was closed – just the way he'd left it. So was his window. The bedding appeared to be the way he'd left it. And…he walked closer. This could take some getting used to…she was still in bed, but from what he could see, she was completely invisible. As in the blankets on his side were pushed back as he'd left them. But on the other side the blankets raised in the air over her missing form.

So was she still sleeping?

And how come he couldn't see her now?

He desperately wanted to ask Stefan some of these questions. He could see her head lying on the pillow and could hear her breath rising and falling in her chest. She slept.

He quickly texted several questions to Stefan.

And got dressed.

Not sure it was safe to leave her but not really having much choice, he walked downstairs to his kitchen and put on coffee. As it started to drip, his phone rang.

Stefan.

"She's sleeping but appears to be completely invisible." Quickly he explained what he'd seen last night in the middle of the night and the way she looked now.

"Why the hell is she able to do this?" he asked. "It makes no sense. No one can go invisible."

"She's not going invisible as much as her energy is taking on the look of the energy beside it. It's a cloaking method she developed to hide. She could do it somewhat before her attack, but now it seems like she's beyond capable."

"I don't know about capable because she's not in control. In the middle of her nightmares her body was in and out of whatever state this is."

"Interesting. She hasn't had enough time since waking from that coma to assimilate the changes to her system. The attack was horrific but only on an energy level. So it needed time to recharge. A six week rest like that meant her system was busy doing something. Healing in some areas. It could take her a week or two to incorporate the changes and possibly months to understand how they affect her abilities. It could even take much longer for new abilities to show up."

Dean couldn't imagine. "You were going to help her before, can you help her now?"

"If she'll let me."

"Hmmm." He didn't know what to say to that. "Do you want to come over here? Or meet us somewhere?"

"She needs to see a doctor. Her system is shorting out."

"There's a doctor for this?" He'd never heard of such a thing.

"Yes. A couple. One in town. I'll have to contact him."

"Okay, get back to me as soon as you can."

"Will do."

He hung up and turned to pour a cup of coffee. And stiffened. Slowly he turned around to see an empty room. But…not an empty room.

Casually he poured a second cup and set it down on the table. "Here's one for you, Tia."

He felt the nervous start, the anger. "No, I don't really see you. I hear you somewhat. I see something off from the corner of my eye. But I can't *see* you." He placed the coffee on the table. And faced her directly. "It's more sensing you."

A chair was pulled back by an invisible hand, and suddenly she sat down fully visible.

He breathed a sigh of relief.

"There, that should be easier on you."

She shot him a dirty look and tugged the coffee toward her.

He grinned. "I gather you need caffeine to start your day."

That earned him a second dirty look, but so far she hadn't said a word. That worked for him. He busied himself making a large omelet for breakfast and, without asking, split it in two and delivered hers on a plate with the cutlery to go with it. "Add that to the caffeine for your stomach to have something to work with."

"I have no caffeine," she muttered, tugging the plate closer.

He laughed and retrieved the coffee pot. He filled both cups again then sat down across from her. She was eating like she hadn't had a decent meal in weeks. He stopped his fork halfway to his mouth. She *hadn't* eaten in weeks. And that would account for the wan skeletal look to her. She really did need fattening up.

They ate in silence. He wanted her to finish before he brought up Stefan and a doctor. He suspected both wouldn't go down well.

When she was done, she pushed her plate back and tugged the coffee closer. Slouching down she sighed and closed her eyes. "Thank you, I enjoyed that."

"You're welcome." He got up and retrieved the dirty dishes, rinsing then adding them to the dishwasher. "Do you need more coffee?"

No answer. He turned to find her head resting on her arms on top of the table. She was sound asleep. Again.

No wonder. She'd been through a lot and her body was on overload. Did he leave her there to sleep this off? Which could be hours yet. Or did he take her back upstairs?

Undecided he stood and watched her for a long moment.

And damn if her body parts didn't start to flick off and on again. One minute he could see her forearms and shoulders, the next they were gone and her head appeared to be resting in mid air. Then the arms and shoulders reappeared and her head disappeared.

He jumped back. That just looked…wrong.

Thankfully her head reappeared quickly.

Shorting out, Stefan had said. Yes, that made sense. He

didn't understand it but could see that if this was electrical impulses then there was something definitely wrong. Stefan's doctor might be the best person for her to see. He doubted she'd agree.

Just then her head reappeared and seemed to stabilize. He walked a few steps forward, thinking maybe she just needed rest, before he realized only the back of her head had reappeared.

Her face was blank.

Like a jagged line cutting off the back of her head, he could see where her face should be and the rest…was more or less, gone.

This was too much.

He reached for his phone – again.

CHAPTER 11

S HE WAS SO tired.

Like in the old days when she'd been running forever with no end in sight. Not tiredness after a long workout knowing you'd done something good for yourself, that you'd recover and do well in an hour or two. This was long-term exhaustion that came from being in a stressful situation for way too long and knowing it didn't matter what you did, it wasn't going to change any time soon.

She was at the end of her rope.

Which made no sense.

She'd been sleeping for six weeks. What was the problem? Why hadn't her system recovered? It needed to. She couldn't keep doing this. She needed to get away. Having no strength, and all her energy going to heal her damaged system meant she couldn't run. She was as weak as a newborn kitten.

Look at her. She'd fallen asleep at the kitchen table. Even now, lying in the same position for so long, her body hurt. Her toes ached. She'd been so hungry she'd inhaled the food and now her stomach wanted to revolt. Lord, she was a mess. Somehow though she'd landed at a place where someone appeared to not only hear her but see her – at least enough to know where she was. And he wasn't freaked out by her fatigue and disappearing act.

Maybe that was a macho male front instead.

With her head still resting on her arms, she tried to assess the damage to her system. The shock over Simone added more stress. In the background she could hear sounds somewhere else.

Voices. A conversation.

She wanted to listen.

But the words weren't making sense, it was like the sentences were backwards. She gave her head a shake and tried again. Now the voices stopped talking. She sat up and pushed her hair back off her face and stared bleary-eyed around her. She was alone in the kitchen. Dean's kitchen. Reassured that she recognized the place but unnerved at the jumble of words in her head, she pushed her chair back and stood up.

Instantly the room swayed around her. Jesus. She grabbed for the edge of the table and hung on until her world stopped spinning.

What the hell was wrong with her? She stuffed the fear that something major was going on back down deep inside.

She was just tired, just needed time to rest. That was all.

Bravely she took one step. Then another. Okay, that was better. A few more and she was almost confident all was well again. The living room was through the wide doorway in front of her. She managed a couple more steps and saw the couch. She made her way over to it and collapsed down. Maybe a nap. If she could just sleep a little longer she'd be fine.

Surely…

And she closed her eyes.

And dropped back under.

"SEE WHAT I mean?" Dean felt vindicated. Stefan and Dr. Manson, a friend of Stefan's, had arrived right after Dean had called. They'd been watching Tia sleep, their conversation low and modulated so as not to wake her.

She'd woken anyway.

But it was the way she'd woken, obviously dizzy, moving in and out of visibility in a way that had the air crackling with electricity but more than that…she hadn't seen them. And they'd been standing right in front of her.

Like what the hell?

Now she was asleep again.

"I'd like to have her back at the hospital," Dr. Manson said.

"Ha," Dean said. "Good luck with that. If she doesn't want to stay you know she's just going to walk out."

"She might, but we have a few ways to keep her in," Stefan said quietly, his gaze locked on Tia.

"But she'd have to be willing or it would be a fight every minute."

Stefan nodded absentmindedly. "She'd need to be willing."

"She's not." Dean made that clear. "I don't think there's anything you can do to make her willing either."

"I don't know about that. She's not in good shape."

"Actually, she's in great shape," Stefan said. "But her synapses are off."

Dr. Manson said, "That would be very unusual."

"Hmmm." Stefan sighed. "We need to run some tests."

"If she's feeling bad enough she *might* be willing to undergo some," Dean said. "She's not very trusting."

"With good reason. She was tested a long time ago. Fascinated, the specialists ran every test possible and then some." Stefan turned slightly away. "Some of the tests were uncomfortable. Others downright painful."

"What about her parents? Didn't they do something to protect her or at least limit the time she was a lab rat?"

"Her parents tried when she was young, but she was too much for them. After she entered the program they, along with their son who had none of the same issues, literally disappeared into the night and left her behind."

Dean stared at Stefan. "What? Isn't that abandonment?"

"In theory, but in truth they signed papers to give her to the project and the head of the project. *Ansell Wilhelm*. He was a highly decorated doctor who'd done cutting edge research on genetics, but mostly with animals."

"So what? Tia became his first human test subject?" Dean asked incredulously. "That's not legal."

"No one knew," Stefan said. "There was a minor scandal when the world found out but no one cared. Paperwork disappeared and there was a lot of innuendo but no proof. Still, his funding was cut off when the hint of scandal happened and he more or less went off the grid, taking several of his patients with him."

The doctor said, "Likely went underground. Possibly even a third world country. There is lots of money available if you aren't too worried about where or why."

Dean hated to think of Tia's childhood as a test subject. "She must have had a horrible life."

"Actually, it was worse than you think. That trailer you were at yesterday," Stefan said, "was her childhood home."

"What?"

"Yeah, it took a bit to run that down. I actually got the confirmation from her then ran it through the database. Her parents owned it for seven years. Along with signing her over, they might have been paid to disappear."

The doctor threw out his arm suddenly as if to silence them. They all paused to stare at Tia. Her body was illuminated in a weird gold.

Stefan caught his breath and quickly moved forward. The doctor followed. Dean stood in place wondering what the hell had happened. Her body, instead of disappearing one chunk at a time, now lit up in one area at a time, but it was a luminescent glow like from the inside out. It was crazy.

He watched both Stefan and the doctor walk around Tia, studying her energy, her body. They were acting almost as crazy as she was. When Stefan dropped to his knees and peered from a bent over angle at the area where her foot glowed, Dean realized they were looking for something on her…or in her.

Lord only knew which. And why.

Surely this was an organic kind of issue. No, they said something about electrical. What he knew about electricity was minimal. He could change out plugs and fix a lawn mower cord after being run over but not much more. The principles were easy though – if you were talking about normal electricity.

He understood electrical currents flowed through the body. And she appeared to be "shorting" out. He just never imagined such a thing was possible.

In fact, he'd have said it was completely impossible.

Besides, if there were interruptions in her electrical impulses, she might feel weird but none of that should affect how she visually looked as in disappearing body parts.

The electricity wasn't affecting him. He should be able to see all of her like a normal person.

But he couldn't.

He had to admit it was fascinating.

And it was easy to imagine how a scientist might be willing to do just about anything to study her.

But what kind of tests had they performed? Ones to see how much power she had and what interrupted it? What could make her problem worse? Or how low her energy could go and she could still function?

None sounded like fun to him.

After a moment, as the other two men studied her intently, he asked, "Well? Any idea why she's doing this?"

"Several ideas," the doctor muttered. "Truly, she is unique. This must be a result of her individual abilities being shorted."

Stefan said, "Yes, but is the shorting happening because she's doing it, someone is doing it to her or is she injured in some way?"

"If she wasn't…she will be soon. This is affecting her organic systems."

"So you see her heading for a whole body failure?" Stefan asked, his forehead creased. "I was thinking she's been doing something like this for years – probably while asleep – only something has set it off now in a big way that she can't control."

"What?" Dean stood beside Stefan, staring down at the young woman who'd become a little too important in his nice neat orderly world. "Are you saying someone has done this to her? As in trying to hurt her?"

"Quite possibly." Stefan stood up and brushed his pants off. "In which case we do have one chief suspect."

"The guy who attacked her earlier?"

"I'm presuming so." Stefan turned to study the room around them. "Now if only we knew who that was."

From the other side of the room, the doctor said, "I need to run some scans to see if there are any implants hidden in her. It could be microchip size, and I think it's sending a pulse or something to disrupt her system."

"Or maybe it's not on all the time, as that would make it easier to detect, but something might have set it to go off accidentally. You know, like a smoke alarm when the battery is dying or a CO2 alarm when there is gas."

"Maybe this is an alarm system," Dean suggested.

Stefan turned to stare at Dean. "That's a very good possibility. This could be her body sending a message. These being the symptoms of the bigger problem."

"I need her back in the hospital," the doctor said.

They all jumped back slightly when Tia opened her eyes and said in a hard tired voice, "I'm not going back there."

CHAPTER 12

TIA WANTED TO bolt up from the couch and run as far and as fast as she could from the three men. But she didn't move a muscle. In fact, she wasn't sure she could. Her body was starting to seizure but her muscles didn't appear to move. Energy seizures? Was such a thing possible?

People with abilities seemed to have two systems. One physical and one energetic. If a person could get sick on the physical system, in theory it should then be possible to get "sick" on the energetic level.

Great.

Just what she needed. Was there an equivalent to cancer on the physical system? 'Cause it would be so typical of her to be the first one. Damn.

The doctor studied her with a narrow gaze that made her wonder if he could see right through her. But there was no intrusiveness. Just a practitioner's assessment. Stefan looked at her with an unfocused gaze and she realized he was studying her from an energy level.

Deciding she'd had enough of being stared at, she shifted to a sitting position. Then, using the armrest for support, she stood up – a little shaky but at least she was vertical. She studied the room. As far as she could tell she was still in Dean's house, but everything was foggy. As if she was looking through a light rain.

"Where's Dean?"

"Right in front of you." Dean's voice came through a weird cloud.

She rubbed her eyes but she still couldn't see him clearly. "I can't see you very well," she muttered.

Instead of a shocked exclamation, a warm hand landed on her shoulder, grounding her. Instantly, her vision cleared. He stood in front of her, a worried look on his face.

She smiled. "Thanks, now I can see you."

"I didn't do anything, but you're welcome." His smile gentled, but his gaze narrowed as he studied her features. She could feel the power of his concern. It was…disconcerting.

Feeling stronger, she took a step forward. With a mental shake, she reached up and rubbed her temple. "I wish I woke feeling like I'd had some rest. Instead, every time I wake up I feel frazzled, frayed at the edges. Terrible feeling," she muttered. She should go to the washroom, wash her face, maybe it would wake her up, but she didn't want to move.

Dean stepped back, letting his hand fall away and as if a connection had broken she suddenly felt worse. Weird. She felt better touching him. Still, she could hardly hold his hand all the time. Besides, she was better than before she'd collapsed. She excused herself and went to the washroom. She didn't want to look into the mirror, but she knew she had to. She felt so disconnected from everyone, everything. She hadn't even asked for an update on Simone. God, what was wrong with her?

She used the facilities, gave her face a good scrub, tried to run her fingers through her hair. Thankfully there was mouthwash in a cupboard. Stefan had brought her meager belongings from the hospital, but apparently toiletries had not been among them. Still, she was grateful to have her purse back.

Finally, she pushed open the door and walked out to the living room and to the men who waited for her. She heard Dean say something to her but where he stood was only a blur of energy. Turning toward the sound of Stefan's voice, she realized he was no longer as clear as he'd been either.

She whispered, hating the fear snaking through her, "There's something wrong with me."

Then she fell to her knees.

The men rushed to her side.

But not in time.

She toppled face forward to the floor.

"DAMN IT. WHAT'S wrong with her?" Dean asked after moving her to the couch. Stefan and Dr. Manson checked her over while he watched.

"We don't know," Stefan said. "I wish she'd given us some of her symptoms before collapsing."

"There's something going on between Dean and her," the doctor said quietly.

Stefan nodded. "I saw that."

"Saw what?" Dean cried out in frustration. "What are you talking about?"

"When you placed your hand on her shoulder, her energy strengthened as if you were stabilizing whatever was off with her system."

"I didn't do anything but try to offer my support," Dean said. "Who'd have thought something like this was possible?"

"We didn't. And we've seen some crazy things." The doctor turned to Stefan. "Your call."

He nodded. "We need to take her in."

"She doesn't want to go anywhere," Dean protested. He didn't know how he felt about any of this, but he knew she didn't want to go to a hospital. And given her delicate condition, he couldn't imagine a hospital helping her.

"She can't stay here," Stefan said gently.

"If we move her, she'll feel betrayed." And damn if it didn't feel like he was the one doing the betraying.

"She is hurt, sick. She needs help and before we can do that we have to know what's wrong," the doctor said. "Therefore I have to run some tests."

"Do them here." Dean hated that he was starting to sound belligerent but, damn it, someone needed to speak up for her. She couldn't so it was up to him. And that made him feel like a fool. Again. She'd made him feel that way from the first meeting, but now he was doing it all by himself.

"We can't. I'm afraid first and foremost that during her attack she was given something that is disrupting her energy. Because her system is so chaotic I can't search effectively. I need equipment to look for such a thing."

"She won't survive the standard tests like an MRI," Stefan said quietly. "Her energy is too far off the grid. It's likely to send her completely off the wall. Maybe even cause a heart attack."

"Then she's not going. Done." Dean sat down on the floor beside the couch. He reached out and stroked her arm. Her body had taken on a cool tinge as if she was chilled. It was a hot summer day so he didn't get it, but she obviously wasn't like anyone else. More... Alien. At his own stupid joke he had to wonder if that wasn't part of the reason someone was after her. "She's cold."

"Yes, her body is going to respond to this stressor in

many ways."

"So we need to find out how to stop it." Unable to help himself, Dean reached out and gently massaged her shoulder. He couldn't keep her here – not with his son around. He needed to protect his family too.

But neither did he feel like he could abandon her.

"Solutions?"

Stefan grinned. "Maybe." He pulled out his phone. "Maddy, how is the bed situation at your place? I could use a spot for someone for a few days. Not to mention your help."

Dean frowned. "What is he doing?"

"Trying to help Tia in the best possible way."

The doctor listened intently to the conversation, but it didn't make any sense to Dean. "If she needs a place to stay, she can stay here. She doesn't need to go to Maddy's place, whoever that is," he muttered. "That's hardly a step forward." He wasn't sure his place was a good option either, but he couldn't stop himself from offering to help her. He had to think of his son, but there was just something about her… Maybe he could help keep both Tia and Jeremy safe.

"Yes, it is." Stefan put away his phone. "Maddy has a bed free at one this afternoon for two days only, then it's full and she can't change that. So we have two days to make a miracle happen."

Dean stood up. "Two days? Is that all? Maybe I should be asking what kind of a place this is and if Tia's going to be okay there."

"Hopefully she'll be much better, but if not we'll have to find another place for her." Stefan's gaze turned inward. "I do have a few other places to check. But Maddy's Floor is definitely the best option."

"It's also a gift that would be impossible for most other

people as it's very hard to get in there." The doctor nodded at Tia. "She's a lucky girl."

"I'm going to have to do some work on her as we head over," Stefan said. "Then stay and see if I can get her energy to integrate with that of Maddy's Floor. If not, and her energy starts to short out the system in place at Maddy's, then I'll have to isolate her. I need to help Tia but not at the expense of those already on the Floor."

None of this made any sense to Dean. "If she wakes up and wants to leave, she can come back here."

"It could be dangerous," Stefan reminded him. "She's being hunted."

Just the term hunted made his anger flare. "In that case, she really needs us."

"Yes, she does." Stefan's voice lowered and he motioned toward Tia. "In more ways than one."

Dean glanced down to realize his hand was back stroking her arm and shoulder. She was fully visible at the moment and there was a peaceful repose to her features. "She looks much better."

"She does." Stefan's gaze went from Dean's face to Tia's face several times. "What are you doing for the next few days?"

"I was going to pick my son up in a little bit." There was a heavy pause. He looked up. "Why?"

The doctor answered, "Because she needs you. You are helping to stabilize her energy."

"What?" How did any of this make sense? "I'm just letting her know she's not alone. Comforting her like I would my son." Okay, it was a little more than he'd do with his son, at least mentally. "She's been alone a long time. It's hard to live like that. I'm just letting her know – where ever the hell she is – that she's not alone anymore."

Stefan's phone rang. He spoke for a few moments then hung up. Dean waited for him to speak. "That was Maddy. We're to bring her over right now."

"I thought not until this afternoon?" Dean frowned down at the young woman on his couch. Torn. He didn't want to leave. How had life gotten so complicated?

"Dean, any chance you could stay with her for today at least?"

Dean looked up. "Why?"

His own phone rang then. "Hi, Mom."

His mother chattered quickly, "I know you want to come and get Jeremy, but I somehow promised him a trip to the zoo. I know you said you'd be by to get him anytime now but really, I don't get to see him very often, and I'd love to have him longer. He wants to stay too."

In the background Jeremy yelled and cheered, "Dad, say yes. Dad, we're going to go and see penguins."

Dean rolled his eyes, his son was obsessed with penguins – anything animal related but penguins topped the list this week.

"Mom–"

"No, I know. You need to spend time with him too, but after realizing how precious life is…we need a little time together."

"How much time? And you saw him last weekend, remember?" he said humorously. "And you'll see him next weekend."

"But those are short visits. He stayed overnight last night, but you dropped him off late so he went to bed right away. We didn't get time together. Now, if you left him overnight again, we could stay up and watch movies and eat popcorn," she said in a wheedling tone.

In the background his son chanted, "Popcorn. Popcorn. Popcorn."

"You did that on purpose," he said with a laugh.

"Of course. You're busy or you'd have been here by now. Go find yourself a nice girl." And damn if she didn't hang up on him.

He stared down at his phone.

The other two men laughed. Stefan said, "I'm not sure what just happened, but I gather you're free now."

"Apparently. My mother has stolen my son for the rest of today through tomorrow. Lord only knows what she'll try tomorrow in order to keep him."

"Is she always like this?" asked Dr. Manson.

Dean looked over at the doctor. "She lived back East until a few weeks ago. After getting a clean diagnosis from breast cancer, she decided that being in remission meant being given a second chance at life. There's just the two of us so she moved closer."

"Sounds like it was the best decision for both of you."

"It was. Jeremy adores her."

"And she's a great babysitter," the doctor added with a grin.

"True enough." Dean stared down at his hand still resting on Tia's shoulder. What had his mother said? Something about finding a nice girlfriend? He hadn't been trying for a long time. Not since his son moved back in with him eight months ago. As his ex-wife was going to the Middle East for her career, she decided Jeremy needed his father more at this time. The change had been heart wrenching for all of them, but the Internet made keeping in touch easier.

Still, being a single father definitely changed his dating

habits.

As in – he didn't anymore.

Now, as he stared down at the strange and wonderful person in front of him, he was tempted for the first time to change that.

CHAPTER 13

IF SHE'D STUCK her finger in an electrical socket, she couldn't have been more shocked and frazzled. She hurt. Inside and out. Her bones ached and her mind just wanted to cringe and not see or talk or think of anything.

But someone kept poking at her.

She'd kicked out once or twice, but they'd been feeble. Ineffective. In fact, she'd begun to doubt her kick had her body moving at all. It was like little bursts of energy being shot off to the side but the leg hadn't actually moved.

"Stop it," she muttered. "Leave me alone."

"No." But the voice was kind, caring. Female.

That made her suspicious. There was no one in her world that was kind. People were either dead or callous. She was a nice person, but hadn't ever been able to make much in the way of friends. Except Simone.

Tears burned her eyes. Simone was in trouble. And it was all Tia's fault.

This sucked. She should be the one dead. Dead would be so much better.

"No, it wouldn't," said the same voice. "You're alive and we're going to keep you that way."

That's when she realized she'd been speaking aloud. She tried to roll over but something was restraining her. She wasn't strong enough to resist.

"Am I a prisoner?" she whispered.

"No, you aren't," the voice rushed to assure her. Then the tone changed, became more confident, assured but also filled with relief. "There you are, Dr. Maddy."

"How is she?"

Tia listened to the new voice. A gentle voice filled with caring and light. She sighed happily.

"Confused, scared, fighting."

"All normal," the one called Dr. Maddy said calmly.

Dr Maddy – and what kind of name was that? – stepped into view. Except Tia couldn't see all of her. And what she did see didn't make any sense. "Why did you remove your head," she asked in shock. "How can you function without one?"

"Is that what you see? My body stopping at my neck?" Dr. Maddy asked curiously.

"Just weird colors where your head should be. My head is hurting. Damn headaches."

"How long have you had these headaches?"

"Weeks, maybe years." She wanted to roll over, and not being able to became the one thing she couldn't stop thinking about or trying to do. "Can you remove the restraints please? I really need to roll over."

A cool hand came down to land on her forehead. "You aren't restrained. Try to roll over now."

Tia tried hard but nothing moved. "I can't," she cried out in panic. Then hands lifted and turned her body in the direction she'd been trying to roll and she sighed in relief. "Thank you."

"You're welcome," Dr. Maddy said. "Tia, I'm going to run some tests and see what's going on here."

"No," she said, starting to shake. "No more tests."

"Tia," Dr. Maddy said firmly, "I won't hurt you." A smoothing hand stroked down her shoulder and arm. "You aren't seeing properly and you can't move normally, so unless you want to return to the hospital you were at before, I need to check you over."

"Okay," Tia whispered. "But no one else. I can't trust anyone."

"Got it."

Tia waited, tense. But there was only a gentle stroking on her shoulder and arms. When the soothing motion shifted down her back she relaxed. Maybe the tests were going to be done later today. Tomorrow. Sure, that made sense. Had to take time to book the machines for her. She relaxed, enjoying the soothing feel on her frazzled nerves.

With her eyes closed she let herself slip into a light peaceful state.

"Is she awake?"

Tia heard Dean's voice from the doorway but didn't want to move. She had never felt so peaceful. So easy in her body.

"Yes, she's just resting."

"She looks better already," Dean said.

Tia wanted to smile. He sounded so worried. That was nice. She couldn't remember the last time anyone cared. She'd been alone so long. Simone had been her best friend. The only one who'd known her history. The only one she could relax around. Talk to. Be normal with. Be herself.

It wasn't even a friendship, given their crazy different backgrounds and the distance between them, but a reconnecting with her past. As if by remembering her past she'd be able to keep a better eye on her future.

It hadn't happened that way. Instead, she'd lost Simone.

"Easy." The hands on her back stopped for a brief moment. "What are you thinking about?"

"Simone," she whimpered, tears flowing down her face. "She's in trouble."

"We're looking for her," Dean said from somewhere.

"Too late," Tia said. "I can't sense her anymore. I think she's dead."

The hand on her back increased the pace slightly, but Tia was barely noticing the beautiful mantle of care as it had been replaced with painful memories of the friend she felt sure she'd lost.

"You can't trust your senses right now," Dr. Maddy said. "Your energetic system is constantly being disrupted. It's not connecting in a flowing stream like it should, so it's always spluttering out of juice."

"Why?" Dean asked.

"Not sure yet. I can't see anything on the surface to account for this. I'm trying to stabilize her, so I can run a few different tests and hopefully get more answers. A lot of things could be interrupting the synapses."

"Such as?" Dean asked, his voice insistent. Tia liked that about him – especially when it wasn't turned her way. She wanted to twist slightly so she could hear the answer better, but she couldn't move.

She wasn't paralyzed, but there was a disconnect between the orders given and the actions followed. An interruption.

"Hard to say at this point. Could be minor like an injury on the energetic level. Could be anything."

Tia heard a tiny strangled gasp, then pain. Like waves and waves of greasy pain. An ocean of it rolled over her, through her and underneath her.

In the background she heard several people crowded around. "Go away," she whispered. "Leave me alone." God, she just wanted to be left alone to die.

Not going to happen.

The voice rolled through her mind and her head. She cried out at the strange pressure inside, the newness, the shock of the invasiveness.

How was this possible? It wasn't. It couldn't be. No one should be inside her head, her body. But the waves of agony had her curling up in a tiny ball and rocking protectively in place, whimpering.

Lord, she hurt. She needed them all to go away.

She hurt too much.

"Please," she whispered. "Stop. It hurts so much."

DEAN STOOD BY helplessly. Stefan, Dr. Maddy, who wasn't anything like he expected, and nurses all bustled around, all had a job to do. He'd picked Tia up and brought her to Dr. Maddy in Stefan's car. Carried her up some elevator in the back and had her in a private room within minutes. He didn't think he'd ever seen anything like it. No paperwork, no forms to fill out, no wait.

But since arriving, Tia had gone downhill. He hated to say it, but he wanted her back in the normal hospital that he'd been guarding just last night. She'd been in decent shape then.

As he considered the issue, he realized she'd been going downhill since she'd woken up. Not good.

He'd never seen anything like it. Or like the treatment she was receiving right now. Such strange movements and motions. He'd seen Stefan pull off some weird stuff when saving his son, but it had been easy to ignore back then. He'd been so overwhelmed with his son's miraculous recovery that Stefan could have danced nude, covered in blue paint, and he'd have been okay with it.

But these weird arms in the air, sweeping down her body looked like a bad voodoo session.

He wanted to say something. Desperately wanted to jump into the middle and carry Tia away to safety. Before he could think of anything to help her, she groaned, rolled onto her back under her own power and opened her eyes.

"Why do I feel like shit," she asked, her voice thin and thready. "And who are you people?"

The tall slim woman standing over her laughed. "I'm Dr. Maddy and you probably don't remember me, but I saw you when you first arrived."

Tia shook her head. "I don't remember anything clearly. It seems like I just had a weird and horrifically bad acid trip, only I have nothing to compare it to as I've never done acid."

The doctor laughed again, her voice light, warming, caring.

Damn it. How did Stefan find all these people? Dean usually lived in a world of nastiness. To think there was an equally positive and happy side to that same world was a bit disconcerting. He was a crime fighter. He walked the dark side most the time. Here they walked in the light. Maybe if he could spend enough time with people like this he'd remember all the good things he was fighting for.

"Any idea what's wrong with me?' Tia asked.

"Let me ask you a few questions." Dr. Maddy proceeded to ask her some of the damn oddest medical questions Dean hoped to never hear again. Questions about shellfish. Questions about type of diet. About her friend Simone.

About where and when had she eaten last? About what it was. About the attack and what did she remember?

The answers were simple, plain and seemed fairly unhelpful.

The next question Dr. Maddy asked was how Tia felt during the attack. And where the pain was centered.

When both women quieted, Stefan stepped in. "Maddy? What are you thinking?"

She ran a hand gently across her temple. Everyone, nurses included, watched her. She shrugged and said, "I know this is going to sound right out there, but... First I was thinking implant, and now I'm wondering if something wasn't removed."

Everyone stared.

"Removed?" cried Tia. "Are you serious? As in organ donors? As in someone took something away from me?"

"I can't be sure yet," Dr. Maddy said. "So until I am, I'm not going to give any details." She frowned at Dean. "Did you find anything in your truck, your house that might have been hers?"

He stared, his mind a blank. "Not that I remember seeing..."

She shrugged. "Okay. I'll spend some time thinking about this."

Tia struggled to sit up. "But you can't leave me with that little bit..."

"I have to." Dr. Maddy started to walk away. "I'll be back in an hour or so and I'll do more tests. Run a scan. See what I might find."

Dean shoved his hand into his jacket, his fingers encircling the metal chain he'd found awhile ago. He frowned. "Wait." He pulled it out. "I don't know about this... I found it somewhere around the time she was attacked. Something weird happened. It's like I was attacked too, but there'd been no one else there at the time. I forgot all about it."

"My bracelet," Tia cried. "Oh thank you."

Maddy walked closer. "Interesting. It's metal balls ringed together."

"One of the kids gave it to me," Tia said with a smile. "I've always worn it."

"Well you might want to change that." Maddy reached out a hand to touch it and drew back. "My energy doesn't like it. And there's a good chance, Dean, that your energy didn't either. Could account for much of your medical problems keeping you off work too." She studied it, frowning, then did something in the air above the bracelet. "There, that's better." She glanced over at Tia. "I think when you lost this, your energy had a chance to shift again. You've been living with it for a long time."

"Is that a problem?" Tia asked hesitantly. "It was uncomfortable when I put it on originally, but John just teased me about it." She stared at the one thing she'd kept from that world and realized it was likely the worst thing she could have taken.

"As a general rule, this is not good for our energy. You, however, seem to have adapted to the iron and steel. I'm not sure just what it is."

"If I've adapted then why did it affect my energy?"

"When you lost it."

"Oh..." She turned away. "I don't want it. Not anymore."

"Good. I wasn't going to give it back to you," Dr. Maddy said cheerfully. She walked out of the room.

Dean stared at Stefan. "Is she for real?" he asked. There was only one nurse left and the dirty look she shot him left him in no doubt about her opinion of his question. Well, this was the first time he'd ever met the doctor, and the words out of her mouth didn't inspire confidence.

"She's the real thing, and the best in the business." Stefan's voice was distracted, the look on his face introspective. Dean couldn't tell what he was thinking.

"I have to think about this. Go over the last few weeks. See what might have happened."

"Does that mean you believe her?" Dean asked incredulously.

Stefan pulled back and shot him a sharp look. "I absolutely believe her. She is Dr. Maddy." And he turned and walked out.

Leaving Dean to stare at a shattered Tia still lying in the bed.

CHAPTER 14

TIA TRIED TO sit up and get her body to follow through on her orders. She needed to leave, but how when all she could do was lie here, useless?

Dean reached down, tucked his hands under her arms and pulled her upward. "Is that better?"

She nodded. "Thank you," she said, her voice a bare whisper.

He sat down beside her and picked up her hand, his gaze intent. "I don't know Dr. Maddy but I do know Stefan, and he saved my son's life when the doctors couldn't."

"He's legendary," she whispered. "I'm glad to be here with people who can help but this is scary. It's like my body isn't getting the signals from my brain. I can barely move and my mind wants to just sleep. Not fun."

"No, but Dr. Maddy seems to know and understand. At least she has a direction to check out."

She smiled. "I know. I'm just trying not to panic. I'm starting to wish I'd never left the hospital."

"Ha. Doesn't that figure." He grinned at something secretly funny.

She frowned at him, not understanding where there was anything funny in this. "It's been a downhill slide since I left."

"Maybe now that you're finally awake and placing so

many demands on your body, it can't handle it. Maybe it's not recovered from the coma yet."

Mildly interested in that hypothesis, she said, "I hope it's something as simple as needing bed rest and time, but it doesn't feel like it."

"Doesn't matter. Dr. Maddy will figure it out."

"Dean, can you come here for a moment?" Stefan stood in the door, motioning him.

He squeezed Tia's hand and said, "I'll be right back."

STEFAN MOVED BACK out of the doorway and closed the door firmly behind him. "Dr. Maddy is going to run an internal scan, and it's easier on her if you aren't touching Tia."

Internal scan. That didn't sound good. In fact, it sounded downright horrible. "Is it going to hurt? She's in pretty rough shape already."

"No, in fact, it should make her feel much better."

He wasn't sure about that. An odd sound came from behind the door but with Stefan standing firmly in front of him, he realized he wasn't going to get in.

He studied the door, worry in his voice. "I don't want her hurt anymore."

"None of us do."

Dean's shoulders slumped, he leaned against the wall and tried to ignore the odd sounds coming from behind him. "She's been failing since she woke up, hasn't she?"

"Yes."

"Is this likely to kill her?"

"Oh yes," Stefan said somberly. "And quite possibly soon."

"As in months?" Damn that wasn't good.

Stefan shook his head decisively. "Possibly hours at the rate of deterioration. That's what Maddy is trying to stop. See if we can find out why."

"Hours?" he exclaimed. "Is this normal for you psychic people?"

Stefan laughed. "There is nothing normal about anything. And psychic people have the same system you have. In fact, as you are psychic, you have the same system and potential problems she has."

"Wait, what? No way I'm psychic. I'm just normal old boring Dean. Only son. Single father and I have a mother. All the rest is my work world."

"We all have the ability to be psychic. Some of us are more aware, more open to the center and work with the energy more. You have the same ability she does."

"Uhmm, no. My body parts all show up all the time."

Stefan laughed. "Hers do too. If she wasn't injured you'd never know."

"I'm not so sure about that." Dean shook his head. "I think she's used this technique of hers to stay hidden a long time."

"She has indeed. But you shouldn't be able to see her in her invisible state."

"I don't see the missing part as much as there's a weird sensation that something should be there but isn't. When I look out of the corner of my eye, I see her best. So it's more like a defect in her masking system. At least that's how it all started. Now it seems her whole system is off."

"Very true. That you can see her is great."

"Maybe, but I hear her better. I guess being invisible doesn't affect the noises she makes."

Stefan looked at him with an odd expression on his face. "Are you saying you can hear her even when she was invisible?"

Dean nodded. "That's how I first understood what she'd done. I couldn't see her, but I could hear her breathing. I just didn't want to believe it."

"Easy to understand," Stefan said in a distant voice as if he wasn't really listening to the conversation.

"Why? I've always had good hearing, just not crazy good at anything else."

"Except that you appear to be able to help stabilize her energy. Help ground her."

"That doesn't make any sense." Dean thought about what ground meant. "Unless it's something everyone can do."

"No, you calm her down. She doesn't spark or have bits and pieces flare off her body when you are holding onto her."

"If true, that would be odd and disturbing. It's not like I can sit here and hold her hand all day."

Stefan laughed. "If only…"

"Yeah, I wish." Dean grinned. "Now if that were to keep a hand on her in a bed…"

Now Stefan really laughed. "Trust you to think of that."

"Hey, if you weren't a newly in love male, you'd be thinking of it too. Besides Tia looks like she could use a little loving."

Stefan's tone turned serious. "I think she could use a lot of it. I can't see that anything in her history was easy. Or kind."

"Was she abused?"

"Not sexually. At least I don't believe so. But she was

kept in the study and given many tests, so abused in that way, yes. Not being allowed to go to a normal school, have friends, birthday parties, yes again. But that wasn't her whole life. She was living a normal childhood so she understood how the world worked and knew what it was like to go to school and have family and friends originally. But that all changed when she was put into this program. Since she escaped, she's been on the run, and there is nothing normal about that either."

Dean sighed. "Do we know if there was ever a missing person's report put out on her? I'm trying to work this from the cop angle, and none of it makes any sense. She shouldn't have been put into a program like this, and neither should her parents have abandoned her to it."

"*Shoulds* in this world aren't going to make a bit of difference. When her family ditched her, she didn't have a support system. It was up to her to make it through that mess on her own."

"Not fair." Actually, plain shitty.

"No. But she's not alone. There are many people in trouble in one form or another all over the world who, like her, have no one to help them. There's nothing fair about any of it."

He started to walk away.

"Wait, where are you going?"

"Home to my beautiful Celina." Stefan turned and smiled. "Keeping those we love close is the saving grace for all of us."

"And in Tia's case?" Dean stood there hating to think of abandoning her. "She has no one." He couldn't leave her, but neither could he stay to be with her. She was a sad case. Surely, that's why his heartstrings were being tugged. Surely.

"She needs all the love she can get." Stefan kept walking. "I'll be back in the morning. Or in the night if something major happens to her. Call me if you need me. Although I'll probably know beforehand."

"How?" Dean asked, only Stefan was too far down the hallway to hear him. Damn.

Dean walked back to the door that was between him and Tia. He opened it and peered in. His jaw fell open.

There was a beautiful glowing light in Tia's room, hovering over the bed, over Tia. The light was thin and easy to see through, but it pulsed with power. He'd never seen anything like it. He wanted to go in and touch it, take pictures of it, experience whatever it was. But it was there for Tia. He let his glance slide over to the beautiful woman. Her body was relaxed and her face, well, she was smiling in sheer joy.

Whatever was happening was making her happy. Making her feel good.

Damn this was odd.

Just when he'd decided to slip inside and sit down to watch, a wave of that green energy slid toward him and the door slammed closed in front of him.

Well, as a message that was pretty clear. As to what he'd seen and thought he understood about reality – that was as clear as mud.

CHAPTER 15

TIA'S WORLD WAS a kaleidoscope of color. Heat. Visuals she'd never seen before. And pain. But a pain she didn't understand. It held a muted quality to it. As if someone had shoved cotton batting between her and it. Nice in a way, but there was always that sense that if she moved wrong, did something in an off way, that pain would rise up and there wouldn't be enough cotton batting in the world to stop it.

At the same time, some of her was hot and some of her was cold, as if there was a wall between parts of her system.

There is.

She froze.

Who said that?

I did. Dr. Maddy.

And I'm here too, Tia, said Stefan.

Where is here? she asked in a low voice.

We're speaking with you telepathically.

How could the three of them be having this conversation? Tia wanted to laugh but didn't want to hurt the beautiful woman's feelings. However, no matter how this sounded, there was no way any of this was clear.

There was a distant rumble in her head. Laughter. She smiled.

So what was that about a wall? Stefan asked.

Not a wall so much as a short, Dr. Maddy said. *You ap-*

pear to have something in your belly region that is stopping the transmission of some electrical pathways.

Belly? Tia asked cautiously. *Why would something there affect everywhere else?*

It's likely not in your belly as much as in your 3rd chakra. In which case it would have the power to affect all the chakras in your body, Dr. Maddy explained.

Hmmm. Chakras. Sounded like something out of a bad movie. Kind of like herself. *So can this thing be removed?*

We hope so, but so far we haven't been able to identify it. It's not physical like a foreign object, nor is it organic to your body like a tumor.

So…what does that leave for options? she asked.

Dr. Maddy, her voice slow and thoughtful, said, *I'm not sure but I think it is energy. Someone has placed energy at a specific spot in your system, and they are still attached somehow. Maybe even yanking your chain at will.*

What? she cried out, barely hearing their slight groans. *Sorry,* she said, toning down her voice. *Are you saying someone has done this on purpose? If so, why?*

That's what we need to find out, Stefan said smoothly. *And for that we have to go back into your history a bit.*

No, she said absently. *You need to find the asshole who attacked me and knocked me out for six weeks. He's the one who likely did this to me.*

That's possible but this seems old. There's got to be a reason why it's affecting you now, but I suspect it was placed into your system when you were much younger. And probably when you had no idea.

Of course I had no idea, she said. *I'd never have allowed it.*

What about a long time ago when you were first involved in all those tests? You knew some were done while you were asleep, right?

Yes, she said, her memories opening up to those nightmares. *A terrible time in my life.*

And what if this person implanted this energy back then? Stefan asked.

Only from one moment to the next, he was gone. So was Dr. Maddy.

She was alone. The voices in her head were gone.

She might have slammed a door in front of them – she kinda felt that way, but the abruptness of it all made her wonder.

She'd never done anything like that before. But the thought of someone having implanted energy what…an energy bomb? In her system a long time ago was damn scary. As scary as those shitty years she'd lived at that "hospital." Hospital, my ass. It had been a secret testing facility, and that's all she knew. Except she hadn't been alone.

There'd been other victims with her.

Faded names and faces filled her mind as she remembered a very aggressive male who hadn't wanted anything to do with the doctors. They'd done something to him to make him more agreeable. It had worked, she recalled. Considering he'd scared the bejeesus out of her, she'd been delighted with the change. It was only now she had to wonder what they had done. But she didn't want to remember. It had been years since she thought of the other people in her group. They'd all left over time until, at the end, she'd been the only one still there. Either she wasn't a success and hadn't been released or she was the only one without family. The others had all been moved out of the institute while she'd been locked up. She'd done her best to avoid even letting the memories surface.

And in the back of her mind was always the worry the damn doctors had done something else to her. Something irreversible. Something irreparable. Something permanent.

Why?

And why her? She'd never done anything to anyone. She'd been a child. An innocent child who'd turned into a wary and very streetwise teenager. Now an adult, she could look back that long road and wonder that she'd made it at all. And where did she go from here.

Oh wait, she couldn't go anywhere. Because those assholes from her horrible childhood were still yanking her chain.

DEAN SLUMPED IN the hallway, head leaning back against the wall, eyes closed.

"Dean?"

At the woman's voice, his eyes flew open and he bolted to his feet.

"Easy, I didn't mean to wake you." Dr. Maddy said gently.

"I didn't mean to fall asleep," he muttered, giving himself a shake. "How is she?"

"She's holding. But there's definitely a mystery surrounding her condition." She hesitated for a moment, and then said, "You're in law enforcement, correct?"

Not sure where she was going with this, he nodded. "I am."

"Is it possible for you to track the studies she was put into when she was a child? I could use the names of the doctors involved. It might give me an idea of what was done and why." She smiled apologetically. "Normally I'd ask my partner to chase the information down, but he's out of town."

"That's fine. I can search her history and see what I can come up with." He looked around. "Is she staying here for tonight?"

"Yes."

"Then I'll go to the office and start searching right away." He said goodbye and took off, glad to have a clear job to do. A nuts and bolts type of job. His kind of job. This damn fairy dust was hard to be around.

CHAPTER 16

TIA SLIPPED OUT of bed and walked to the doorway. The place was unlike any hospital she'd ever been in, and she'd been in more than a few. She'd been in way too many all through her young years.

There was carpeting on the floors, beautiful paintings on the walls and some wall hangings that appeared to be hand stitched. She glanced back at her bed and realized it had real blankets on it, handmade quilts. How could this be?

Taking the opportunity she turned left, tugging her housecoat over her shoulders, and walked down a few doorways. Bedrooms lined each side of the hallway, small but complete and lived in. Most of the occupants were middle-aged adults. One held a child who sat cross legged on her bed, a puzzle spread out in front of her.

Tia smiled down at her. She wondered if she should speak, but the child looked absorbed in what she was doing. That was fine by her. She was too upset and out of sorts to do so anyway.

She walked to the closest window. Beautiful gardens were down below, she was on what must be the 4th or maybe 5th floor. There were small sitting rooms and balconies. Easy chairs and comfortable looking couches. This was her idea of a perfect living room, it was very comforting being in it.

"And that is the way it's supposed to be," Dr. Maddy

said from behind her. Her voice was tired but calm.

"You could read my thoughts?"

Dr. Maddy nodded. "It saves time."

Tia studied her. "How does this place exist? It must be a private hospital."

"What it is, is unique." Dr. Maddy smiled, her gaze assessing. "Shall we sit and talk?"

She motioned to a deck with double French doors open. "I'm going to have a coffee, would you like one?"

"Yes, please." Tia brightened. "Any chance it's not regular hospital coffee?"

Maddy laughed. "No, it's not hospital coffee. Just as we take healing seriously here, we don't joke about our coffee. Go sit outside and I'll grab two cups."

Delighted at the idea, Tia walked outside and chose a chair close to the edge so she could look over the railing.

She hardly noticed when Dr. Maddy arrived with two cups of foamy coffees. "Whoa, nice."

"My own coffee maker," she said with a small smile. "I damn near live here, so I have the few pleasures that make my day that much more enjoyable."

"Smart." Tia reached over and blew the top gently. She loved coffee and lattes especially, but the thought of waiting for it to cool enough to drink was irritating. It smelled so good.

Dr. Maddy picked up her cup and had a sip. Her gaze was clear, peaceful and yet intent.

Well, she could study Tia all she wanted. She wasn't trying to hide anything. She went to pick up her cup and couldn't grab it.

She frowned and tried again. Her hand went right through the ceramic and hot liquid. This was just so not happening. Stunned, she slumped back into her chair and turned her gaze to Dr. Maddy.

"You didn't know?"

"Know what?" Tia said in a faint voice. "That I can't pick up a cup of coffee?"

"That you aren't in your physical body."

AS SHOCKS WENT, this one was big. Dr. Maddy studied the first major case of disconnection she'd ever seen.

That Tia had no idea made it even more interesting. She really didn't understand she was wandering around in her etheric body and not in her physical body. Maddy wondered how long she'd been able to do this, and if those around her knew.

She had the unique ability to look solid when wandering too. Most people would be fooled until they came closer. And when she was in contact with Dean, she became solid.

Something Stefan and Dr. Maddy had never seen.

Dean's energy somehow helped her.

It's one of the reasons she'd given him an errand and sent him away. To see what would happen when that connection broke. And she was seeing it now.

Tia stared down at the cup on the table. "I'm not going to be able to drink that, am I?" Her voice was so forlorn, Dr. Maddy laughed. "Not until you wake up. I promise you a cup when you do."

"Wake up?"

"Yes," Dr. Maddy said firmly. "Wake up."

Tia stared at her. "No, see I *was* asleep. Then I woke up. I'm awake now."

"You were asleep. Your etheric body woke up, left the

bed and wandered the floor."

"Not possible." Tia shook her head. "I saw people here. They saw me."

"Of course. So did I." She took a sip of coffee. "Did anyone notice you though?"

Silence.

Reluctantly, Tia shook her head. "No," she said softly. "They didn't. I thought I was just being really quiet."

At that Maddy's eyebrows shot up, and it was all she could do to hold her grin back. "And you were."

Tia rubbed her arms wrapped around her chest. "Where's Dean? I'd like to see Dean." Tia looked around as if searching for him. Her energy started to fizzle.

Maddy watched carefully at the proof of the connection between Dean and Tia. The bracelet was another big one. It would have affected them both – yet in different ways.

She really wanted Dean to be here right now too. So he could see Tia.

She'd bet a million bucks Dean didn't know the difference and wouldn't take the news kindly.

STEFAN WAS WAITING for Dean in the lobby when he returned to Maddy's Floor several hours later.

"Hey, Stefan. I didn't expect to see you here." Dean hadn't been able to stay away. He came back as soon as he could.

Stefan smiled. "It's necessary. I, we, Dr. Maddy and I need to speak with you for a few moments."

Dean's back went up. "Is Tia okay? Is she worse?"

"She's holding for the moment. Dr. Maddy spoke with her earlier. There was news that came as a bit of a shock to her, but she's taking it as well as can be expected." Stefan's voice turned wry. He turned and walked to the old style gilded elevator. "Let's go up."

"Sure, I only left because Dr. Maddy asked me for more information on Tia's background."

"And did you find anything?"

"She spent five years as part of a different kind of paranormal study. They likely already knew about some of her abilities. According to the brief I read, they were trying to duplicate her abilities. But what they put out there for the public to read and what went on behind closed doors are probably two different things."

"True enough. Does it give any other details about who was in the study with her, and where she went afterwards?"

"There'd been an accident and the study shut down apparently. But again, no details."

"No, there wouldn't be," Stefan said. "She believes that Dr. Ansell Wilhelm, the head of the project, died in an attack at the lab. I'm not so sure he did. If we could confirm that, it would help. Did you live anywhere close to that trailer park where Tia lived as a child?"

"No, thank heavens. That wouldn't have been a great childhood. A rough neighborhood that one."

"Hmmm."

The two walked into the elevator and pushed the button to go up. Dean looked at him. "Why all the questions?"

"Just wondering if there is a connection between you and Tia."

"No," Dean said in surprise. "I never met her before the hospital."

"Okay. I just wondered."

Dean paused. "Of course she looked familiar, but I

didn't really see it until later when she was in my house. She looks like a girl I rescued a few months back. Before all the crap in my world happened."

Stefan hit the stop button on the elevator panel. "Looks like?"

Dean frowned at him. "I doubt it was her. She appeared to have been attacked. I tried to talk to her, but she wasn't all there." He closed his eyes for a long moment. "She wore a hoody and had the hood over her long hair so I couldn't see much. It was also in the evening and it wasn't a clear sky. Honestly, she gave the impression of being a runaway teenager in trouble. Seemed to be in major distress. I called for an ambulance and never saw her again."

"That must be it." Stefan hit the button and the elevator continued its creaky climb. "I'd bet that was Tia. It only makes sense that there'd be a prior connection."

"Must be what?" Dean said in exasperation. "You're weird most of the time but since Tia, you're downright bizarre."

Stefan laughed. "If you only knew."

"Knew what?" And why wouldn't he just come out and tell him. It might have been Tia he'd seen. The more he thought on it, the more possible it became. Still, what difference did it make? "You're just as bizarre. You just don't know it."

The double doors opened to see Dr. Maddy waiting for them. "Good, you found him."

She turned and led the way back to the balcony.

Seeing Tia, Dean smiled with relief. "Hey, I'm so glad to see you awake and up. You look great."

Tia gave him a half smile, her gaze curious as she stared back at him. "I'm glad to be awake this much at least." Her comment confused Dean even more. Then she added in a low voice, "Thanks for caring."

The truth and pain in her words reminded him of her lonely childhood. He sat down on the chair beside her, reaching over to pick up her hand and smiled. "I do care. You're not as alone as you think."

She stared at their hands for a long moment, raised that shocked gaze to his then looked to Dr. Maddy and Stefan.

Dean knew something was wrong. He just didn't know what. "It's really irritating when you all know something I don't. I'm not used to feeling dense but around you two…"

"We don't want you to feel that way," Dr. Maddy said. "In this case, you are showing us something we've never seen before. And we don't know what to think. So it's for you to teach us."

He stared at the two of them. "More riddles."

Tia laughed. "They mean you can see me as if I were solid and real in front of you. Feel me as if I'm flesh and blood. Hold me as if I'm solid."

"What the hell does that mean?" He pulled back slightly. "What? Are you trying to say you aren't?"

She nodded. "I'm here in my etheric body only. My physical body is still in bed."

At his look of incomprehension, she added, "Something like being a living ghost."

Oh hell.

CHAPTER 17

"I WANT TO see my body." Tia stood up and ran. Straight past them. Dean unsuccessfully reached out a hand to stop her.

She stormed down the hallway back to her room and came to a screeching stop in the doorway. She looked in and saw herself sound asleep. In bed.

Not standing in the doorway like she thought she was.

"Actually, you are both. Remember it takes both to survive," Stefan said behind her.

"Easy for you to say," she said bitterly. "It's not like you're standing here without your body on."

He gave a bark of laughter, walked over to the visitor chair and sat down.

Then he stood up.

Leaving his body behind.

Oh shit. Oh shit. Oh shit.

She could feel her nonexistent heart pounding inside her nonexistent chest. She closed her eyes then opened them wide. He still stood in front of her and his body still sat in the chair beside her bed.

"This is so not happening."

"Of course it is."

"You never knew?" Dean said beside her, his voice curiously detached as he stared at Stefan seated on the chair. "I presume Stefan just did something odd."

"He left his body so he looks like Tia in ethereal form," Dr. Maddy said. "If you can see her, then you can see him."

"But I can't," Dean said in frustration. "I see him sitting beside the empty bed only."

Silence ensued. As one, all three people turned to look at him. He groaned. "Now what did I say?"

"Is that bed empty to you?" Tia asked in shock. "Really?"

He turned and studied the bed. After a moment he shrugged his shoulders. "I'm not sure what I'm seeing. The bedding is pulled up and sitting at an awkward angle, but there doesn't appear to be anything underneath. It's like you're invisible again."

"I'm underneath," Tia said. "How weird is that? He can see me in ethereal form but not in physical form right now."

"I don't know how," Dr. Maddy said, "but let's find out." She turned to Dean. "Walk over and hold both her ethereal and physical hands."

"How?" He looked at her, and then said dryly. "Remember I can't see her physical hand."

Tia watched as he followed Dr. Maddy's directions and eventually managed to pick up her physical hand.

"Now, Tia, go and hold his hand. Make sure you hold him with your right hand, the same hand your physical body is holding."

Tia stepped to Dean's side and placed her right hand in his.

Crackle!

"Whoa, what the hell was that?" Dean cried out.

"Now look at the bed and tell me what you see." Dr. Maddy said, her voice raised slightly, curiosity and excitement in the air.

But he was staring down at the hand in his. The nonexistent physical hand. "Holy crap. I can see her hand."

His gaze flew to the form on the bed and he swallowed – hard.

"This is some weird shit."

Stefan spoke from the far side of the room, "Dean, when you thought you saw her being attacked and you stepped up to help her, how long ago was that?"

"Just before I went off on physical leave myself."

"Physical leave," Dr. Maddy asked sharply. "What do you mean by that?"

He turned, but his gaze stayed on the bed. "I started having trouble with my vision, digestive problems and fatigue. The doctors thought I'd picked up a virus somewhere but couldn't pinpoint it. That's why I was doing a security stint at the hospital – I need the extra money. I'm no longer getting my full pay, but the bills didn't reduce with the income."

"And now?"

"And now what?" he growled. "What do you mean?"

Tia spoke from beside him. "She means do you still have those symptoms or have they improved?"

She watched him turn to face her, and his gaze grew wider. He dropped both her hands and bolted backwards. "Holy shit," he whispered. "What the hell is going on?"

HE STRAIGHTENED AND glared at her. He hated feeling like nothing made sense. But that was how he felt right now. Nothing. Made. Sense. "What happened to you?"

"What happened to you?" she asked curiously. "How do

I look to you now?"

"Like…" He stopped, at a loss for words, then continued in a rush, the words flying out of his mouth. "Like a ghost."

She grinned, at least he thought that was a grin. "Okay, so now things might be back to normal."

"How," he waved a hand at her, "is this normal?"

"We all have the ability to leave our bodies," Stefan said quickly from the other side of the room.

Dean cast a glance his way and caught his breath. His heart pounded against his ribs. What the hell was going on? "You too?"

Stefan nodded. He motioned to where his physical body was sitting. "Me too. I just do it consciously."

Dean shook his head. "This so can't be right."

"So now you see things normally again." Dr. Maddy's voice was thoughtfully curious.

"If *this* is normal," he snorted. "How you could figure that doesn't make any sense to me. But okay."

She laughed. "*This* is very normal."

"Why would holding her hand," he looked down at his now empty hands, "make any difference?"

"I'm not sure. But there is something about your connection to her."

He bypassed everything else and went to the heart of the matter. "What would have caused this disturbance in the first place? And is this why I spent the last month going from specialist to specialist without getting any help?"

"Quite likely, but until I know more I can't say for sure. But as your vision was affected, your perception would also be affected. Your balance and sleep patterns could be off, and you'd definitely be tired as your body struggled to right itself." She paused, then nodded. "For whatever reason, your body couldn't but would of course continue to try, and that would set up all kinds of issues inside."

He was shocked, relieved, delighted and incredibly confused. "I'd love to think I was back to normal. Hell, this is the first time I've ever taken a sick day, and I went down for weeks."

"Could you place the start of the problems after you helped Tia?" Stefan asked.

Dean shook his head. "Not that day, maybe not the next, but soon after I started to notice things weren't right. But they weren't necessarily very wrong. It was a slow decline until I couldn't function at work and at home. As nothing improved I did the rounds and rounds of doctors." He looked over at Dr. Maddy. "Are you taking on new patients?"

She laughed. "My patients are all here on this floor, but I do occasionally help other people."

"More than occasionally," Stefan murmured affectionately. "She's yet to turn anyone away who is in need." He motioned to Tia on the bed. "Tia is a good case in point."

"You called. I helped." Dr. Maddy gave him a special smile.

"But have you helped? Am I okay now?" Tia asked, her ghostly voice more of an echo than the clear ringing bell voice Dean remembered.

He gave a tiny head shake to clear his mind. "This is going to take some getting used to."

"Yes it will, but just think – your body can heal now. You should notice a visible improvement today."

He started. "That fast?"

Dr. Maddy nodded. "We still have to find out why this happened. But given that some things are starting to revert, we need to make sure it doesn't happen again. I did a scan on Tia's body looking for anomalies. Sounds like I need to do the same for yours. Maybe there was an energy switch in the visual cortex."

"Scan and energy switch along with visual cortex in the same sentence do not sound like something I want anything to do with."

She laughed. "Relax. It's painless. And harmless." At his look she smiled. "It's a visual scan. Nothing more. Honest."

Not sure if he believed her, he relaxed only slightly.

"Energy switch?" Tia said. "Are you saying when I was attacked, the attacker actually hurt Dean?"

"Quite possibly," Stefan said. "He might have intended to hurt you, but Dean got in the way."

"Or he was pissed at me and deliberately targeted me." Dean shrugged. "If we're talking Sci-Fi already then we might as well do Sci-Fi theories."

The others grinned.

An alarm sounded out of the hallway and Dr. Maddy bolted. "Sorry, have to do it later." And she was gone.

Dean looked over at Stefan to find him sinking into his body. He did a double take and watched as Stefan opened his eyes.

He gave a tiny wiggle and grinned. "That feels better."

Jesus.

Dean turned to Tia, but she wasn't making any move to her body. Lord, that sounded so wrong. "Are you going to do what he did," he asked, motioning toward the bed.

Tia shook her head. "I can't.

"Can't?" How the hell did that work? Stefan had managed easily enough. "If I hold your hand could you?" he asked, feeling like an idiot.

"I don't know," she said in surprise. "Maybe."

"Then let's give it a try." He held out his hand again and she placed her weird ghostly one in it before he reached across to pick up her physical hand. "Do it now," he said.

She shrugged and awkwardly lay down on top of her body.

CHAPTER 18

"I FEEL LIKE an idiot," she muttered as she lay on top of her body. She couldn't really feel anything.

"What happens if I let go," he said and dropped her etheric hand. "Is that easier?"

She closed her eyes and tried to sink herself inside her body. After a moment, she opened her eyes and realized she was still lying on top of herself.

They quickly tried various hand holding options, but the end result was she couldn't seem to rejoin her body. She caught Stefan grinning at them. "What's so funny?" she asked.

"You two. Returning to your body isn't physical, it's mental. Just think yourself back inside."

She glared at him. "That's not very easy you know."

"That's the trick actually," he admitted. "It is easy. You're making it difficult."

She snorted, lay back down, closed her eyes and thought, *let me be one with my body.*

And damn if the room didn't erupt in cheers.

She opened her eyes to see the same room but from a slightly lower position. She lifted a hand and saw the skin and nails looked right. She laughed. "I'm back."

"You are indeed." Dean grinned down at her. He reached out and held her hand, studying it. "This is what I thought I saw all along. Who knew?"

She grinned up at him, threw off her covers and sat up. "Whoa, dizziness."

"You need to assimilate slowly," Stefan said. "Adjust to the extra weight."

She shifted a little on the bed, more of a butt wiggle that had Dean smiling, and realized Stefan was right. "It is heavy. And clunky. And awkward."

"Life, this physical experience is all of those things, but it's also a gift. A precious experience you need to remember to appreciate. Too many people only realize the value of this gift when it's too late to fully experience it."

"Understood. Body, I need to take care of you." Still grinning, she hopped to her feet and walked around the room, stretching and twisting. "Damn that feels good."

"And just in time," Dr. Maddy said from the doorway. "I have a request to move up the arrival of my incoming patient."

Stefan stood up. "We can take our leave now."

Dr. Maddy nodded. "Let me know if I can help."

"If you get a moment, do a remote scan on Dean, and let's see if he's got something missing or added like we assumed Tia had."

"Understood." Dr. Maddy smiled at the three of them. "Glad to see things are back to normal now."

Tia walked over to the beautiful doctor. "Thanks so much. I don't know anyone else who could have helped."

"I think you need to thank Dean. He seems to have had the biggest impact on your healing."

Tia nodded. "Thank heavens. I'm sorry he was hurt when I was, but I'm very glad to see him here with me now."

She reached out, delighted when he reached back.

LOOKING DOWN AT their hands, Dean asked, "How much does any of this mess have to do with her body parts going missing. Is that still an issue?"

There was a collective silence for a long moment before Stefan shrugged. "No idea. She's all there at the moment. With any luck she might stay all there."

"What a ridiculous conversation," Tia said.

"And one you'll need to take outside." Dr. Maddy grinned and shooed them out of the room. "We have to get the bed ready, and I'll be busy doing the intake and initial assessment. If you want to talk still you can go back out on the balcony and visit."

"No, you've been wonderful. Thanks as always. We'll leave now," Stefan said.

With Stefan leading the way, they quickly went down the elevator and to the parking lot. It was the early hours of the morning. The sun was rising, but the world was still asleep.

"My place?" Dean asked.

"Sure. At least until I know what's next," Tia muttered. "Much of my world hasn't changed. I was attacked and I'm still in danger. My only friend is missing and could possibly be dead."

"Maybe, but now at least you are healthy enough to deal with what comes next." He looked over at Stefan. "Are you coming back to my place?"

"I'm wondering about going home and doing some research. Why don't you both come with me?"

Dean really just wanted to go home and rest but knew that wasn't likely on the agenda. He pulled out his phone to check the time and saw four new messages from his mother.

He quickly dialed her. "What's the matter?"

"Jeremy wasn't in his bed when I woke up at six this morning, I searched the house. He's nowhere to be found." She sounded hysterical.

Shit.

CHAPTER 19

TIA'S HEART SANK at the curt explanation as Dean cut off the first phone call then made a dozen more. He turned from being a warm caring individual with his own oddness to a flat stared, cold incredibly intimidating cop before her eyes.

In a way it was reassuring. When the situation demanded, he stepped up. His son was in trouble. Because of her? Surely this guy – whoever had messed her up – wouldn't go after a child to get back at her. Or was he paying Dean back for helping her? Different possibilities ran through her mind.

He'd have no problem hurting a child to get the results he wanted. He'd done it many times before, so if he was behind the kidnapping then there was a hidden game plan. He never did anything the simple way.

Dr. Wilhelm had been very particular that rules were followed correctly. Grant money depended on results, he'd say. Real money depended on real results, and the only way to get those was to have the protocol rules followed. He'd fired more than one tech over this.

She used to laugh over it because it made her feel superior to know that the crazy doctor had to follow someone else's bidding as she did his.

Not much fun at the time, but then she'd thought it was only short term and that he was trying to help her. Her parents were supposed to pick her up that first summer for the holiday, and she'd planned on never coming back. Only they never came. There'd been no contact since Christmas, and they'd missed every holiday in between. Still, there had been hope, until the doctor made it clear she didn't count. Her parents didn't want her. He was the only one who wanted her, and she was so much better off with him.

Like hell.

All she did all day long was get her arm pricked for new blood tests, and do demonstrations. Play with his stupid toys, even the fancy ones from some labs. Wilhelm had spent thousands of dollars on items that would affect her abilities. Sometimes her abilities changed, and she often got too tired to control her energy the way he wanted her to.

She tried to hide her abilities but it didn't always work.

He truly believed her quality of life improved with him. Maybe it had, at least in the beginning. When she entered puberty, her abilities had been erratic as hell. They'd also increased tremendously. She had to admit that as much as she hated him for what he was doing to her, he did it because he believed in her and that he could replicate the results artificially. He wanted to create applications for military use, medical use – although how her stupid ability to blend into the world around her would help anyone who was sick she didn't know.

But he figured the interests would be global. Unfortunately, he died before he achieved that goal.

Good thing for her.

He'd died in the lab. A kid attacked him, she'd heard. Chaos had reigned. When she'd finally managed to get the hell out of there, no one was left. She had walked right out of the damn place and never looked back. Over the years she'd been afraid that maybe that had been a rumor, and Dr. Wilhelm was still alive. Her biggest nightmare, that old fear that he'd somehow survived and would find her.

The only one she missed was John. She'd connected to him in a way she hadn't been able to others. He'd had some weird ability, but she didn't know exactly what it was. All she knew was that Wilhelm had been excited when John arrived.

John had been older than the other kids. And more developed. He'd been cute, approachable and for a hurting teen like her, he'd been a rock star. She'd crushed on him for weeks. He'd given her the bracelet she'd lost in that fight for her life. She'd been delighted, then he was gone.

She wondered what happened to him.

She remembered various names of the people who'd worked in his lab, but they were all students and she only knew them on a first name basis. They'd been much nicer than the long-term technicians, but just when she was at the point of being friends with them, they were gone the next day. It gave her quite a complex until she realized the good doctor was doing it on purpose to keep her isolated so she would stay close to him.

That wasn't possible. She already knew her life was never going to change if he had his way, so why get closer if he'd never let her go? Better to make friends with others and hopefully find someone sympathetic to her plight. Hell, people were letting animals out of testing laboratories all the time. Crazy groups were going in and breaking them out if there was no other way.

Why was no one breaking her out?

It took her years to understand the answer.

It was because no one knew she was a prisoner. They all just thought she volunteered.

She turned to look at Stefan. Fatigue had wrinkled the skin around his eyes. Also now there was a hum to his features as if something was alive she hadn't seen before. His eyes were brightly focused. He was in working mode.

He was looking for answers to the disappearance of Dean's son. He used his abilities to help others. Her abilities on the other hand were ridiculous. Oh wow, she could look like a wall.

So not helpful.

Her glance fell on Dean, once again back on the phone calling his mother.

"Good, I'm glad they are there already," he said. "I'm on my way." He was already walking toward the door.

She figured his whole world had collapsed. And she'd been forgotten. Maybe that was a good thing.

"Dean," Stefan called to him. "It's all related."

Dean carried on towards the door as if he hadn't heard. Tia looked over at Stefan, but his eyes were closed and he appeared to be relaxed, sleeping even. She frowned, not sure what to do. She stood, ready to take off after Dean and tell him what Stefan said, but he hit an invisible force and came to a shuddering stop.

He spun around. "What the fuck!"

"The energy in this mess is connected to Tia. We knew there was always a chance of him finding out about your involvement. But we hadn't considered they could easily track your mother and therefore find your son."

Dean looked at Stefan. "You helped my son before. Can you track him now?"

"If I can't, I know someone who can," he said. "He's a relatively new addition to my group, but he's a hell of hunter."

Tia looked at him closer. "Group?"

Stefan tossed her a casual look. "Group."

She was desperate to ask more questions, but Dean was already talking. "How do we get his help?"

"I've already contacted him." Stefan headed to the door. "I need to see the inside of the room Jeremy was taken from."

"I'm coming," Tia said, running after Stefan. "If this is because of me, I want to help."

"You're not going to be able to," Dean said. "You're just going to be in the way."

"We don't have time to argue. Let's go." She opened the truck door and hopped into the back seat. Stefan jumped into his car.

Dean threw up his hands and raced to join them.

WHAT THE HELL? Why were they all coming? Dean needed to focus on getting his son back. Not on all the rest of this shit. He knew that was important, but his son came first.

"We'll get him back, I can track his energy. He's in good health and relatively happy. At the moment he thinks he's on an outing with one of your friends."

Dean shook his head. "None of my friends would do this to him."

"No, but he doesn't know that."

"Damn it." He pulled the truck onto the main road and took two turns to find the road already blocked with cops. His spirits brightened. "Good, they're here already."

"Has an Amber Alert gone out?" Tia asked.

"Doing that right now. I have to confirm the description of the clothes he'd been wearing."

Stefan smiled. "Spider-Man pajamas."

"How did you know?" Dean glanced over at him warily. The things this man could do were freaking scary, but he was damned glad to have his help. "Where do we meet your hunter?"

"Hunter is on his way. He won't bother you. He needs to get the scent, then he'll take off again."

"Oh, he uses dogs."

"No," Stefan said with a smile. "He's just very smell and instinct oriented. Trust me, he's good at what he does."

Dean wasn't going to argue. If he had everyone out looking they'd find Jeremy easier and faster. Every moment counted. He pulled into the driveway and parked.

His mother detached from a large group of people and ran towards him, waving her hands, tears running down her cheeks.

"I'm so sorry," she cried out. "I don't know how he got in. The doors were locked, the security system was on, but this morning I found it off and the door open. I don't know how anyone could steal a child."

Dean took her in his arms. "It's not your fault, Mom. If someone wanted to get in, they'd get in regardless. I'm grateful they didn't hurt you in the process."

But that's not what she wanted to hear. "Maybe if they'd hurt me they'd have left him behind." The floodgates burst, and she buried her face against his chest.

He wanted to do the same thing but couldn't afford to indulge. The longer it took to find his son, the harder it became.

"I have to go inside," he told her gently, giving her a hug. "Tia is going to sit with you while I talk to the men."

TIA STEPPED UP and wrapped an arm around the woman, leading her inside to the living room of the small bungalow. The woman let herself be seated, although she curled up into a ball and rocked herself back and forth. "I'll make us a cup of tea," Tia said, not knowing how to help but needing to do something. Was there anything but tea to offer? She figured a hefty shot of brandy might do the trick, but if one wasn't used to it, it could be hard to get down.

Dr. Wilhelm had run a series of tests with her and various alcohols in an attempt to determine what helped and what hindered her abilities. None hindered the abilities, but too much affected her ability to control them. Duh.

He'd been consistent though in figuring out what affected her and what didn't. She couldn't do hard liquor at all. She'd gotten violently ill. A glass of wine was fine. But she didn't drink alcohol so none of it was a problem.

While the water was boiling, she stared out the window, watching men search the property and the neighborhood around her. Small picket fences dotted the backyards and every yard was being systematically checked.

Stefan walked into the kitchen. "Are you okay?" he asked. "We can't forget your own health in this emergency."

"I'm fine." She snorted. "Sure, as long as I don't focus on the fact that this happened because of me."

"Not because of you. He'll do whatever he needed to do to get at you. If this works, he's happy. If it doesn't, he'll try something else."

"Then let him have me," she whispered. "Use me as bait to get Jeremy back. I can't live with that on my conscience."

"It's too early for that, let Hunter do his thing first."

She stared at him in surprise. "Hunter is his name?"

Stefan nodded. "It's the one he's used for a long time."

"And he does this for a living?" Her curiosity of the man who hunted and belonged to Stefan's group piqued. Disgruntled, she realized she wanted to belong to his group. Or might if she knew what it was.

"It's for people like us," he offered as if understanding her thoughts, or had he read her mind? "We help each other and learn from each other. Several work with me on cases, and others I call on when I need a specialist."

"Like Hunter."

"Like Hunter." Stefan gave a small smile. "In truth Hunter would be pissed if he wasn't in on this one. It's right up his alley. He's on a mission to eradicate assholes like this one from the world."

"Then he has no family," she said. "There's no way he could do this kind of intense work if he had a wife and children."

"True. That would be a weakness to him. Something others could use against him."

"And he'd be right." Dean glared at Stefan. "That's exactly what's happened here."

"It is, but Hunter has already tracked them away from the house." Stefan waved an arm in the direction of the search going on around them. "This needs to happen just in case, but Hunter is already moving toward his target."

Tia gasped. "You mean he's found Jeremy?"

Stefan shook his head. "Not yet, but he's tracked them to Minion Mall."

"Why there?" Dean asked, pulling out his phone. "I need to talk to the captain. Get a team to go."

"Sure you do," Tia said. "But you also have to trust in Stefan. If he says Hunter is on the trail I'd be inclined to believe him."

Tia glanced over at Stefan. "We can go there, can't we?"

Stefan nodded. "And we need to go now."

Dean shook his head. "No. I'm bringing a team." He glared at Stefan. "No way is this guy getting away with this."

"You're forgetting something, Dean," Tia retorted. "I can go places most cops can't. I could go in and get out without being seen."

DEAN SPUN AND stared at her. His heart in his throat. It never occurred to him she could do something like that, but that was, in fact, exactly what she'd been doing all along.

"Holy crap." With a question in his eyes, he raised his gaze to Stefan.

Stefan nodded. "Yes, she should be able to do that just fine."

Hope bloomed. "That would be huge." Then reality set in. "But only if we know where he is."

"I'd trust Hunter if I were you." Tia said.

"Why is that?" he said, his voice dry. "I thought you didn't trust Stefan."

"I'm getting there," she muttered.

Stefan turned away. Dean watched as his gaze defocused as if he'd been talking to someone telepathically.

Then Stefan straightened. "McDonald's. They are in the restaurant at the mall."

Dean stared, his mind slow to process, and then he got it.

CHAPTER 20

TIA WATCHED DEAN rush toward her and Stefan. "We're taking my truck. Let's go."

They packed into the truck and took off with gravel spitting behind them. The mall was only a few blocks away. At the entrance, Dean slowed down and crept to the restaurant.

Stefan said, "Easy. We don't want anyone to know we're here. Hunter is inside. He needs time to scout out the place."

"Is my boy there?" Dean's voice was thin, thready.

Stefan hesitated, Tia turned to look at him. Then he gave a decisive nod.

"Do you have a photo of him," Tia asked quietly.

Dean shuffled papers beside him. He picked up his cell phone and held it back for her. His son's bright smile shone from the background. He was missing a front tooth. The twinkle in his eyes as he hugged his stuffed rabbit made her grin.

"Okay, I'll go see what I can see."

"Don't do anything stupid. If Hunter is correct and he's there, we have to stop this from becoming a hostage situation."

She snorted, hopped out and slammed the truck. Walking casually up to the side door she realized this guy would be looking for her so incognito started now. Up against the side wall, she rested her back to the wall and closed her eyes.

It helped to be able to pull her camouflage trick in private. Someone might be watching her, in fact, she sensed both Dean and Stefan's gazes. She frowned. Stefan was a whole lot closer than the truck. She shifted and opened her eyes. Stefan stood beside her, waiting.

Ready, he asked in her mind.

Surprised but willing she nodded. *I am.*

Let's go.

He waited for the next people to arrive at the door and both slipped inside behind them. Standing at the entrance Tia studied the packed restaurant. *I can't see him.*

Hunter said they are in the corner by the washroom.

They moved through the restaurant, her gaze darting from side to side. *Is Hunter here?*

Yes.

Can you see him?

No one sees Hunter unless he wants to be seen.

Sounds like my kind of guy.

Very different abilities.

Hmmm. She couldn't image. *There!*

She could see the little boy, he was stuffing a french fry in his mouth and trying to share with the rabbit. *He's got his bunny with him.*

According to Dean, he takes it everywhere.

Good, it helps identify him.

She froze. *I don't see his kidnapper.*

Stefan sucked in his breath. *It could be a trap. Don't move.*

I'm not, but you know the choices are limited.

No. We have more than you think, he warned. *Don't do anything stupid.*

Not going to. But she had to save the little boy. He'd

been taken because of her. She studied the other patrons. *He's on the other side, about four booths behind Jeremy. I think I saw him on the street six weeks ago when I was attacked.*

Must be him.

Or a coincidence.

No such thing, Stefan said flatly. *I'm telling Dean.*

Good, you do that. I'm getting Jeremy. And she slipped away.

DEAN HATED WAITING. This was too damn important. It was his boy. Guilt ate his insides. He should never put his son in danger. He pounded the steering wheel. This shouldn't have happened. His family should have been safe. It was never a problem before. Until he met Tia.

It wasn't her fault.

I know that. But damn it…if anything happens to Jeremy.

I'm thinking this is almost a done deal.

What's a done deal? All of sudden he froze inside the truck and turned to face Stefan. *Damn it. You know that freaks me out when you talk to me inside my head. Yet here you are sitting like a zombie beside me. But you're not here, are you?*

Yes I do. Get used to it, Stefan snapped. *I'm inside the restaurant with Tia. Hunter has just gone outside.*

Dean peered through the windshield. *What does Hunter look like? I can't see anyone.*

And you won't. He's only seen if he wants to be seen.

Easy to say. Damn it. How the hell are you doing that? He groaned. *Never mind,* he said. *How's Jeremy?*

He's fine and is sitting alone at a table eating fries.

Alone? he asked incredulously.

Yes. Tia thinks a man sitting back four seats was there the night she was attacked.

What? Enough of this shit. He needed to have a face for this asshole. Better to punch his fist through the guy's jaw if he knew which was his. The team pulled into the mall. Shit. They were here already.

Tia is beside Jeremy.

What about the kidnapper? We need to grab him or no one is going to be safe.

Hunter is on that.

Dean hopped out. *I'm walking in.*

No.

He froze. *Why not?*

The asshole is on his way out. There was a pause. *Hunter says to go to the other side. He's heading there.*

And Tia? He asked as he bolted around the back of the restaurant.

She's approaching Jeremy now.

IDIOTS.

Like he was going to hang around and wait for them to tap him on the shoulders and say, "Gotcha." Better he disappeared and for them to get the message. *I can access who I want anytime I want.*

Not that they were smart enough to do that. In fact, he might have to leave them a bigger message next time. He wanted Tia. He'd do what he had to do to get her, but he wanted her willing.

The two of them had unfinished business.

What the hell did that damn cop have to do with anything? Why cops? Tia would never have gone to them. Not willingly. She'd been honed and conditioned against them for years. They all had been.

This didn't make sense. She couldn't have changed that much over the years.

Then he shrugged. So what if she had. He'd just beat it right back out of her.

He had a lot of bones to pick with her.

But there was time. He'd get to them all eventually.

First he was going to get the hell away from this place.

Cops gave him the hives.

CHAPTER 21

TIA STOPPED BESIDE the little boy and casually draped her arm along the back of the chair. "Hi, are you here alone?"

Jeremy's eyes grew wide and he nodded his head. "He's coming back, he said."

"Oh good." She watched him shift slightly closer to his bunny. "What's your pet's name?"

"Dozer," he said gleefully, giving him a big hug, continuing to chatter. "He's mine, my dad gave him to me."

"He's cool." She smiled. "Sounds like you have a great dad."

"He's awesome," Jeremy shouted. "He's the best."

She laughed. "Are you ready to go see him? He's outside."

Jeremy looked outside, craning his neck to see his father. "Really? How come he's not in here?"

"He's talking on the phone and it's too noisy inside."

"Cool." Then his lower lip trembled. He lowered his voice and said, "The man said I have to stay here."

"And the man said I could take you outside."

Jeremy brightened and held up his arms.

Her heart aching, she wrapped her arms around him, bunny and all. She stood up and blended into the interior. Choosing the closest exit, she walked carefully forward, determined to get this little boy out safely.

Holding her energy tight to her chest, she made it to the door in record time.

Outside she could feel her body tremble with the effort.

You're doing great, Stefan said calmly inside her head. *Take a left and head for the truck. Dean has gone after the kidnapper.*

I think he's ditched us, she whispered, trying to preserve her strength.

Maybe, but maybe he didn't ditch Hunter.

She crept forward trying to avoid any scenario that would involve the boy seeing his father attack a man or be attacked. He'd been through enough already. Only her strength wasn't holding.

Slowing and scared, she knew she still had a distance to go, and her heart pounding, she knew she was in danger of not making it.

Something is wrong, she whispered. *I don't know what or why.*

Wrong how? With you? With Jeremy? With the area around you? Stefan snapped, looking for answers.

With me, she cried. *Where are you? I don't feel so good.* She started to run. To Stefan. To Dean. To anyone who could take care of Jeremy.

Fast.

I'm falling, she cried out.

I've got you, Stefan said, strong arms grabbing her. *Drop the shield.*

Instantly her senses reasserted themselves. She looked around, trying hard to stay on her feet. Stefan held her and Jeremy.

Jeremy took one look at who held them and cried, "Stefan."

"Hey, Jeremy, nice to see you again. How are you feeling?"

"Awesome sauce," he cried and reached out to grab Stefan and hugged him hard.

Dean came running.

"Hey, Jeremy."

"Daddy."

Then everything went woozy and Tia sagged hard against Stefan.

Can't make it.

And she succumbed to the darkness.

DEAN CAUGHT HIS son as he launched himself from Stefan into his arms. He shuddered, his arms closing tightly around the tiny body. Tears burned his eyes. God it had been close. Too close. He didn't know what was going on, but if there was ever motivation needed to hunt this asshole down, the kidnapper had given him the perfect one. Put his family in danger, would he? It was not going to happen twice.

He'd kill the bastard before he got a second chance.

"Dozer doesn't like french fries," Jeremy announced. "But I bet she would."

"Who's she?" he asked, having trouble following his son's train of thought.

"The nice lady who carried me out here."

Dean smiled. "You know something, I bet she does. Maybe we should invite her to have some with us."

Jeremy grinned. "We're going to have to wait until she wakes up from her nap first," he announced with his typical aplomb.

Dean spun around looking for Tia and found he was alone, except for the gang of cops heading his way. "Did you see her fall asleep?"

"Yes, she looked so tired, she just closed her eyes and fell, but Stefan caught her." Jeremy laughed. "That's how I'm going to go to sleep from now on." He giggled. "And you can catch me and carry me to bed."

Dean grinned. "I'd love to – once. After you give me lots of warning. Otherwise, I might not catch you."

"Ha. Stefan caught her," Jeremy complained. "And she didn't warn him."

"Sure she did," Dean said, looking around the parking lot for Stefan and the sleeping Tia. He hoped they were in the truck. "You just didn't hear her." Motioning to his buddies, Dean casually carried Jeremy over to his vehicle. He should probably have his son checked over by the medical professionals to make sure the kidnapper didn't do anything to him, but given his alert, happy disposition all he'd have to contend with was an overdose of french fries in his small tummy.

At the truck he saw Stefan standing on the far side. He was talking on the phone.

"No, it's not a normal sleep. She's out."

Dean raced over, Jeremy bouncing in his arms. "How is she?" he asked in a low voice as he set Jeremy in the front of his truck.

"Out cold," Stefan muttered.

Damn it. He peered into the back seat. She was stretched out on the seat, her knees hanging off the end. They'd have to shift her upward to be able to close the door. Her skin had a waxy pallor. He reached down and grabbed her hand. "She's really cold," he said in surprise. Jeremy popped up on his feet, a blanket in his hand. "For the lady."

Dean gave his son a warm hug. God he'd never get enough of those chubby arms around his neck and said, "Thanks, Jeremy."

He took the tiny blanket and spread it over Tia's chest. He glanced at Stefan and mouthed, "What's wrong?"

Stefan shrugged. "No idea. Why don't you grab her hand and see if there is an improvement."

Dean searched his features. "Okay." He reached down and picked up Tia's hand. The coolness of her skin was concerning. As was the laxness. He understood unconsciousness but in this case it was as if there was a lack of substance to her.

How that could be, he didn't know. It was concerning. Holding her hand in his, he watched her features, hoping for a change.

"She's here, right?"

"She's here," Stefan murmured. "But she said her energy was failing before she went down. As if too weak to do what she was doing. I caught her just before she collapsed."

"Did she do anything different than any other time?" Dean asked. "Use any different energy. I know that sounds crazy, but…"

"Nothing is crazy in this business," Stefan said. He glanced over at Jeremy and smiled…and froze. "Shit," he said under his breath.

Dean glanced from Stefan to Jeremy and back again. "No shits allowed, tell me what's wrong and it damn well better not involve Jeremy."

Keeping his voice low, Stefan said, "Let me see the stuffed animal."

Dean looked over at Dozer. He looked as normal and ratty as ever. He'd tried several times to separate Jeremy from the animal but he hadn't succeeded. "What about it?"

"I'm thinking there is something…off with it."

"Off? Off how?" Dean reached over and picked up Dozer as an unconcerned Jeremy played with the coins in the pocket on the dash. He gave the stuffy a quick search over but there wasn't any tears or repairs to it that he could see. In fact, he looked normal.

He held it up to Stefan. "Looks fine." He glanced over at Stefan only to see an odd look come over his friend's face. "What is it?"

"It's got a negative energy on it. It will damage anyone's energy over time, but in this case, with Tia. It's doing its damage now."

"How?" Confused and worried, Dean looked at the stuffy and back at the comatose woman. "Surely this thing can't be doing that kind of damage."

"I can feel it from here," Stefan said. "Now that I know it's energized that way, I can protect myself for a little bit at least."

"And Tia?" Dean said. "Jeremy loves this thing."

"Which makes it a great weapon," Stefan murmured, staring at the stuffed animal like it was a viper about to strike. "Oh…"

At the change in his voice, panic reached out and pinched his stomach. Dean said, "Oh, what?"

"The energy is changing. It's balancing back out again."

Dean snorted. "None of this made any sense to begin with, but now it really isn't making any sense. How could it do that?"

"You. You're doing it. You're saving Dozer for Jeremy."

STEFAN COULD FEEL the energy pulsing, searching as the

changes that Dean had unknowingly made weakened. Waves of weak wrongness drifted in his direction. He deliberately pulled his own energy in tighter, snug up against his body.

This energy had a foreign atmosphere to it. Something damaged. Yet also seeking to heal. He frowned at the undulating waves drifting from the bunny. They weren't strong. They weren't specific. They were…pathetic.

Wondering, he pulsed a little healing energy into the center of the waves. Instantly his energy was absorbed. And the other energy strengthened. But was it strengthening in a good way or was he adding good energy to be converted to bad? He hadn't added enough to see. He pulsed a little more. The energy flared then settled slightly.

Interesting. He pulsed more into the center of the bunny. What could take energy and turn it to something bad? Energy was energy. If this was a switch from positive to negative then an actual breakdown of the energy molecules must have happened.

Therefore, positive energy once applied should shift the balance back again.

Did he know how to do that? And even if he didn't, all nature seeks balance, all nature seeks to heal. So in theory if he gave it positive energy, then it should rebalance and re-heal itself.

But it was a gamble. He didn't know what caused this so if he didn't have enough of what it was looking for, he could be making the scenario worse.

That was fear talking. Closing his eyes he tracked the energy back to the bunny and found an odd metal ball shoved deep inside. He carefully wrapped the ball in energy, gifting it with strong healing vibes and love. Always love. Fear was the absence of love and in that situation all negativity thrived. Fill the void with love and all turned to glorious positivity.

A hard lesson to learn.

He carefully imbued his wrapping with joyous love of all things. Then slowly unwrapped the ball.

It pulsed in a normal manner.

The energy had reversed.

So Dean's overwhelming relief and love for his boy had affected the ball, just not enough to heal it fully.

But it still needed to come out. Using his senses, he tracked the slight trail the ball had made as it was shoved deep inside the bunny. It was tiny, like shot from a shotgun. Unnoticeable in most scenarios. Certainly for most people, unnoticeable in this situation.

He opened his eyes and reached for the bunny.

And damn it if it didn't send out a shock wave.

"Shit," he murmured, shaking his fingers. "That stung."

"What did?" Dean asked, frowning at him. "I can't feel anything."

Stefan opened his vision to include Dean's energy, and sure enough, he'd been surrounding the bunny in bright positive energy so it wouldn't hurt Tia. He likely hadn't known and now that the ball was fine, he hadn't turned down his output.

"Shut down the energy a little, will you please," Stefan asked as he watched the frown on his friends face and the automatic lowering of the power he'd used to keep Tia safe. Very interesting.

"I don't know what you mean," Dean said, staring at the bunny. "I'm not doing anything."

"Yes you are, or were rather, as you've corrected it now." Stefan laughed. "Take them home and look after them." He turned toward his car. "I'll follow."

CHAPTER 22

T IA WOKE UP with her back sore and her muscles aching.
She groaned and tried to roll over.

"Easy. We're almost home."

She reached up with both hands and rubbed her face. Memories of Dr. Maddy, Jeremy and the seriously bad morning filled her brain. "That's nice." Whose home?

She knew she didn't have one. She'd been staying with Simone. Now she had nowhere. Before leaving Land's Edge, she'd given away all her stuff but the few items she'd carry with her. She hadn't owned much. Possessions didn't mean anything to her. And given that she'd lived a nomadic street life, she'd learned to live light and stay that way. So far nothing had changed.

Except now these bastards had gone after an innocent boy.

That was enough. First Simone and now Jeremy.

Opening her eyes, she stared at the roof of the truck.

Her body had that "drained" feeling after a horrific emotional shock, only worse. Why? She remembered getting Jeremy out of the restaurant and finding her energy evaporating quickly. She'd barely made it another couple of steps. She vaguely remembered Stefan grabbing for her and Dean taking Jeremy. Now she wondered how she was supposed to stay safe if she kept passing out.

She'd end up in the hospital and then in a psych ward. Then back on the streets, without family or medical insurance. And in tougher shape.

Not the future she'd envisioned for herself.

The truck came to a gentle stop. Dean turned off the engine. She wondered if he had pulled off to the side of the road and was ready to ask her to leave.

Leave the truck. Leave his life. Leave his son well the hell alone.

She wouldn't blame him.

Shoving the regrets deep inside, she sat up then grabbed her head for the dizziness. With a stifled moan, she slid to the side of the truck and the open door.

Dean waited for her. He helped her down and steadied her while she gained her feet.

They were at his house.

His mother was there, bawling buckets over having Jeremy safe in her arms. Tia could relate. She felt like crying herself. Dean held her close for a moment. She wished she knew what was wrong. She was weepy, tired, feeling off. And that so wasn't her.

She'd always had a clear plan, even if that only meant hiding and staying hidden.

She had no idea what to do now. Surely that was why she was feeling like this.

"Take it easy, you were out cold for at least fifteen minutes."

She nodded. "Seems like I'm doing a lot of that lately."

"Not a problem," he said easily with a gentle smile. "You can stay here as long as you want until you feel better."

Surprised, she stared up at him. "What? I figured you were going to ask me to leave now."

"You saved my son. Why would I be so callous as to ask you to leave now?" Anger filtered into his voice. "That's a hell of a way to say thanks."

"I'm responsible for that man coming after him in the first place," she said in astonishment. "I did what I could to fix the scenario, but no one in his right mind is going to want me to stay around."

His jaw clicked closed and a tick played out on his cheekbone. "I don't desert those in need, and I never forget something like someone saving my son's life."

"Then you need glasses because you aren't seeing the cause of the problem in the first place," she muttered.

"I know exactly who is responsible and it isn't you," he snapped. "That's enough of that. We'll hunt this asshole down together so both of us can get our lives back."

She stared up at him, relief coursing through her. Did he mean it? She searched those dark unfathomable eyes wondering if he was too good to be true. She hadn't met very many men she'd trust and none that would have helped her like this. She hadn't known they really existed.

And did she dare trust him now that he was in front of her? Maybe.

Then he did something that blew her away.

He lowered his head and kissed her.

As he raised his head, she stared at him in shock. "Why did you do that?" she whispered.

"Because it seemed like the right thing to do," he answered with a shrug, a lost look to his face as if he truly didn't know what impulse had driven him.

She smiled. "It was nice."

Light flared in his gaze and he lowered his head again. She leaned into the warmth of his arms. The safety, the caring, the novelty – at least for just a moment.

Warmth spread through her body, heating the chilly spots inside. Sad to think there were more cold spots than anything else. But her life had been a mess. Lonely and alone for so long, she'd forgotten the joy of being held. The joy of belonging to someone. To know she was loved and cared for.

And Dean made her want it all over again.

She pulled back.

"Daddy, did you kiss her owie better?"

Dean grinned. "I did. She's feeling much better."

He turned, slung an arm over her shoulders and tugged her toward the house. For some reason – most likely the revelation of what was being dangled in front of her with the knowledge she couldn't have it – she slowed her feet. She had no business being here. Putting his family in danger. The best thing she could do was run. She knew how to do that. She'd been doing it for a long time.

His hand firm on her shoulder, tugged her forward. "No more running. You need a place to regroup. Create an action plan. Let the cops do their thing. You have a place here. A safe place."

"No, it's not safe," she muttered. "He will find you here."

"Good. Let him. We'll be ready."

There was something in his voice that had her looking at him intently. "Are you thinking to set a trap?"

"Sounds like a plan."

It did. Just not a great one. She'd always found running worked best.

SHE LOOKED READY to bolt. He just had to coax her inside.

Let her relax a little. Convince her to trust him. Not an easy thing to do given that his son had been kidnapped and she'd been knocked out a time or two.

But they were all safe for the moment, and that gave him a second chance. To secure his family. To help her. To get the asshole that endangered them all.

Because he'd had enough of running. He was all about going on the attack and taking care of business before business took care of him.

But he had to find the bastard first.

An unmarked police car pulled up as he walked to the front of his house. He pushed Tia forward. "Go and have a cup of tea, a bite to eat. You need to rest."

He waited until she climbed up the stairs and entered. Then he turned and walked to where his partner waited, leaning against the car. "Jones, what have you got?"

"No fingerprint match so far. We have him on video. He's been identified as Torrence Vladrong. He was a student with Wilhelm's program."

"So he was there with Tia?" Dean frowned. "Then why go after her?"

"Is he going after her?"

"I don't know what else he'd want." Dean stared at Jones. "Sorry, not sure what I'm saying. It's been a long morning. All I know is the asshole could have hurt my son. He could have taken him and run. He didn't. Why?"

"He didn't want the boy. He didn't want to hurt him," Jones said.

"I think it was a message. That he could take what he wanted when he wanted."

"Why? What does he want?"

"That's what I want to know."

The two men leaned against the car, both deep in thought.

"Any news on Simone?" Dean asked.

"No. And Brennan was killed by a single gunshot to the heart," Jones said. "No sign of a fight. No defensive wounds."

"And no gun left behind?"

"Not that we've found yet."

"So Simone has either been taken or is in the wind." Dean hoped for the latter.

"We're searching for her but no leads yet."

Dean frowned. "Two vehicles were available in the garage, and yet she didn't take either."

"No. So she either couldn't or realized they'd be tracked and went under the grid."

"Where? And why? Is she part of this or playing her own game?"

"Or did she take an opportunity to get out of a bad situation and disappear," Jones said.

"We aren't going to know that until we find her."

"If we find her."

"And Vladrong." Dean frowned more fiercely. "What are we doing to find him?"

"Everything we can. We have his picture, his name, it's out everywhere. But until we get a lead then we're all waiting for the status quo to change."

"Why would he have allowed us to identify him? To see his face?"

"Because he doesn't care?" Jones suggested. "He has a place to hide. A way to get underground? He was sent by someone else? He doesn't understand the danger?" Jones threw up his hands. "I don't know. I'm just throwing out ideas."

"Any and all of them could work." Dean hated the unknown. The questions without answers. The too many pathways and no direction. When they caught their man, they could usually figure out the answers but often it wasn't that easy. Often there wasn't an answer. Often it was backbreaking work to fill in the answers as to what had really happened and why.

Life didn't always cross the Ts and dot the Is. But they had to figure out why Tia was so important to this man – or else they'd figure out this man's motives. Without that, there was no way to know what drove him. Or predict what he'd do next.

Or when he made a mistake.

And Dean needed him to make a mistake.

"How are you feeling these days?"

Dean knew what he was asking. "Much better. I should be back to work soon."

Jones straightened, a big grin on his face. "Awesome." He high-fived Dean. "That's freakin' awesome. I've been waiting for you to get back to the job for over a month now. Sucks being without you."

Dean laughed. "Glad to hear that. I still have to get the clearance from the doctor, but I feel much better these days and all the weird symptoms are gone."

"Damn, that's good." Jones rubbed his hands. "So what, a day or two? A week? I need something to look forward to."

"As soon as we find this asshole that kidnapped my boy." He shook his head. "I can't leave him now."

"Nope, but you have more resources to hunt him down from the inside."

"That's why I have you," Dean said. "And you can do

that while I protect my family."

Jones motioned to the doorway of Dean's house. "Stefan is here? How the hell did you manage that?"

"Yeah, he's been helping." Dean looked toward his house. Stefan stood in the doorway searching the street and looking at the house. "What is he looking for?"

"I was going to ask you that question," Jones said. "I've got to go back to the office. There's a hell of a lot of paperwork to take care of now. I'll be back to get your statement. If you could write it down in the meantime that would be huge. You know how this works. You never know what you know until we get all the information together."

Dean nodded. "Right. I'll get the others to write down everything they saw too."

Jones nodded and headed around to the driver's side of his vehicle. "We're on this. Keep your family safe."

Dean nodded as his buddy drove away. "That was the plan from the beginning," he said softly to himself, "but apparently I didn't do so good."

"You did fine," Stefan said from behind him.

Dean spun around.

"I'm heading home. I need some rest. I've put up a guard around the house. As long as you are all inside, you should be safe from this guy. But that protection can't ever be a hundred percent as more and more abilities keep coming up and we never know what people can do."

"Got it." Dean looked to the house. "They're all inside?"

"All three of them, yes. You might want to consider sending your mother and son away for a week or two."

"If they'd go."

"They'd go. It's safer out there than it is here right now. Your mother has also been through a huge shock. She needs time to get over this. Your son has no idea how close he's come. Keep it that way. He needs normal for a long time."

"Right." How the hell was he supposed to give his son normal in a world gone crazy? He had to protect him. That meant get him out of here. "I'll send my mother and son back East. She can go visit her old friends and extended family."

"That would be good. And book the tickets under someone else's name, right?"

"Christ," Dean said, wiping the sweat off his face. "I need to catch this asshole fast." Remembering his conversation with Jones, he looked over at Stefan. "Any idea why he wants Tia?"

Stefan shook his head. "Not yet. I'm not even sure he's working alone."

"I'm wondering if he is a dupe in all this. Sent to retrieve her any way possible."

Stefan stared at him, his eyes defocusing. "Quite possibly. But then why didn't he? He just left. Without any of us. So more of a message? A warning? And with Wilhelm dead — you said he is, right? — then who is pulling his strings?"

"That's the question, isn't it? And more importantly, why? What could they possibly want with her that they haven't already gotten?"

CHAPTER 23

"**I** DON'T BELONG here." It was like the fourth time Tia had said that same thing out loud. No one had listened to her before. And they still weren't listening to her. "I need to leave."

"Nope. Not going to happen," Dean said.

She picked up the sandwich he'd made for her and took a bite. She needed the food, the energy, but she really didn't need the cold implacable silence over her statement. She didn't belong here. She'd stay for a day or two and get a handle on what was happening, but after that she was done. She'd sneak out and disappear. Just like she'd always done.

"I know that look. No, you aren't sneaking away. No more running. We put your running shoes away officially now."

She stopped, sandwich slowly lowering. "Sorry?"

"No more running." He took a big bite and stared at her, the look in his eyes firm yet humorous. "So stop coming up with excuses to make your exit graceful."

"She doesn't have running shoes, Daddy," Jeremy said, giggling. "We can't hang them up."

"Quite true." And he smiled, his gaze never leaving her face. "Right, Tia?"

She narrowed her gaze. "Not fair enlisting help."

He grinned and took another bite. "I'll do whatever it

takes."

She rolled her eyes. "Why do you care?"

That gaze narrowed. "Because I do. And so do you. You don't want to keep doing this."

"No, I want to be normal. But normal doesn't happen to people like me."

"It can."

Tears welled up in her eyes. "No, it can't."

With a warning glance over at Jeremy, Dean said, "We'll talk about it later."

"No, we won't." She bit into her sandwich. "This is really good. Thanks."

"You helped make it." He grinned.

Jeremy giggled. "She made all of them."

Dean laughed. "So she did."

The rest of the meal finished quickly. Then Dean excused himself and went to his office to make some phone calls.

She wanted to go with him but knew she wouldn't be allowed. Besides, she was going to hang with Jeremy for a few hours while he napped. She was pretty exhausted. She'd also heard a little of the conversation from Dean and his mom, Gillian, that she and Jeremy would be leaving soon. Going back East to visit friends and family.

That was the best idea she'd heard yet.

So she'd keep Jeremy occupied for a few hours while Gillian recuperated and Dean got plans together. She stood up and collected the dishes. "Jeremy, what do you want to do for the next little bit? Play some games, watch television…" She left it open ended.

"Cartoons," he cried at the top of his lungs. "Now. Can we go now?"

"Sure thing." She grinned, loving his enthusiasm. "Give me a minute to finish cleaning up."

"Kk."

She wiped the table. Dean was in the office and appeared to be on the phone. He'd likely be there for awhile. "Okay, take me to it."

He giggled and dancing all the way, led her into the family room and a huge television with a big sound system. The biggest set of speakers she'd ever seen stood on either side of the television and glancing around the room, she saw two more. She snorted. Typical male.

The TV was on within minutes, and she settled down for a couple of hours of cartoons. While watching, she wrote up her statement of the morning's events.

Hours later, she shifted her position to realize Jeremy had fallen asleep on the couch beside her. She grabbed a blanket and covered him up. Then she got up and went in search of Dean. There was such a normal atmosphere to the day now. As if the morning had never happened. She knew different, but this casual family atmosphere made her want something more. Something for herself. Something like this.

And it so wasn't going to happen.

She walked toward the office and heard Dean in conversation. "I know I've been off for a month. But I'm fine now. I can go back to work full-time. I need to be on this case."

"You need to let us handle it."

"Not going to happen." Dean's voice was hard, defiant.

"Damn it, Dean, I know this is your family and I know this is you, but we have teams of men working on it. We'll get him. You focus on keeping your family safe. So go East with them and we'll take care of Tia."

And then silence. Tia strained to hear more then realized

the other voice had been on speakerphone. And had now been muted. Shit, had she made too much noise? Let him know she was here? That wouldn't be good. But at least she knew the department wanted him to leave too. She was in full agreement. As for the same department keeping her safe. Like hell.

She walked around the corner and saw Dean and a stranger sitting in his office. How had he gotten in without her knowing? But it did explain the reason for the speaker-phone. She nodded at the newcomer and gave Dean a tight smile. "He's right you know. Leave with your family and keep them safe."

He snorted. "Trust you to listen in on conversations when you aren't supposed to."

"It was a little loud, sorry," she said in a cheerful voice. Well, she wasn't sorry and there was no one in that room who would mistake her tone of voice for anything else. "So what…are you going to go into protective custody and let them look after you?" she asked. "See, I don't trust the cops anymore than I trust the assholes who kept me locked up. I'll never forget it was a cop who delivered me back to the lab in the first place."

"What?" Dean roared, standing up. "What are you talk-ing about?"

"I'm talking about having escaped while in Wilhelm's program and the cops returning me. Excuse me if I don't put too much faith in them now."

The stranger stood up. "My name is Jones and I work with Dean. You do realize he's a cop – right?"

DEAN WATCHED THE mix of emotions cross her face. He

hadn't known her very long, but the expressiveness of her face was endearing. From shock, to horror, to sheer disgruntlement. She shot him a dirty look, spun on her heels and walked away.

"Uh oh," Jones said. "I guess I shouldn't have told her?"

"Don't worry about it. She knows but is having trouble with the concept. We just haven't had much time to talk."

Jones snickered. "So what have you been doing since you met her?"

Dean rolled his eyes and chased after Tia. She'd returned to the couch and dropped down beside his son. She stared at the ceiling as if trying to process the information and not liking the outcome.

"Hey, I'm sorry I didn't tell you. It didn't occur to me you didn't know."

"I did know but I tried to forget it. Besides, you acted like a cop at the hospital, but you were a guard there," she accused.

"At the time I was working as a guard for Stefan. I wasn't a cop in that role."

She nodded. "And when you said you'd been on leave it had been from the force?" Her head rolled to the side, looking for a visual confirmation.

He nodded. "Since not long after you were attacked."

"And that night weeks ago, when I was attacked…" she said bitterly. "What the hell was that all about?"

"I was trying to save you. You were alone on the street corner and having some kind of psychotic fit. What was I supposed to do? You were frozen on the spot and looked like your whole world had collapsed. Of course I came and helped."

She stared at him. "I was under attack."

Dean glanced behind him but couldn't see his partner. Jones wasn't into drama and the full extent of his relationships were humps and bumps in the night with not even a greeting the next morning. That's the way he liked them. Dean couldn't imagine anything worse. He turned his attention back to Tia and nodded. "Remember, I was also attacked. I didn't understand anything I saw or heard. You were in so much pain, but there was no one else there with us."

"Now you know better. But you were there though, right?" she questioned him as if she had to reexamine everything she knew about him in light of his career choice. As long as she came down on the side that all was good then he was fine with it.

"I was. I thought I saw someone following you. Then another man walking past you but soon after – as in right after – you had this weird frozen-can't-move-and-my-life-is-over event."

She snorted. "That's pretty damn close. Then you called for help and were attacked at the same time. Now six weeks later we find each other again. I'm in a psych ward and you're my guard. How do you think that makes me feel?"

He had no clue. "I didn't know it was you I was guarding," he said, quietly. "Stefan didn't give me any details. Just said you needed protecting and if I saw anything unusual to take it in stride."

A broken laugh slipped out. "Yeah, weird, that's me."

"No, but I did see something weird," he said in a low voice. "I saw a beautiful woman who'd been dealt a rough hand in life and who had some crazy abilities to go with it. I didn't recognize you. I didn't know you but in a way I knew you."

"That would be the energy stuff. Whatever hit you was a part of what hit me and our energy will automatically recognize each other now." She shot him a warning look. "And just in case you have any ideas of knowing me, you're wrong. You don't know anything about me."

"And you know nothing about me," he said, his voice cooling. "I'm a cop. Inside and out. But I'm not a bad guy." He took a deep breath. "And there could have been many reasons why that other cop took you back to Wilhelm. Not all of them because he and all his cohorts are assholes."

She glared at him. "Maybe not, but I think he was paid to return me. A reward or a payout. I don't know and I don't care. Cops are dirty."

Now he was getting pissed off. "No, a few, a small number of cops are dirty. The same as a few, a very few psychics are bad. If you can become invisible and walk into a bank and walk out with as much money as you can carry, you might not do that, but you know perfectly well there are other people out there who would." He was on a roll now. "And just because this cop was wearing a uniform and driving a cruiser doesn't mean he was a cop. He could have been an ex-cop."

She glared at him.

He glared at her.

Jones broke the silence from several feet behind them. "So when's the wedding? You two are acting like you're married already."

She gasped and color washed up her neck.

Dean groaned. "Shut up, Jones."

He chuckled. "Yeah, I'm heading back to the office now. Unless you two have anything to add?"

Both Dean and Tia shook their heads. "Everything is in

the statement I gave Morgan already," Tia said. "Thanks for coming."

Jones grinned at her. "No problem. Keep this big goof safe."

She nodded and said very seriously, "I will."

Dean groaned. "Like hell she will. Keep me in the loop, Jones."

"Will do." Jones raised a hand and walked out the front door. "I'll call with an update."

And he left.

Dean turned back to face Tia and found she'd disappeared too.

CHAPTER 24

TIA WALKED UPSTAIRS, wishing she had a bedroom so she could throw herself on her bed and cry. Not that she was the crying sort but damn it, today just felt like that type of day. At least to hide away and be alone for awhile. She could try to sleep but it wouldn't work with her head all messed up.

How could she be hooked up with a cop? God she was an idiot.

She was also a fool for making it matter so much.

He was right. Not all cops were bad. Just because she'd had a horrible experience didn't mean they were all like that.

Dean certainly wasn't. But he might turn on her and do something to screw her over eventually. She hoped that was her history talking. Seriously, he'd bent over backwards to help her so far. So good cops did exist. And she shouldn't be mad at him. She sat down on the bed and buried her face in her hands. What the hell was she supposed to do? She had nowhere to go and this was a waiting game that would never end. The asshole had to be connected to the lab. No one else knew she existed. No one ever had. This had to be related to the lab. And she couldn't squelch the fear that somehow Wilhelm had faked his death and was after her himself. He'd never forgive her for escaping a second time.

The man she'd seen at the restaurant was vaguely familiar, as if he'd been at the lab with her, but had he been Wilhelm's assistant? A grad student or another patient?

She frowned, letting her hand drop away. Was it possible to gain Wilhelm's records? A list of who'd been put through his program. Those who stayed. Those who failed out? That would at least give them a list of where to start. Hell, the cops should know who he was by the damn fingerprints he'd left behind. Her prints were taken when she'd first arrived at the lab. The process had terrified her. She'd done nothing wrong. They'd said they needed them for their security clearance process.

It had been minor to all the other infractions. Not the least of which was to keep her a prisoner for all those years. Like what the hell? How had that been legal? Or okay with society? She didn't even want to think about her family and their responsibility in this. She had a brother – were her parents still alive? Her brother? Did she care?

Mostly on a curiosity level but other than that, no.

At least she didn't think so…

She groaned. All of that had been taken away from her a long time ago. It was stupid to care. Stupid to wonder. If they'd wanted anything to do with her, they always knew where to find her. Except her brother.

He likely didn't know she existed.

Sad. For both of them.

"Are you okay?"

Dean. Damn.

"I'm fine."

"Well, you look more than fine to me."

At the note of humor in his voice and that little bit of something else…she opened her eyes to realize she'd laid down on his bed.

"No, don't move." He came around to the other side – his side – and sat down beside her. "There's so much going on I just wanted to make sure you were okay and not worrying." At the look she sent him, his grin widened. "Yeah, I know. It's not something you can't *not* worry about." He reached over and lifted her hand to cradle in his. "I was hoping you'd come up for a nap."

"I won't be able to sleep."

He nodded. "I know the feeling. I keep walking past my son and reaching out and touching him to make sure he's really here."

"When are they leaving?"

He glanced down at his watch. "In a couple of hours."

She nodded. "Good. I'll feel better when they are safe." She studied his face. If anyone should nap it was him. "You look tired."

"I've been racking my brain looking for angles we might have missed. Threads to pursue."

"I was too. Can we get access to Wilhelm's project? Maybe the list of people he tested, worked with, hired? The ones who didn't stay in the program?"

"Jones is looking into it as I'm not back to work yet, but so far the material is very slim. We did find out who the man was from MacDonald's. A Torrence Vladrong. Jones is digging into his background. A lot was kept off the books."

An idea percolated. An ugly idea but at what point did she have to do something much uglier? Abruptly she said, "What about an unexpected visit to the lab?"

He stopped then leaned over. "What do you mean? I thought it was closed down?"

"The building was his own. The estate was a trust set up by his parents for paranormal research. I'm sure the records are all there." She frowned. "His lab might still be running under different management. Under a different name."

He slowly straightened. "Do you know where this building is?"

She slowly nodded. "It's not exactly some place you ever forget."

"Do you have an address?"

She shook her head. "No, but I should be able to find it if we drive around."

"It's in your old neighborhood, isn't it?"

Tears threatened. "Oh yes. It wasn't far away at all. In fact, I could see my roof top from my window. I always wondered if that had been on purpose. So I could see but not visit my home."

"Bastard." Dean stood up and walked to the window. "Did you ever go home?"

"After I moved to the lab I never saw my friends, my brother, or my parents again." She gave him a teary-eyed look. "I never ever left that place until I escaped, and then when I was returned, I was a permanent resident – forever."

DEAN FROWNED. HOW did a child live through that betrayal? The very people who should have cared for her, loved her…walked away from her. Like, how did people do that? What was in their genetic marker that allowed them to give away their flesh and blood? There was supposed to be a special bond between parent and child. Not one that could be tossed aside so casually.

What would make supposedly loving parents do something like that?

Unless the bond between them and the child was broken. What would break such a thing? Hate? Disgust? Disappointment? Fear?

And the first three led to the last one. He glanced over at Tia. "When did your abilities start showing up?" he asked casually.

"No idea. I was well into them by the time I was ten as my parents were beside themselves trying to figure out what to do with me. They'd originally run me past every doctor they could get me to, and somewhere along the way they got to the point of realizing I couldn't be helped, that the doctors didn't want to see me and if they admitted I was missing the appearance of limbs for an hour or two their own mental health was called into play. Apparently I had that uncanny knack of missing an arm only to have it show up just before the doctor would be called in to see me. Considering the type of looks they might have gotten, I can see how distressing it might have been. Honestly, I think Wilhelm was likely a Godsend for them. It gave them someone who was interested in helping me."

"Helping you?" Dean asked incredulously. "They believed that?"

"I think they wanted to believe that. It was packaged that way and for the longest time I believed it too." She gave him a tight grin. "It was easier to believe that than the truth."

Now that he could believe.

"And when did you find out the truth?"

"Which truth? That my parents had left me behind permanently?" At his nod she shrugged. "Somewhere around the time I realized the phone calls were not being returned. The letters I sent out were never answered." She stared off at a distant point. "To be fair, I'm not sure those were ever sent out." She sighed. "Then summer months came but they didn't come with it."

He couldn't imagine the little girl sitting there and waiting for her family to come.

"For the longest time I was afraid they'd had an accident and that they'd all perished. It made it easier to see why I was still there."

It was hard to swallow. He focused on his own son for a long moment, letting the love fill him. It was unfathomable to think of what she'd been through.

"Then I knew for sure because as I started to fight the system, getting more and more uncooperative, Wilhelm used my family as a weapon against me. How they'd never come for me. I was a freak of nature. No one was ever going to want me." She threw out a hand. "You know. Think of all the nasty things people say to each other in the hopes of getting them to do what they want."

"Surely that only made you madder?"

"At the time it made me very quiet. I cooperated again because he was all I had to live by. If I wanted out then it was only going to happen with his permission. He used to offer me day trips as treats and gifts as rewards. Anything for him to be able to do the tests he wanted to do. And when I refused…"

She broke off and rubbed her temple, but he was sure there was a sheen of tears on her face.

"What did he do then?" Anger, slow building but with a force he'd rarely felt, surged up. He waited for her answer, hoping it wasn't the one that had jumped into his mind.

She shrugged and in a flat voice said, "He did them anyway."

Yeah, if that bastard was alive, Dean was going to kill him, if he was dead…well he'd find a way to kill him again.

CHAPTER 25

WHILE WAITING FOR Gillian and Jeremy to board the plane the atmosphere had been deliberately light-hearted and fun. Gillian was anxious to leave, and Jeremy was excited about his first plane ride. Dean appeared to be in control and that was a good thing – she certainly wasn't.

Outside Tia stopped and stared at the overcast sky for a long moment. "We need to go to the old lab." This sucked big time.

"We'll drive past now. See if there is anything left."

They walked the short distance to the truck and hopped in. The traffic getting out of the airport was heavy. She couldn't help but wonder at society's ant-like existence as she watched vehicle after vehicle turn left and right and feed in and out of the airport. Everyone moved in orderly procession at top speed. Everyone had a plan and a direction.

Unlike her.

The truck took a hard right with a raw squeal of tires. She straightened and stared out the window. And found her heart jumping into her throat again. They were driving past her old home. She stared with sadness and grief as they made it all the way past. It looked horrible. Lost. Deserted. Rundown. Kind of like her memories.

"What a sad place," she murmured.

"Several other families lived in it since you were there

last. It was bought from your parents and turned into a rental unit."

"It looks like it." That accounted for the desolate air surrounding it. The lack of love.

"Yeah, and the owners likely recouped their cost many times over without reinvesting back into the property again." He took the truck around another corner adding, "Typical."

With a curious sense of detachment she watched her old neighborhood go by. The scraped knee when she'd tripped falling onto that curb. The fire hydrant that used to be completely hidden by weeds and wildflowers was now fully exposed. Not even those found a warm enough environment to survive today.

"It doesn't look the same," she murmured. "Yet at the same time, it does."

"It's older, more run-down and you are now older with a whole new perspective."

"True." The truck pulled up to a gas station and stopped. She glanced over at him. He was staring at her with a questioning look on his face.

"Where to now?"

Oh shit. She'd been so lost in her walk down memory lane she'd forgotten she needed to give him directions. She peered out the window and tried to orient herself to the lab. It hadn't been walking distance, but it wasn't that far either. "Go ahead a couple of blocks and take a right."

It took several more blocks and a few more turns, but eventually she caught sight of the building rising in the sky.

There was a deep silence in the vehicle when he pulled the truck onto the shoulder of the road across from the place. They both stared at the run-down building.

"It looks deserted."

"All the records indicate that the lab was shut down

around the time you left."

"Hmmm." She didn't trust much about that good doctor. If he'd been able to keep his work moving forward from the grave he would have. Dean parked the truck and turned off the engine. And looked at her expectantly.

"What do you want to do?"

"I want to look inside." Suddenly determined to do just that, even though it was the last thing she wanted to do, she opened the passenger door and jumped out. The door slammed harder and louder than she expected. And echoed in the night.

Shit.

"You okay?" Dean asked, his gaze intent.

She ignored him and stared at the three story monstrosity. Yet for all its size, it had seemed much bigger in her nightmares. There were busted windows and bars on a few others. The gate held a Private Property Keep Out sign that now hung drunkenly off to the side.

The little girl inside whimpered. *Don't go. Don't go. You'll never get out.*

"There's still power in the place so someone is paying the bill."

She froze. "You mean there might be people still there? A functioning lab still in operation?" Her voice rose in shock. She wanted to scream in pain and terror. And she wanted to race inside and knock the shit out of the first person she saw. She needed a target. Someone to pummel for all the years of abuse she'd taken.

At the same time, she wanted to turn around and hide.

Like she always had.

She straightened her shoulders, aware he was doing some search on his cell phone – probably looking for the company who was paying the bills on the property. She strode across the deserted street and through the gate. She breathed slowly and carefully.

She'd made it this far. She could do this.

What did companies do with buildings that had served their time and had their day? Did they bulldoze them to the ground? Sell them off for property value? Someone had to pay the taxes on these places.

As long as this particular lab never was a fully functioning prison again, she'd be fine with it.

With Dean trailing behind she headed to the door. Off to the side she read the small sign. Psyche Laboratories. She didn't remember that at all.

In her mind, she could see herself entering this building so long ago. Twice. She'd not looked back when she'd escaped the second time. Not until today.

The knob turned under her hand. She frowned. "Shouldn't this be locked?"

"Not if there's nothing inside. Think about it, if there is something inside and people want to know what's inside, they will break a window or break down the door to find out. If you don't lock anything and they can walk through and see it's empty then they can't cause major damage in the process."

"I suppose." The open doorway yawned in front of her. She winced. "I never thought I'd see a day where I'd willingly step back inside this place."

"That just goes to show that you couldn't imagine such a positive future." He pushed the door open wider and stepped around her. "Let's go. We could be home in an hour."

That brightened her spirits. She wasn't still a prisoner here. Life had changed for her. She could walk back out again.

She stepped inside then turned and looked back. Deliberately, she walked back out. She turned, a grin on her face and explained to a very confused Dean. "I was just proving to myself I could leave. That I wasn't going to be locked up again."

Understanding lit his face. "No worries there. I'd never let that happen to you."

She studied his face, and for the first time in a long time she realized – she was alone no longer.

SUCH A SIMPLE movement. She'd entered and left to prove she could. He was only just realizing how much pain and fear she'd had to overcome to be here. That she'd entered on her own was fantastic. Now to make a quick search to prove to her that the place truly was empty, that there'd be no answers to find here and then they could go home. He had pizza on his mind. Maybe a couple of beers and her.

Maybe, just maybe, he'd manage to get her back into his bed.

This time for a whole different reason.

But first he had to get her through this. And if there was information to find, they needed to find it. Jones was doing his level best to dig up the information on this property, but the corporation that held the title, a biomedical company, hadn't used it for years. They were holding onto the property until the area regained some of the value it lost when the economy crunched. It had recovered slightly but not enough to make it worthwhile to sell. The property was derelict and the building deserted.

Dean knew that.

But convincing Tia was a whole different story.

CHAPTER 26

S HE WALKED SLOWLY down the hallway, wondering at the reception room that sat securely behind walls with just a glass window that opened and closed to allow communication between both parties. She didn't remember that part. She didn't remember the institutional white, the long stretch of uncompromising entrance. Doorways that played off from side to side. But she did remember that bank of scary elevators. She knew they went both up and down. God help her. She'd taken them in both directions many times.

"I suppose the offices would have the most promise?" Dean asked.

"Maybe. We certainly need to check." But inside she knew it wasn't where they'd find the stuff she was looking for. She couldn't take her mind off the elevator. Even in the semi-darkness it had enough power to gleam in the weird light. A beacon.

Painfully she ripped her gaze away to watch what Dean was doing. He'd gone into each room and systematically searched the offices as he came to them. Six doors down he popped back out again and said, "Everything is empty."

She nodded and walked to the elevator. She stared at it. It had frequented her nightmares for a long time. Even though it was old and likely broken it still had power over her subconscious.

"This is a big old thing," Dean remarked, pounding his hand lightly on the metal front. The noise gave a dull throb that echoed downward. "Is there a downstairs to this place?"

"Several," she said painfully. "First I want to go upstairs." She turned to the stairs and started climbing, wondering at her impulse to see her old room. The window she'd stared out of for years, hoping, wishing for a better life.

She kept climbing, Dean silent at her side.

At the third floor, she opened the door and walked out. She studied the long hallway and realized it was still the same dingy color as before. There weren't as many doors here. She turned left and headed to the third one down. She stood in front of the door, slightly ajar and took a deep breath. She pushed it open.

Beside her, Dean gasped.

Her old bed still sat there. Steel frame that she'd been tied to when she'd misbehaved. The window with the bars that had been attached when she'd threatened to jump out and end her life – and his research.

The lack of personal effects because she wasn't allowed anything to remind her of the family she no longer had.

She shook her head, releasing the memories and forced herself to look around with a detached mindset.

"I wonder if anyone else stayed in this room after I left."

"Does it still look the same?" he asked, a banked rage in his voice.

She nodded. "Exactly the same."

"Then likely not."

"Good." She did a quick search, including the closet, found it empty and turned back to the hallway.

"Do you want to check the other rooms up here," he asked quickly. She spared a glance his way, realizing he was being patient and strong at her side. Letting her do what she needed to do when she needed to do it.

She appreciated that about him. "Thank you, but no. This floor was empty for most of the time I was here."

He started. "Why?"

"Who knows? They certainly had the space. Maybe it was punishment for me. More isolation." She shrugged. "At the end, Wilhelm wasn't the most rational."

"Jesus."

Back at the stairwell, she took one last look down the hall then walked down the steps forever. At the main floor she kept going. There were two more floors below. She went down to the first one and opened the door – or tried to. It was locked.

"Oh, this is promising." He stepped in front of her and did something with his hand. Before she could figure out what it was the door opened. Surprised, she walked through and stopped. To the right were the treatment rooms, but in front of her was the glass wall to the observation room.

"What went on here," Dean asked in a hard voice. He reached out and rapped the glass wall. "Not glass."

"Supposed to be something unbreakable." She shrugged, her gaze lost in the room she'd spent days in. But he wasn't there anymore. She could leave now. Dean had helped set her free – at least in her mind. She turned to Wilhelm's office. The first door on the right – where he could see her in the observation room.

Bastard.

DEAN STARED AT the layout. This most auspicious room with its walls of glass had likely belonged to Wilhelm. The asshole could sit there all day and watch those imprisoned in the observation room. In one way that was likely a good thing. It was an observation room. However, in another way – it was really creepy.

"How often were you in here?" he asked, absently noting the bathroom with only part walls offering the barest of privacy. He couldn't imagine how that lack had affected a traumatized young girl.

"Sometimes daily, sometimes only monthly. Depended who else he had to pick on at that time," she said, her voice hard, cold. "When he was bored, I was his favorite pet."

She turned and walked to his office door and pushed it open. "There could be stuff in here, but if not he had a warehouse downstairs where he kept the old stuff."

The room, he could see from over her head was a little less empty than upstairs. There was a scarred desk in the center and an office chair turned on its side. A couple of papers lay crumpled on the floor with footsteps crushing them flat. It had been deserted a long time ago. The only windows were to the hallway. No filing cabinet and no closet. It was dismal.

"Next," he said. "Where else do you want to look?"

But she'd wandered over to the desk, straightening up the chair. An odd look on her face. She sat down in the chair and pulled it to Wilhelm's desk. There she stared out at whatever he'd stared at all the time she'd been here.

"Are you okay?"

She lifted her head and smiled. "I am." She motioned to the desk in front of her. "I spent a lot of time wondering what he saw when he sat here and watched me. Now that I'm in this same place..." She shook her head and stood up. "It's all so crazy. And foolish." She walked out the door adding, "And a long time ago."

He watched her give the observation room one more brief look then turn her back on it and walk purposefully back to the stairs. He followed. She had a goal.

All he could do was see she reached it.

CHAPTER 27

THE FILE STORAGE, or the warehouse as Wilhelm called it, was downstairs in one of the locked rooms. Wilhelm had originally had a partner, but they'd parted ways a long time ago. He'd hung onto the other man's research just in case he came back. He'd often told them that one day he'd be famous, but his partner wouldn't because he hadn't believed in him anymore.

She wouldn't be at all surprised if he'd done something to his partner. No, that wasn't Wilhelm, but that the partner never came back had to mean something. Still, as her doctor, he'd had a ton of power over her and she hadn't had a choice while young. Now…

He was dead and life wasn't fair but at least she was out of that hellhole.

Dean kept up beside her as she strode down to the next level. She'd escaped through here the first time but knew the other patients and some of the staff were scared of this area.

Hell, they'd all been scared.

She pushed open the door to the lowest level and walked through. The hallway was dark. Ugly. She shivered. Her hand instinctively reached for the light switch. A harsh white light bulb hung drunkenly on wires. The light above her stayed dark.

This hallway, identical to all the others above had fewer

doors. She stood undecided. "I'm not sure which direction to go."

"Then let's go where the light is. If we can't find what you're looking for there, we'll come back to the other side."

She stared at him. "I suppose you believe in fairy tales too, don't you."

He stopped and shot her a confused look. "What?"

"You know it's not going to be that easy. If there's anything bad here it's going to be in the dark half of the hallway," she muttered. "At least in the movies."

"This isn't the movies," he said in exasperation. "And not everything in life is a horror story."

She shot him a disbelieving look as she walked down the hallway – on the lit side. "Like I said, fairy tales."

Twenty minutes later, having walked the whole length, checked all the rooms, he was forced to concede. "Okay, so we didn't find anything on this side, but that doesn't mean it's going to be really bad on the other side." As they were back at their original position he switched off the light, walked over and unscrewed the bulb that hung off its wires.

"There, now let's see if we can shine some light on the situation." He flicked the switch back on and they turned to the dark side of the hallway. "Let's go to the furthest end and see if I can find a place to screw this in."

She watched him, a smile on her face. She'd never have thought to do that. A smart move. Then again, she wasn't tall enough to reach the damn light in the first place.

The dark gave the hospital the same feeling she'd had in her memories. A shiver rippled down her arms. There were no boogiemen here today, but in her mind that child was screaming at her to run…

"Okay?"

"I am." She could only hope her voice was stable, sure. Inside she wasn't so confident but didn't want to always come across as some weakling. Never that.

His sharp gaze stayed on her face for a moment longer before easing back and moving on. She breathed a little easier. The hallway ahead was exactly the same as her memories. Back when she'd been led from one room to another, sometimes crying, sometimes fighting, always hating the journey, not sure what was to come. Not sure how bad it would be this time.

Always wondering why she just didn't give in and do what they wanted her to do. Why fight.

Because it had been wrong and something inside of her said she had to keep up the fight, and if she wouldn't fight for herself, then who would? No one. Because no one cared about Tia Hanniger. They'd all forgotten she existed – if they'd ever known in the first place.

Life was a bitch and all that.

She straightened her back determined to not let the same damn hallways make her skin crawl with memories. Dean strode ahead of her. He found another light socket hanging down and quickly screwed his light bulb into it.

Instantly cold light flooded the deserted space. The paint peeled off the walls here. The ceiling tiles hung slightly down as if something in the duct work had broken and needed repairing but no one had bothered. That was like a lot of this program. No one had bothered.

She swallowed hard and smiled. "Thanks. That's easier to see."

He nodded. "Let's get this over with." He strode forward and opened the first door he came to. She peered in over his shoulder and gulped hard. Her breath caught in the back of her throat and she closed her eyes.

"Jesus. What the hell went on in here?"

In a detached voice, one she was proud of, she said, "This was one of the punishment rooms. If we didn't behave, he'd bring us down here and chain us up."

The walls still held the padded cushions so the patients could bounce from side to side without hurting themselves. The hooks holding the bindings still hung securely from the walls. The rusty stains on the floor were new. She stared at them.

"Is that blood," he exclaimed, stepping forward into the room.

"Most likely," she said, following him inside. "There was often blood, but they always cleaned it up quickly." She waited a beat. "Mostly fear of infection I suppose."

He stared at her in shock. "Were you ever here?"

She snorted. "All the time. I couldn't seem to stop fighting my circumstances. Lots of the blood on the floor is mine."

"Yours." His voice deepened, became menacing.

She studied him in surprise. This made him angry. Good. She liked to think he'd be upset at the wrongs in the world. "Yeah, mine."

"Did they beat you?"

"Sometimes. Sometimes they gave us drugs that brought on nosebleeds, sometimes they cut us," she said in a conversational tone. "Mostly it was superficial, unless Wilhelm lost his temper."

It took a moment for the heavy silence to set in. She turned to look at Dean. He looked ready to murder someone.

"Good," she replied tartly. "Get mad. Lord knows I did

over the years. You at least have the power to do something about this. Unlike those of us that were here."

"How many?"

"Too many," she answered shortly. "In the beginning, maybe a dozen, at the very end, just me." She laughed but even she winced at the harshness of the sound. "Like Wilhelm said often enough, I belonged to him. There was no other place for me to go."

"Jesus Christ." It was said more as a prayer, but with the force of an avenging angel. She loved that about him.

"He's dead. There's nothing any of us can do to him now. If I could," she said, "I would have many times over."

"Damn good thing," Dean snapped. "I'd have taken this asshole out myself."

"Actually, given the opportunity, I'd have beaten you to it. Several others tried. That's when he doubled up the security on the place." Her face twisted sourly. "Not that it did him any good."

"Meaning?"

She shrugged. "The final straw was when Gord, one of the other poor sods that was here, attacked Wilhelm. Gord was shipped home after that, and for a long time Wilhelm never came into our rooms alone. Gord broke a couple of ribs and maybe something else. I don't remember."

She waved her hand at the bloodstains. "Actually, I don't want to remember. Come on, we're taking forever."

With that she walked back out and opened the door across the hall. "This is it," she called out excitedly. "There're still some filing cabinets in here."

"They are going to be empty, you know that."

She raced across the floor and pulled over the top drawer, empty. The next two cabinets were also empty. The one on the bottom, she pulled it open and pulled the damn thing right out with her need to find something important.

It was also empty.

Shit.

She squatted down and tried to fit the damn drawer back in but couldn't get it to line up properly.

"Forget about it. There's no one left to care if the drawer is put away properly or not."

She nodded but couldn't stop trying to fix it. He took it out of her hands, placed it in the right position and as he tried to push it in, they heard paper crumple. Tia leaned over to find a folder jammed in the back.

Dean, anticipating her need, tilted the entire cabinet sideways so she could reach it.

"There're two files." She snagged the folders and reached for several loose sheets tucked in and around the fat files.

Standing up again, she held the folders aloft. "They must have forgotten about these."

"Probably didn't know they existed," Dean said. "A shredding company likely came in and cleaned the place out."

She gave him a horrified look. "They wouldn't have, would they? That was Dr. Wilhelm's life work."

He gave her a strange look. "I'm not sure anyone gave a shit about his research, Tia. Sounds like he was a crackpot."

"He was." But he was also her crackpot. And she'd hated him – but he'd also been a mainstay in her life. In a twisted way she'd depended on him. He'd been father figure and mentor, then after she'd tried to escape the first time, he'd just become her prison warden.

For the first time, standing there in the empty room staring at the last of what she could find of his research, she wondered if he'd seen her attempt to escape as a betrayal. If he'd bonded with her, then he most likely did.

That might account for the viciousness of his response. At least in his demented mind.

She gave her head a shake. It was all old news. Dead news. Just like the doctor. He was gone and she was alive and well and doing better than ever. And just think, for the first time, she wasn't alone.

Sliding a sideways glance at Dean, she had to wonder just how alone she was. And just how attached she was.

"Now what's rolling around in that pretty head of yours?" He caught up to her and slipped an arm through hers. "Are we leaving? Do you want to check the other rooms?"

She stopped and turned, realizing now that she had something from here, even if it wasn't what she really wanted. Instinct told her to get the hell out. Or was it remembered fear, panic? She had enough of those old memories rising up to make her panicked now. But she shouldn't be so fast to leave. She couldn't remember what was in the other rooms, but there had been something.

And she was never going to come back so she'd better look now. "Damn it. I don't want to, but I think we should check them." She turned and walked back. At the next room, the door was open and it was empty. "Good. Hopefully the others are the same way."

He opened the next one, took a good look inside while she waited in the hallway and said, "It's empty."

She nodded and walked to the next one. Glancing down the hall, she realized they were almost done. "Three more."

"Good. Let's get this done and get out of here."

"I want pizza," she said, opening the next door to find

another bare room. "Empty."

"And empty," he said from slightly ahead of her. "One last one."

She nodded and walked up to the door. "I don't remember these rooms."

"Good. Sounds like you remember way too much from here."

"True enough."

With a deep breath, she opened the last door. Maybe it was that whole nightmare thing again saying she'd find something horrible behind the door, but as she gazed inside, she realized the last room was empty too.

"Thank heavens for that," she muttered as she walked back toward the stairs.

"You really thought you'd see something?" he asked.

"Not necessarily. It's more a case of my mind always said there was something here based on what it knew from before." She shrugged. "I know it probably sounds stupid, but I needed to update my memories. To see this place derelict, empty. Harmless."

"It doesn't seem stupid to me." He frowned. "Are you good now? Can we leave?" They walked up the stairs to the main floor and out the front door. There she turned and looked back at the big slice of her life so far. "Yeah, I'm good."

She walked out to the edge of the property where the broken gate hung. With one final last look, she turned back, and standing with hands across her chest, stared at the building. "It doesn't look the same."

"Why would it? It was a long time ago."

"Yet, there is something…"

He shifted impatiently at her side. "Something what?"

She shrugged. "Almost a presence there."

"I don't think so. It's broken glass and sagging beams."

She nodded. "It must be my imagination."

DEAN WAITED FOR her to be done. Whatever it was she was doing. Saying goodbye maybe? He'd have kicked his heels at returning to a place like this, happy to never set his eyes on it. But in her case, there was something…off.

Still, it was late and darkness was settling in. And he was starving.

"Do you need to go back in again?" He waited, trying for the patience required.

"If there is something there," she said almost absently, "it's more energy than substance."

"Huh?"

She shook her head and smiled. "Nothing. Let's go, I'm starved."

Still carrying the folders he noticed she hadn't looked at yet – something else he would have done differently, as in he'd have looked inside them immediately. She appeared afraid to open that door – like Pandora's Box – it could be something she didn't want to start.

"Pick up pizza and home?" he asked.

"Absolutely."

She remained silent the whole trip back to his son's favorite restaurant. They waited the ten minutes for their order to be ready then completed the last of the journey back to his place.

The house was empty with his son gone but with Tia there, it was full of life, warmth. His last relationship had been a long time ago. He dropped the pizza boxes down on the table. "Let's eat."

She tossed the files on the table and sat down.

He opened the boxes. Heavy Italian sausage filled the air. "Oh, that smells good."

"It does." He sat down and shoved the files back slightly. And picked up a piece rich with meat and cheese. "Seems like hours since we ate."

"It was," she mumbled around a mouthful of hot pizza. "It's almost ten o'clock."

He stared at her. She nodded to her phone on the table and swiped across the top of the screen. Sure enough it said it was nine-fifty. He shook his head. "Where the hell did the evening go?"

"Lost like all my years in that shit hole."

Taking another bite, his gaze wandered over the top of the pizza and back onto the folders. He could see names and scribbles all over the outside. They were both thick. Sad. Then he caught sight of one name. His heart lurched. Not wanting to go there, he flipped open the other folder.

CHAPTER 28

"DO YOU KNOW a Billy Massey?"

Tia paused, a third and so not necessary slice of pizza staring at her from the box. "Billy was one of the kids at the center."

"A friend of yours?"

She glanced over at him, a wry expression on her face. "You are assuming we were allowed to have friends."

His gaze widened. "Didn't you have social contact with the others there?"

"Sure we did. During some of the experiments. Sometimes over meals. The odd occasion. But it wasn't exactly what you'd call a nice scenario. Several of the kids there were happy, thinking they were special and had won some kind of accolades." She shrugged. "They learned otherwise very quickly." She really didn't want to talk about this right now but with those files sitting on the table in front of them...

"To hell with it," she muttered and snatched up the third slice. With her first bite she closed her eyes and let a happy moan escape. "It's been so long since I had pizza."

"What kind of food did you eat at the center?"

"Regular institution food. In other words, disgusting. I got skinnier and skinnier. Especially during my later teen years. I couldn't eat the crap they were serving, I didn't care to live the life I was living and the combination was deadly."

She waited, knowing he wasn't going to be able to let it go at that.

"And…?"

"And I escaped. It wasn't well thought out. It was more an accident or happenstance. I realized after I was returned that if it happened once then chances were good it could happen again." She glared at the stack of papers in front of them. "I wanted that second chance."

"And you got it," he said in a soothing voice. "You're fine now."

"Not quite," she muttered. "Someone is still after me."

"Do we know for sure that this person is related to the lab?"

"Has to be," she said. "How can it not?"

"It's a really fucked up world out there," he said, reaching for the last piece of pizza in the first box. "And we need more than guesses at this point."

"We do know that the guy at McDonald's was possibly there when I was attacked. That means he's likely connected to the lab."

Dean nodded his head. "Right. So there is a connection to that extent." He pondered for a moment, eating in silence. "What about Simone, did she have a connection to the lab?"

Tia smiled. "No. Given the shape I was in, she asked. But how could I explain about the tests 'to make me healthy' again." Her voice took on a mocking tone at the end.

"Wait." Dean leaned back. "I assumed the tests were parapsychological in nature."

"They were. But most parents were of the opinion that there *was* something wrong with us. And they wanted us 'fixed' regardless of how."

"Did Dr. Wilhelm pass his lab off as a place where people like you could be treated and become…hell I don't know…normal?"

She nodded. "I think so. Then when he figured out what we could do, he wanted to do more and more tests. With me there all the time, he could do more in-depth tests."

"What kind of tests?"

She laughed. "In the beginning they were everything from the type of food we ate, the type of music we listened to, the colors we wore."

He grinned. "I gather that didn't produce the results he was looking for?"

She shook her head. "Not at all. By the end, he wanted us to be better, stronger, have more abilities."

"Whoa, I had no idea." Dean stared at her in shock. "I can't imagine that went over well."

"At the beginning he always tested to see what made us stronger, then weaker, and poor naive us thought he'd meant to weaken our abilities so we were acceptable in our parents' eyes. Instead, he was cataloguing our responses to see what made us stronger." She shoved the pizza boxes back off the table and pulled the thick folders forward. "He pulled some pretty nasty shit in his attempts to see if there was something that would set off hidden talents. If he attacked, could we attack him back, bigger and stronger so to speak?"

"That sounds highly unethical."

"Ethical and Wilhelm didn't belong in the same sentence." She opened the first folder and raised her gaze to Dean. "Especially after I managed to escape. There were only four kids there at the time, but according to them, they were all punished as if they were to blame for my escape. He always assumed I'd had help."

She kept quiet for a long moment, wishing she could

explain the inside fear that had tormented her for such a long time. "I did have help, but not the first time. Like I said, that was more accidental. But the second time…oh yeah, I had help."

"Who helped you?" he said in a puzzled tone.

"I have no idea," she whispered. "And you wouldn't believe me if I told you."

"Try me?"

She laughed. "All right. It was…I don't know, you'll laugh but it was like a ghost. Or something. I don't know, but it's like there was a whisper saying to run." She shrugged. "Whatever it was, I saw that second opportunity and I took it."

"And the ones you left behind," he asked in a gentle tone. "Did you never worry about them?"

"No," she said shortly. "I didn't have to. You see, by the end, there was no one left. I was alone. In fact, I might have been the only one left alive in that damn building, except for Wilhelm. I figured I'd been forgotten in the padded cell. When the ghost appeared and showed me how to escape, I never looked back. For all I know the place had been deserted for days."

HE DIDN'T KNOW what to think. A ghost? An entity that helped her get out of a locked room from a deserted lab. How bizarre. And what could he say? Nothing. But he had to come up with a response of some kind. He smiled. "Sorry, you lost me at ghost."

"Yeah, that's where I lose most people," she muttered. "Not that I tell many. What about you and your weird symptoms after the attack? Did you see or do anything odd that might make you think there was more to this physical existence?"

He opened his mouth to say no, hell no, only he couldn't. Why. He closed his eyes and sat back, watching her study the very first page in the folder. He had seen some weird lights when he'd first realized there was a problem. After all, when you looked at a person and saw colors around their head, it was an obvious enough problem to go and ask the doctors about, and he'd quickly learned there was nothing physically wrong. The doctors had immediately turned to his psychological health. He'd been quick to learn that lesson. Not fast enough for a few odd notes in his file suggesting time off and that his mother's illness might have had something to do with his mental stress, not to mention being a single dad and maybe he should look at getting some help at home. Like that was an easy option. He'd never told anyone else.

"So the answer is yes." She snorted. "See how it feels. You don't know if you should say something or not because I might consider you weird or not quite right in the head."

"It wasn't much," he protested. "But along with the enhanced hearing came enhanced sight, only it was real weird. It's like something was wrong. I saw colors where there weren't any, edges blurred. After the regular doctor I decided it was likely a visual problem and went to see an eye doctor."

"But he couldn't find anything wrong – right?"

"No, he couldn't." Dean smiled. "But the symptoms are diminishing now so whatever was wrong is now getting better."

"Fool you. It's not getting better, you are getting stronger so you are learning to handle the information better, and it's not something you see all the time."

"Information?"

"Yeah, your brain received a lot more information based on the enhanced sight and hearing – way cool that is too – and so it didn't know what to do with it all initially. Now that you've had a few months to figure it out, your brain has been able to compartmentalize the information – store it so to speak."

"So you're saying I'm not healing, the enhanced sensations are just going underground?" he asked doubtfully.

"Absolutely. A good way to look at it." She smiled. "It's all real, you know. The colors around people's heads, around objects, the flares when people get mad, the warm rosy glow that surrounds people in love."

He stared at her. "You see it, too?" he asked hoarsely. "I thought it was just my psychosis."

She shook her head. "Nope, not a psychosis. It's simple. You're able to see auras and are starting to learn to read energy. Way cool."

She turned the page on the folder in front of her. "It's all good. You'll learn to see more as time goes on – provided you are still open to the suggestions. If not it will become an ability you'll draw on at certain times but will lie fallow the rest of the time. That's kinda sad, if you go that way."

"And why not go that way?" It sounded damn fine to him.

"Because this is a good ability. It allows you to read other people. To understand if they are telling the truth. To see if someone is really sick or not."

He stared at her. "How is that possible?"

"Have to wait and see. Use them sometime, and you'll see what information is available." She turned and assessed him. "Considering you're a cop, this could be helpful.

Imagine a runaway teen girl who tells you a story and she's looking so seriously sad that your heart breaks and you'd bend over backwards only to find out she has a couple of nasty pimps in the bushes waiting to beat the shit out of you."

He didn't dare tell her he'd never get into a scenario like that, being who he was, but her point was valid. "How?" he asked bluntly.

"Because energy never lies. People lie. People cheat. People steal. Energy is always energy. If you can read it, then it's a huge life skill. It will always show you who is lying at any given time."

"And you, are you lying to me right now?"

She laughed. "Nope."

"How about this morning when you said, you loved me?"

She gasped in shock. And damn if her outline didn't start fading away.

"I never said that," she shrieked.

He laughed. "Gotcha."

CHAPTER 29

S HE SNICKERED. "YOU'LL pay for that." And she turned her head to the papers in front of her. Inside though, her heart beat like a bird on the wrong side of a window. Why would he say something like that? It's not something she'd ever say. Never had a chance to ever do so before and, given her history, she doubted the opportunity would arise any time soon. But his words stirred something in her.

Her teen years hadn't been normal. She'd missed the chance to crush on anyone. There'd been a guy she'd liked at the center, but he'd not been there long. A few months. Then a new younger kid had shown up, and she'd become closer to him but not in any romantic way. Her entire hormonal life she'd been in that damn lab. Since living on her own, she'd had several relationships. Once realizing she was almost safe, only looking behind her shoulder a few times, she'd found a thirst for life and all the things she'd never had.

She'd gotten a job, rented a small studio and had indulged. In a big way. All the food she'd heard about. All the food she'd thought about. She'd eaten until she was sick. Loving some and hating others. She actually took on a second job so she could eat more – this time on the boss's nickel. The small restaurant had been known for its good home cooked food and she'd learned. First by doing dishes, then doing prep work and finally doing some of the simpler dishes and helping with the rest. She'd enjoyed eating and they'd enjoyed teaching her. They'd kept the questions to a minimum. Maybe she'd made it very clear in the beginning, maybe not. She couldn't remember. It was a long time ago.

She'd also had an affair. Several of them. She'd inhaled romance books and thought the words on the paper would mimic real life. That hadn't worked out so well. Groping in the dark, sweaty hands, smelly bodies and bad breath.

Gross. She'd given it a fair sampling with three men, and that had been enough for her. At one point she wondered if she was more in tune with other women and should go that route.

But she never felt the urge to follow it up. In fact, she wanted to read the romance novels – they were much better.

She'd made friends but never close friends. After all, you shared things with friends. Simple things like your history, where you went to school, first kiss. How did one say all three of those had occurred while in an institution?

Not exactly a conversation starter. Besides, she was a private person. She didn't want to be viewed as an escapee from a mental hospital.

"Heavy thoughts?"

"Sure. Like sex, romance and death." She snorted. "Especially the last one." She tapped the papers in front of her. "This patient died."

He reached over and plucked the sheet out of her hand. He narrowed his gaze. "This was twelve years ago."

"Yes, I was there at the time."

His gaze zeroed in on her face. "He died while you were there. Did you know him?"

"I don't remember him," she said shortly. "I heard rumors of a death, several, in fact, but it was never confirmed." She shrugged. "But I didn't know him."

"Was he the only one?"

"I don't know."

"What killed him?" Dean wasn't going to let it go.

"No idea. Maybe these papers explain it. They are all about him." She handed over a paperclip full of papers. "I thought this file was on one person, but each clip is a different person." She riffled through the folder, counting. "I think twelve people. Hell, there weren't that many people in the lab at any time."

"Likely over the dozen years it was operational. Twenty-two participants is hardly anything. You need a lot of people to show viable results for treatments."

"Not many of us weirdos out there. He was damn lucky to have this many. Am I here?" Her fingers flicked through the stack. "Jason. Michelle. Roberta. Bobby. Jerome. Sergei. Calendar." She went silent as the memories of all those people rippled through her psyche.

"Jesus. So many." She went to the second to the last file and pulled it forward. She tapped the top paper in the clip. "He was a pain in the ass. He hated being there, and he'd scream at the top of his lungs for days. We all hated it."

"How did they stop him?"

She paused and looked over at him. "No idea. But he stopped. From one day to the next he was silent. Actually…" She frowned. "He might have just been kicked out. I remember it was a constant noise in the background and then it was suddenly gone.

Dean flicked through the papers and came to the last sheet. "Or maybe they killed him. According to this, he was dead six weeks after arriving. Are you sure he wasn't the one who died."

She reached over and grabbed the papers. "No, it was Calendar. I think that was his name." She frowned as she read the form on the last page. "He was the only one I knew about."

Dean tossed another packet in front of her. "This girl died too. And this one and this one." He dumped the stack in front of her. "Your name doesn't appear to be here for a very good reason – you're the only one still alive."

THE SHOCK ON her face made him want to laugh, but there was nothing lighthearted about the subject matter. If he was correct, all these people had died. And they'd been just kids. Children. Teens. In theory she'd crossed paths with all of them. At one time or another she'd likely met these people face to face, maybe whispered about their crappy lives together. "No," she whispered. "It can't be."

"Why is that?"

"Because I saw some of them leave." She lifted her shocked gaze to Dean's. "As in I saw the parents come and take the kids away."

"And you're sure it was the parents doing that?" Dean waited for her to understand. When she stared at him blankly, he added, "Maybe it was someone else other than their parents."

She blinked. "Why would anyone do that?"

"I don't know, but the thing is we now have something to go on. Something golden. There are names and dates here. We need to get this off to Jones. Have him track these families down and find out what the hell happened."

"Wait." She reached for the pages. "Does it actually say

what happened to these kids? Given the way they died?"

"No. It just says deceased."

She shook her head. "This is wrong on so many levels."

"Yeah, that's one way to put it," he muttered. He reached over, grabbed a stack of papers and took a closer look. "This is an intake form. And then dietary restrictions, medical history. There are a few notes as to how the patient settled in. But nothing on the treatment. Nothing on medications given. Nothing on meetings and impressions from the doctor about each new arrival."

"He was a rabid note taker," she exclaimed. "There's a lot of information missing here."

"Sure, but then why this condensed version of events?"

"I don't know." She grabbed the file. "Billy arrived on June 17th. Okay, then he was allergic to dairy. Hey, I didn't know that." She pondered that information as if trying to match it up to her memories. "It's possible I suppose."

"You don't remember?" he asked her curiously. "How well did you know these people? Did you have a cafeteria where you could all hang out and talk?"

"Oh no. That wasn't allowed very often. We saw each other in passing, when someone had a fit, while in the observation room. Occasionally we'd get to talk in the hallways. We whispered at night to each other." She gave him a crooked smile. "Prisoners do find ways, you know."

"I'm glad to hear that," he said forcefully. "I wish you'd had the skills to break free and beat the hell out of your warden."

"You forget, we were conditioned to think we had no choice. That we were there because we had to be there. And we were kids. We weren't exactly docile, but for the most part we were accepting."

"Sounds like a horrible way to live." And it pissed him right off.

"Oh it was, but it was the only way we had to live. We were always jealous yet hopeful when someone got to leave." She smiled with memories. "It gave us hope that we would make it out of there too. That our families would come and pick us up."

"And you never saw your family again?" He'd pulled out a notepad from his back pocket, instinctively needing confirmation on these details. He quickly asked her a few more questions. "I'm going to contact Jones right now. See if I can scan in some of these pages for him to use as a basis to track down the families of these kids. Maybe there are others who lived. Maybe find some who would be adults now."

She nodded. "Is there something I can do?"

"Well, you're avoiding looking at the second folder, any reason why?"

"Because it feels like a serpent waiting to strike. It's so fat and obnoxious looking," she said, an odd note creeping into her voice.

"All of that from one look?"

"One peek," she muttered. But she stared down at the empty pizza box and picked away at the melted cheese, her gaze solidly *not* on the folder. Although he wanted to rush away to Jones and hand over all this material, he needed to see what bothered her about this folder.

He pulled it toward him and took a look inside. "More intake, more pages of dietary care. Yet this one is thick." And the writing is more illegible than the others. Older. This one barely closed for the stack of material inside. Some of it crumpled. Some of it folded and other pieces just stuffed in. "This isn't a condensed subject folder. This is all one patient," he said, his voice rising. "This is excellent. We should be able to track this person down."

"Oh yeah, you should," she said, shoving the pizza box back against the far end of the table with more force than necessary. "Hell, if you can't, you can't really call yourselves cops."

He snorted. "Okay smarty pants, why is that?"

She turned and glared at him as he stood up, the second folder in his hand, ready to take it to his office.

"Because it's my folder, damn it. Everything in there is about me."

CHAPTER 30

S HE COULDN'T STILL the shakiness inside. Dean had been flicking through the folder since she'd told him it was on her. Every once in a while she'd look over at him worried at what he'd see. She'd lived it. Did she really want to read about it? Then again, these notes and documents were from others. Their impressions, perceptions. Not hers.

Did she really want to not know how they felt about her? How she'd responded. The results they'd formulated. Was it normal to want to step back and completely miss out on learning more? Just because she'd had a horrible time there? No. That was just stupid.

"Damn it." She plunked down beside him and snatched up the beginning part of the file he'd already skimmed through. She caught his concerned gaze and said, "I need to know."

He nodded and shifted the file so it was between them.

She went through the intake form, noting she'd been twelve on the day she'd arrived. Shitty day. Still, there were no notes on her condition or mental state. She flicked through the first couple of pages and read the cold institutionalized type of information. No dietary restrictions. Not yet in puberty. No physical issues. No allergies.

Dropping the first pages, she snagged up the next set. There were initial notes from Wilhelm on her mental health and parental concerns. "Nonconforming. Belligerent. Willful." She snorted. "What did they expect when they yelled at me to stop all the time? Stop what, for heaven sake? It's not like I was having an easy time of it."

Dean reached across and grasped her hand. He squeezed gently but didn't lift his head from the paper he was reading. "I got the impression he started with the intention of helping you, but somewhere along the line he became fascinated."

"Exactly. I'd already been through every doctor in town. In fact," she thought back, "I guess they did try."

"Until your parents found Wilhelm. But why would they have walked away at that point?" Dean's tone was harsh. "Even if you had been found to have mental health issues, surely walking away wasn't a good answer for someone in that situation."

"My brother," she said pensively.

He turned to look at her. "Sorry?"

"My brother came along. And I think they figured they had a second chance, but if he picked up any of the same traits, they'd lose him too. So they cut all ties."

"That's ridiculous."

"That's fear," she corrected quietly. "If all they wanted was a normal family but got a freak first time out and a perfect example the second time around, many people would ditch the first one and try to wipe the stain out of their lives permanently."

"They aren't parents then. You can't collect perfect specimens to have in your family. Your children are a gift – with all the challenges and joys inherent in giving birth."

She liked him better all the time. Actually, she'd gone past like to something so much more. She just didn't know how much more. But damn he was good looking, alpha male, protective and caring. He was a damn good father to his son and a caring son to his mother. Tia doubted his partner would receive any different treatment.

"We see it happening all over the world," she said.

"We do," he said. "But that doesn't make it right."

She laughed. Then her smile fell away as her gaze landed on the sheet titled *Initial Assessment.* And the paragraph Wilhelm had written.

Patient is obsessed with having paranormal abilities. She believes these are factual conditions and is unwilling to consider that such phenomena might be brought into existence by her mental state. Treatment will need to include counseling, drugs and therapy.

"Nice. All three prongs." He shook his head. "Remember you survived. He didn't."

"I'd feel better if we knew for sure he was dead. Everyone says he is but…"

"According to everything we can find, he died just before you left and was cremated."

"Figures." She snorted and flicked through the pages. "Here are the drug treatments he used. Nice. I wonder how many ill effects I'll have over the years from drugs I never even knew I was being given."

"Too many. Most of these drugs weren't likely even tested on people with your condition."

"What condition?" she muttered.

"Exactly." He glanced over at the sheet. "Maybe keep that one out for your own personal history in case problems do develop further down the road. Just to see if something might show up and you need to know what you were given."

"Nice thought. Not."

"Better to never need it than to wonder later."

He was right but it still sucked.

"It's obvious his attitude changed about," he shifted pages, "nine months after you arrived. Then he started to realize you weren't faking it."

"Yeah." She smiled. "I had been very sick. Some kind of flu and strep throat. I wasn't responding to his medicines, and my body was under a lot of stress. I didn't want to be there. I wanted my mother, and he made it very clear that was never going to happen again." She ran her hands through her hair and added, "I went off the wall for a little while. I think that's the first time – likely lining up with the onset of puberty just to add to the tough physical conditions my system was going through – my body started doing weird things."

At Dean's raised eyebrows, she said, "Like you've seen a little of, but in a more minor way. My fingers would just not show up. Then they'd come back and my big toe would disappear. At that point, with him being able to see and touch the evidence, he became a complete convert. It was like night and day. Of course it took time and lots of testing. That's also when the focus on his research changed. He'd always been looking into the paranormal but not the physical anomalies I was presenting. He was looking for signs of psychometry, telekinesis, telepathy, etc."

"So he'd never seen anything like you before."

"Or since," she said honestly. "Apparently I was unique."

"And all these other people?"

"I don't know about the ones who were there when I arrived, but as far back as I can remember they were all supposed to have some kind of ability. If they did or not I don't know. Wilhelm started to get fanatical then he got angry and downright weird. I don't know when sanity turned to insanity." She hated to remember but there was no putting those back in the box. "I doubt anyone but the staff who worked with him for a long time would have seen his mental decline either."

He shook his head. "Unbelievable."

"And those of us who were there long term." She shrugged. "Then again for the last many months I was alone. Or as far as I knew I was alone." She stood up, hating the closeness of the memories. The power behind the words. "Do you have any coffee?"

"How about a glass of wine instead?" he asked, standing up and walking to the wine rack on the side counter. "It's late for coffee."

"I hate wine. But hell, I'm not going to sleep anyway," she muttered, throwing out a hand at the folders. "This is enough to keep me awake forever."

"Hey." He walked back toward her, a bottle of red wine in his hand. "Don't let it get to you. Remember, you beat this."

"I've beaten nothing." She snorted. "I'm a fugitive from some asshole connected to the place of hell I was forced to exist in for way too long. I've managed to put your entire family in danger, and I'm sitting here unable to do much in my life at all. I'd wanted to get an education at some point, I wanted a normal life and I tried it for many years, but I can't have that because I don't know what that is."

"But you *can* find out. We will fix this. You will have a future and one that you created for yourself, not the one you were forced to live." He opened the bottle of wine and poured two glasses of the deep red liquid. "Here, have this. It will help you sleep."

She doubted it, but she accepted the glass and took a sip. Instantly a deep dark dryness filled her mouth as the heady aroma filled her nose, surprising her. "Mmm, that's lovely."

"Not too dry?" he asked, carrying his glass over to the couch. He patted the space beside him. "Come and sit and relax. The paperwork isn't going anywhere."

"I wish it would," she muttered.

He laughed. "That's why we went there, isn't it?"

"No. We were supposed to get information on the others and instead found out most of them had died."

"We don't know that most died, we *think* we know that some died. We don't know that they might not have been part of an earlier study and potentially were all close to death to begin with."

"I hate to say that makes me feel better, but…it does." Her smile was lopsided as she sat down beside him. "I don't know why I said that about not being able to sleep because I am tired. But it's more a physical fatigue whereas my mind is crazy busy. I need to shut it down."

"Have another to help you relax." He opened his arm and waited until she leaned closer before wrapping it around her shoulder. From the shelter of his arms she studied him. This wasn't something she'd done before. But she'd gone into his arms naturally. How did that work? It seemed right somehow, although she didn't know him very well.

Then again, what she did know…

He pulled her closer. Surely he could hear her heart pounding. It was all she could hear.

Until the sounds of his heart filtered through.

And the heat of his body.

It was nice.

Cozy.

Caring. She could get used to this. He reached over, took her glass and placed it on a small table by the couch. She tracked it with her eyes but didn't care enough to protest. In truth she was cold and tired and any effort was proving to be too much. Besides, she was comfortable. Who'd want to move?

She'd close her eyes for a few moments. Just rest a little.

HE KNEW THE exact moment she relaxed. Her body went limp, her arm she'd held close to her chest slid down to his thigh. He shifted back on the couch, moving her slightly into a more comfortable position. The last thing he wanted was for her to wake up with a kink in her neck. She was exhausted, but it was the strain of going to the building, visiting her past rather than a lack of sleep. The bags under her eyes had deepened since they'd made it home. He'd been looking for a way to suggest she go to bed but knew she was too wired to listen.

And the folders hadn't helped. He'd actually brought over the one beside him so he could read further while she slept – if she slept. Now that she'd knocked out, he awkwardly shifted the folder to his lap and flipped it open again.

He didn't even know what to say to the information in here. She'd lived a cold loveless life so far and seeing the details – laid out like that in black and white – made it so much worse.

What was obvious was Wilhelm's fascination with Tia. Right from the beginning. But once he understood she was the real deal, it was like there'd almost been a love affair going on. Hopefully not sexual because that was going to be more than he could deal with. She'd been tortured enough with the shit he'd put her through, and Dean had seen too many cases where sexual activity happened all too often in institutions. Not that it was rape in the most common belief of the world, but more that the person wasn't free to make a choice, often didn't understand the choice and sometimes participated out of fear or as a way to curry favors to make the situation livable.

So far there'd never been any mention of such a thing. He hoped she felt capable of telling him if there had been.

As he flicked through the pages of treatments and notations regarding the reason why each failed, he had to wonder who cared about Tia's whereabouts now. Unless they knew about her abilities, believed in her abilities, and thought she'd be of some use. And what drove people to do something like this? Money, sex, power were the usual suspects. If someone knew what she could do, in theory they might be able to make money off of her – or with her. He had to consider that with a criminal partner Tia could make a killing in corporate espionage. As far as power went, he racked his mind thinking about what she could do for someone – it usually came back to her ability to go invisible and steal information. Political information. She'd help someone go a long way if she'd do that. Not that she would. At least not willingly.

So they'd have to have leverage to force her. Someone like Simone. But then they'd had Dean's own son. And they hadn't asked anything of her. Or him. Not that anyone had given the asshole time. He dropped his head back and groaned silently. This was all bullshit.

There had to be a reason for taking his son. As a message it was clear. "We can get him – anyone – any time, and there's nothing you can do about it."

But why?

He closed his eyes, hating to feel the same confusion he assumed Tia felt as she went around and around this bloody business. Honestly it might have nothing to do with her years at the institute.

He checked his phone. Still nothing from Jones. Damn. He sent him a quick text. "Update?"

The response was immediate.

"Reports on seven of those people so far." Next text came in. "All confirmed dead. All had drugs in their system. All had pre-existing medical conditions. Cause of death is stated as undetermined in each and every case."

Dean raised his gaze to stare around his living room. That was not good. Drugs for what? Knock them out. Keep them relaxed? Numb them to pain. None were good options. Particularly with this energy bullshit.

He dropped his phone, laid his head back down again and closed his eyes. It wouldn't hurt if he relaxed for a few moments himself. Not to sleep, just to rest.

He didn't know how long it was, but an odd rustling sound had him opening his eyes. He stilled, glanced down at Tia, realized she was still sound asleep. The odd sound came again. He turned to the front door to see the doorknob turning.

The door pushed open.

A gloved hand was all he saw before a sudden movement, a bright flash and the room completely disappeared in a brilliant flash.

CHAPTER 31

T IA REACTED INSTANTLY.

She didn't know what woke her, but the flashing bright light was already registered in her brain, her mind and body already following through. She didn't need to be told twice. She woke in Dean's arms, her hand in his, luminescent green flashing through the room.

"What the hell," Dean said, trying to move but he couldn't. She wouldn't let him. "Stop. He can't see you."

Dean froze, looked at their joined hands then at the living room in a green light. "Did you make the lights? What the hell is going on?"

"I'm thinking that someone tried to come in the front door," she said, standing up but keeping a tight hand on his. "And ran into Stefan's security system."

"Stefan's security system? So you didn't do this?"

She shook her head. "Hell no. This is beyond me."

No, it's not. You just don't know how yet.

She froze. And spun around, looking all around her. *Stefan, is that you?*

Yes. My senses were disturbed when the alarm went off.

She shook her head, stunned. Damn. She could *feel* Stefan inside her mind. "That's so personal."

Beside her Dean studied her face. "Say what?"

She groaned. "Thanks, Stefan, for making me odder

than ever."

You'll get used to this – eventually. A ghostly laugh rippled through her mind. *Are you both okay?*

She glanced around at Dean. "Yeah, we're okay."

Did you see the intruder?

"No I didn't. Dean," she turned to stare at Dean. "Stefan wants to know if you saw the guy."

"No, I had just dozed off."

She nodded. "No, Stef–"

I heard.

That was going to take some getting used to as well. Telepathy was one thing but Stefan could not only talk in her head, he could also use her ears to hear. How could that be?

Don't worry about it.

"What do we do now?" she asked.

Dean is already calling the cops.

Once again she turned to face Dean to see his cell phone out and held it to his ear. "Jesus, you're good."

Easy. You can do it, too.

She snorted. "Sure I can."

You can, you know.

She shrugged. "Maybe I've seen worse."

Of course you have. I heard about his program, you know. I was even there once to try and figure out what was going on. I found you alone. I helped guide you out of there.

"What? Really? That was you?" Well, that explained her "ghostly" escape.

"Hmmhmm. A parent asked me to check it out as she'd been contacted about having her son attend."

"Maybe it was after Wilhelm died?"

"I've been trying to figure that out because the letter she received had his signature on it."

"Or someone had forged it or more likely had stamped it with his signature stamp. It's easy enough to whiteout any unwanted ink on the signature line and run it through a copier to get a clean copy. Some of the stamps look original."

Who ran the place after Wilhelm?

"No idea. That's when I thought I'd been left alone. I don't know how long between his death and my escape as I was isolated for most of it."

There should have been something set up in case of his death.

"This man wasn't normal at the end. If he thought there was a way to avoid dying and losing his life's work he'd have tried anything. Hell, he was taking our blood and trying to inject himself with it."

What?

"Yeah." She gave a twisted laugh. "He was that kind of crazy at the end. He'd become a groupie, wanting to be like us, but he wasn't."

Bizarre.

But she could hear *his* mind humming away in the background. Not just his thoughts but his thought processes. She'd spoken this way with him several times already but hadn't noticed the fine nuances in the experience. Why now? Why like this?

Because we're connected mentally. You can hear the energy humming inside my head.

"You know that sounds crazy, right?"

You are saying that? You, who have had how many people say that to you?

"Ouch," she murmured. "It's different when you're on this side."

His laughter rolled out free and easily.

She frowned and turned back to see Dean, phone in hand, staring at her. Listening to her half of the conversation. Shit. She brightened the wattage of her smile and said, "Hey, did you find anything out?"

"I found out you're talking to Stefan telepathically," he said. "That's the only thing that can account for the odd look to you." He paused and looked at her in surprise. "Can you talk to other people the same way?"

What? He knew about Stefan's telepathy? What the hell? She shook her head.

He laughed. "Were you as flummoxed as I was the first time he did it?"

"When did he do that to you?"

"My son was very sick and needed more than the doctors could give him. Stefan's name was mentioned but he's damn hard to get a hold of, so one night I was having a mini melt down at the unfairness of life and railing against the powers that be who weren't helping Jeremy." He grinned. "All of a sudden Stefan stepped into my mind, explained who he was and what he could do. I was pretty freaked out at the time but then decided I couldn't look a gift horse in the mouth, and if I was wacko that was fine as long as my son was safe." He shrugged. "He's spoken to me a couple of times the same way. Now I'm okay with it, but originally – yeah weird."

She closed her eyes. "Why the hell would he do something like that?"

Not to scare people, that's for sure. But it does help cut through the bullshit of trying to get people to believe in what I can do, Stefan said quietly. *I'm not a circus performer, but like you, I can do things. Sometimes it's impossible for people to believe you without a demonstration. And when time is of the essence…this way cuts through that.*

True enough. She reached up a hand and massaged her temple. *I'm getting a headache as well.* She considered what she knew about the abilities of those she'd been incarcerated with.

"Is that headache from you?" she asked Stefan.

No, it was from you keeping the energy block between us. But now that it's gone, your headache is gone too, he said comfortably. *Or it will be when speaking telepathically becomes natural. Easy.*

She stared at Dean. Turned around and glanced back at him.

"What?"

"Stefan is talking about blocks." She walked slowly back to the couch and collapsed down. "If telepathy is natural, why do I feel weird?"

Because by opening the door to our communication you also opened up to a new space and in that space is a lot of healing energy. Energy that your body desperately needs and wants and will do a lot to get — including knocking you out. Stefan's voice started to fade. She barely heard his last humorous comment.

...like it just did.

"OH SHIT. TIA? Are you okay?" Dean stared at her in shock. "What the hell happened?" He tapped the side of her face gently. "Are you awake?" As she wasn't answering, he'd take that as a no. He studied the living room where she'd been standing. "Stefan? Do you know what happened?"

Stefan stepped into his mind. *Reaction from opening the door. Her body needs to heal. Let her rest.*

"And the asshole that tried to break into the house? This isn't exactly a good time for her to be unconscious."

There's never going to be a better time, Stefan said steadily. *Her pathways have been blocked a long time. Her skills should have bounced forward a long time ago. Whether by circumstances or by chemical, physical or psychological intervention, her development has been delayed.*

"And do you know which of those is responsible?" He couldn't imagine how her life had been or that she had more skills to open up inside. "She was damn talented to begin with. Going invisible? Wasn't that enough?"

It is and it isn't. The physical and psychological bodies are collections of various systems. When one is on, it needs the support of the others. In her case the others are blocked so when she's using her abilities, she's pulling from the other systems that are impeded by whatever is happening to her.

"How can we find out? How did I forget she was ill?" He looked at her. Her cheeks were ashen, her lips overly bright.

It's not your fault. We solved a lot of it. Dr. Maddy helped there. But she has to reconnect to her systems. Not an easy thing. And she's resisted having any skills for a long time.

"Why would she do that? She might have escaped earlier." He wouldn't mind having one or two. At least then he'd feel like he had something to offer her.

There was an odd silence. Inside and out. He sighed. "I guess you heard that thought, huh?"

Of course, but more importantly is what you didn't say. You have skills, remember. You could hear her when she was invisible – see her in a way others couldn't. You can communicate telepathically. You have skills and she's noticed. The humor in his voice made heat rush up Dean's cheeks.

She doesn't need help. She needs time in a secure setting to let down her guard and keep on letting her psyche heal.

That didn't sound like much. He glanced over at the front door. "That green light was yours, wasn't it?"

Sure. A security system. But I'd feel better if we moved her to an easier location to guard.

"This appears to be secure considering he couldn't get in," Dean exclaimed. "What else can we do?"

He didn't get in this time. That doesn't mean he won't next time, now that he knows what kind of security system is in place. And has time to figure out how to get around it next time.

Dean stared at the front door and realized Stefan was right. "But if this guy has abilities, surely he can track us no matter where we go." He groaned. "We aren't safe anywhere. Right?"

Right.

"So we need to go on the offensive."

Sure. What are you thinking?

"We could set a trap." The more he thought about it the more Dean liked the idea. Instead of waiting for the asshole to pick and choose, he wanted to make sure this guy came and never left. "What if you left one door unsecured and we get him in, then you secure the door so he can't get out."

That would be fine if he happens to get in while we see him. I won't know what's happening if he doesn't trigger an alarm. If you don't know he's inside then you are in danger too.

"Unless we aren't here," Dean said thoughtfully. "I could get some help from my captain."

You still need somewhere safe to go.

"Hmmm. Suggestions?"

Back to the hospital would be helpful but she'd fight you there, Stefan said humorously. *But a similar idea would be good.*

"It depends if we're talking one day or one week. I can

take us to a hotel for a day, no problem, but I don't have an unlimited bank account so a month is out of the question."

Hmmm

"Stefan?"

No answer.

Stefan had disappeared from his mind. As in here one second and gone the next.

Damn. Dean walked around his living room, hating the idea of being sitting ducks. They needed a safe place that was close by so they could keep an eye on the property and catch whoever was doing this. There was no point in setting this up and having a half hour drive to get back to catch the guy.

He'd been off work too long. He felt like a civilian. That really sucked.

And just like that Stefan popped back in. *There's a hotel only a couple of blocks away if you are interested.*

"There are a lot of hotels a couple of blocks away."

Stefan's voice sounded tired, worn out. *It's owned by a friend of mine. You can have a room for free if you want until this is over. Tell him I sent you. Pack light, move the truck into the garage so you pack up under cover and leave as if you were just out for a shopping trip.*

He knew the drill. "Gotcha."

Making a fast decision, he got the details and wrote them down. "Thanks, Stefan."

Dean – make it fast. He's on his way back.

CHAPTER 32

NOTHING LIKE WAKING up to find yourself in a foreign place with foreign smells and sounds. Tia didn't move. She assessed the brocade on the walls, the huge full-length windows and sheers blowing gently in the wind. Some blankets supported her and a firm bed lay beneath her.

"Feeling better?"

Dean. Recognizing the voice, she smiled and turned to see him leaning up against a strange headboard. "Where are we?"

"At a hotel," he said calmly, that gaze of his assessing. "Stefan set it up."

She frowned, sat up and kicked her legs over the side of the bed. The large room was more like a suite. And there was a bathroom off to the side. She made her way over to it, feeling his gaze on her every step. She had no idea what was going on here but needed a few minutes to wake up and process. She cast her mind back and realized she'd been talking to Stefan, there was a pain in her head, a weird nausea and then nothing.

She hated blackouts.

She used the bathroom and while washing her hands she stared at the image in the mirror. Bright eyes as if she'd had a long rest – what a joke, her hair stuck out everywhere as if she hadn't washed it in a long time – and maybe she hadn't.

But the bruising under her eyes, that was a constant. There was a huge glass shower behind her. And several big fluffy towels.

She glanced down at her clothes and winced. She didn't own much in the way of clothes. Had the little bit she owned come with her? And would it matter if she was in a robe for a few hours while laundry was happening? She rinsed her clothes in the sink and laid them out to dry over the heater. She wanted to feel clean for now.

Making a fast decision, she turned to the marble shower. She didn't think she'd ever been in anything so fancy. Water jetted from the top as she turned it on. She stepped under the hot spray and closed her eyes in joy.

Water had never felt so good. She didn't know how long she stood there but finally realized that if she didn't get moving Dean would come and check up on her. And she didn't want that. Well she did but not because he was worried about her. Sigh. She was an idiot.

She loved having him around, but she wanted him there because he wanted to be there and not because she was a helpless female in distress. She hadn't been that in a long time, and yet, she hadn't seemed to step out of that role since she'd met him.

As she shampooed her hair for the second time she re-membered the attack and green light at Dean's house. What the hell had happened? An intruder obviously, and some kind of alarm system. Stefan's. A knock sounded on the door. "Tia, breakfast is here."

She shut off the water, suddenly famished. Hell, she was always hungry and today it was even worse. Had whatever healing that had been going on burned up more calories? Was that even possible? She barely kept flesh on her hipbones as it was. Too nervy and on the run. She wondered what her mother and grandmother looked like. Was this frame genetic or was she abnormally thin for her maternal line?

She didn't want to dress in wet clothes so grabbed the robe behind the door and walked out.

And came face to face with Dean.

Her nostrils flared. The smell of him. The sight of him.

All she could do was stare. She watched him from under lowered lashes, knowing what was going to happen next unless she stopped it. She was so damn tired of running.

And he offered something she was desperate to have.

Solace. Comfort. Love. Even if only for a few moments.

Something to smile about later when she was alone again.

He'd been so good to her, she couldn't stay. He had family. He didn't need trouble. And all she'd ever had was trouble.

His hands were gentle but firm, he drew her up against his chest. "Did you enjoy your shower?"

The strong scent of male hit her nostrils. Those strong hands gripped her waist, long fingers grasped her flesh. Her gaze locked on his, she nodded. The heat in his eyes lit fires between her legs. Her breath caught in the back of her throat, her eyelids closed as he lowered his head.

Giving in to the urge, she wrapped her arms around his neck and accepted the soft kiss he pressed on her lips. Their mouths moved in synchronization. Her fingers curled into his thick dark mane. Her body softened in his arms and turned compliant.

He guided her down to the bed, their bodies never leaving each other's. Dean grabbed the edges of her bathrobe, tugging it open to spread across the sheets. She shuddered as a cool gust of wind breathed across her heated flesh. Her belly muscles clenched and unclenched from excitement, nervousness and anxiety. Need.

A jolt shot down her body as she lay open to his gaze.

"Beautiful," he whispered. "You are so beautiful."

He stood up, his gaze hot on her heated flesh. Clothes were quickly cast aside until he stood in front of her as nude as she was. More, in fact. She sat up, letting the bathrobe drop from her shoulders. Pressure built up in the pit of her stomach, butterflies emerged and flapped their wings as Dean regarded her.

Multiple tiny scars covered her body. Long healed but still visible in a crisscross network as evidence of what she'd been through. He gently traced several across her belly and her ribs.

She caught her breath, afraid he'd be turned off. She searched his eyes. Love filling her as she saw his eyes were hooded, filled with desire.

With a gentle moan she opened her arms and reached up for him. Her hand closed around him, so big. So hard. She loved the way the breath caught in the back of his throat. The groan that escaped before he could hold it back. She stroked a finger across the tip, her finger sliding through the drop of moisture. He growled and pulled back.

He slid his arms around her, his hands sliding down her ribs to her waist and her buttocks. And he came down on top of her. There was no time to adjust to the feel of his body, so hot and heavy on hers, because he captured her lips and took possession of them in a way she'd never known.

Lord had she'd missed out.

When he finally lifted his head, she lay there still gasping as sensation after sensation rolled through her. Then he slid down her body, dropping tiny kisses…everywhere. On the plump curve to her breast. The gentle hills and valleys of her ribs. Across the dip of her belly, his tongue swirling around inside her belly button. His hands stroked from her ankle to her hip and back again. She tried to reach for him, her fingers tangling in his hair. When she went to tug him upward, he pulled free and slid his hand down to the heart of her and slid one finger deep inside.

Her hips arched up and she moaned.

So he withdrew and did it again.

The second time she cried out. By the time he lowered his head and swirled his tongue over and around the tiny nub she was weeping and chanting his name.

He shifted and moved upward. Growling, he moved until he was positioned right at her tight opening. His gaze locked on hers as he drove deep within.

She cried out, her hips surging upward as he drove deeper. Her mouth parted in a silent moan as her inner muscles expanded to accommodate him.

They groaned simultaneously. He never gave her the chance for her body to get used to him before he was driving more. Her mouth found his, their tongues dueling and tasting one another.

As they started to move in synchronization, Tia found herself unable to look away. Their gazes were trapped as their bodies moved to the oldest song in the world. Accenting their pleasure. She broke away from his intense regard and closed her eyes, her hips rising to meet his strong thrusts. His breath raspy, harder, heavier. Pressure built. She tossed her head from side to side, her hands grasping his arms. She dug her nails into his flesh.

"Ah," he cried, made a quick adjustment to his position then drove down again.

She cried out, her world on fire as the climax ripped through her.

Grinding his hips against hers, he arched his back, a guttural moan ripping from deep in his chest.

And he collapsed down beside her.

Moisture in the corner of her eyes didn't surprise her. It had been so much more emotional than she'd expected. And now that lovemaking was over she felt shy. Insecure. Foolish, considering he was still seated in her body.

Then she remembered. "You said breakfast was here!" she cried, trying to push herself up on her elbows to survey the room.

He gave a shout of laughter and rolled over. "One appetite appeased and another awaits?"

"Damn right."

Within minutes, Dean had a cart sitting beside the table at the window. "There you are. Perfect. Come eat."

She smiled, now dressed in her robe again, and walked closer. Pancakes and sausages and eggs. And with any luck — still warm. "This is great. What are you having?"

He laughed and said, "Whatever you're not apparently. Not to worry, I can always get more if we need to."

"Good," she mumbled with a full mouth. "We just might."

He shot her a disbelieving look and served himself a full plate. "I ordered these all as side dishes instead of ordering two plates."

"Good idea," she said. Then she fell to serious eating. She powered through her pancakes topped in maple syrup and butter then fell into the eggs and sausage. When she was done, she looked up to see him watching her carefully.

"What's the matter?" She reached for her coffee cup to see he'd poured thick cream into it. She gave him a fat smile and lifted her cup in a salute. "Thanks for this." She took a sip. Closing her eyes, she realized if nothing else had told her she was in a high-end establishment the coffee would. Rich, dark, mysterious and full bodied. She almost wanted to cry.

"So good," she murmured, cradling the cup in her hand.

"Glad to hear that. So are you feeling better now that you've filled up again?"

She nodded and studied the remaining food on the cart. "Maybe I could manage a little bit extra."

He scooped the leftover eggs and sausage onto her plate. "There, is that better?"

She nodded. "I'm not sure why I'm so hungry."

"Because you slept the night and the day away. It's not Saturday or Sunday. It's Monday."

HE WONDERED HOW she'd take the news. In fact, she looked like she was still processing. She held onto her cup of coffee again and stared out the window, an odd look on her face.

"You know when I escaped from that damn place, I worried I'd missed out on so much. I swore I never would let that happen again. I wanted to experience everything. Now apparently I missed the last day and a half." She groaned. "And of course there was the month and a half before that too when I was comatose in the hospital."

"After you fell asleep, Stefan said the guy was on his way back with the right tools to fight through the alarm system. It wasn't intended to do more than let us know there was an intruder. Given that and your condition, Stefan offered this place, and I packed up, carried you out and brought you here."

"Thank you."

He searched her gaze but not seeing anything untoward nodded his head and said, "You're welcome."

"What do we do now?" she said, her gaze unwilling to let his go. He could understand that. He'd completely changed her life and now she likely didn't know where she stood.

"I'm waiting to hear from my partner. He's been chasing down the names from the file we found. Hoping to find someone still alive."

As if he'd heard them talking about him, Dean's cell phone went off showing a picture of Jones. "There he is now," Dean said.

He answered his phone, pushing his chair back slightly. "Any news, Jones?" He put the phone on speaker.

"We tracked down two grad students who came into the program later. One had been fired and the other quit. The one who'd been fired said he'd been trying to make the living conditions more bearable for the people in the institution. He was quite aggravated and upset during the conversation. Said it was horrible. The other guy said he couldn't do it. The place was horribly run, and it was obvious that the doctor wasn't all there anymore. He was obsessed with paranormal abilities."

Dean interrupted him. "Did he think the doctor had any abilities of his own?"

"No, I don't believe so, but he was looking to use iron and steel in some of his experiments but would never explain why or how. Particularly small balls."

"But there were still others there at the time. According

to Tia, she was the last one left."

"That's the thing, he was there almost to the end and said there was a lot of hush hush discussion going on — figured that's actually why he'd been fired as he'd overhead something he shouldn't have. They'd told him they were in the process of moving to a new location. Only he didn't know where it was."

Dean's heart slammed against his ribs. "They moved everyone somewhere else?"

"According to the one guy. The other one knew nothing about it."

"Maybe he wasn't there at the same time?"

"No, he was a couple of months earlier." His tone changed. "I did check on some of the parents of the dead kids."

Ah, here was something. Dean straightened. "And."

"I got a hold of Calendar's mom and she was a pistol. Said it was a Godsend that the boy died. According to Wilhelm he was in terrible pain at the end and his passing was easy."

"What?" Dean looked across at Tia who'd been eyeing the last two pancakes on the trolley. But at Jones's words, she sat up. He asked her, "Did you know Billy to be ill?"

Her face twisted in a frown as she thought for a moment then she shook her head. "The last time I remember seeing him, he was laughing and joking." She stared out the window. "No, that's not quite true. The last time I spoke to him he was like that. But the last time I saw him I was in the observation room, and they were wheeling him down the hallway. He didn't look so good then."

"Any physical injuries?"

She shrugged. "Not that I could see but his skin had a

gray cast. I remember thinking he needed a doctor because he was sick."

"According to his mother, he had a terminal illness and Wilhelm said his death was a kindness at the end."

Dean watched her slump back in her seat and play with her fork. It had to be tough to have all these memories not match up with the current information.

Jones continued to speak. "We spoke to a couple of other parents. One wouldn't talk to us, said his boy was deceased and there was nothing to be gained by talking to us about his condition. And another–"

"Condition? What condition?"

"That's the question, isn't it? He wouldn't talk to us. Said if we knew how to find him and ask about his boy then we obviously had the information we needed already."

"Typical." So many people became belligerent when the cops asked questions. "And the other one?"

"Yeah, that's not so nice. She was the girl's aunt and said basically good riddance. The girl was nothing but trouble since she was born and nothing she'd seen that girl do since had made up for her living with her."

"Wow, nice family."

"So I'm getting the idea these were all misfits or unloved or terminally ill cases that no one else could help."

"So far they are fitting into that pattern, yes."

"And his funding?"

"Private. We're still working on that. Keep in mind Wilhelm came from a very wealthy European family and likely had access to the family coffers."

"Hell, they probably paid him to stay over here and do his research and keep him out of their lives."

"Quite possibly. The company was Wilhelm Bros, Ltd.

Although, there were a couple of other administrators in and out, but no names."

"Okay, keep me posted," he said. "We need to find his new location too."

"Yeah, quiz Tia. She likely knows more than she thinks she does."

They hung up and Dean tossed his phone on the small table. He reached over and filled his cup of coffee. Hers was still full. Not sure how to approach the conversation, he stayed quiet.

"Well," she asked. "Another location. Interesting. The place was empty when I escaped. I always assumed I was the last one alive."

"Or maybe you were just the last one to be moved." His tone deepened. "And maybe they are still looking for you to go back and join them."

She swallowed hard. "As in I'm the one that got away?"

"As in, they just haven't collected you – yet."

CHAPTER 33

S HE STARED AT him. Her stomach roiled at the thought, but there was something there…something triggering in the back of her memories.

"There was something about collecting under one roof, but I don't remember much about that. As if there might have been several labs that needed to be combined into one."

"What?" Dean leaned forward. "So there could have been several labs?"

She shrugged. "There could have been dozens. And run by Wilhelm's family for all I know. I saw a man who looked to be his brother arguing with him one day." She smiled. "I was in the observation room again."

"This is the first you've mentioned visitors."

"It's the first you've asked," she said in exasperation. "How am I supposed to know what's important and what's not?"

"Okay, think back. Did you hear a name? See a name tag? Hear anyone else mention Wilhelm's family?"

"Sure, we all joked about it all the time. He had brothers, several of them, and a mother who lived back in the homeland. The sons all came to America in search of a better life." But she added, a mocking tone to her voice, "Instead he found us."

"And he wanted more."

"He wanted much more than he originally thought. I never did hear any of the conversations between the suits that came to check up on his work or between the other doctors that came through. We were kept isolated. The staff talked, but to each other, not so much to us, but we had a great gossip line. We tried to keep each other in the loop but…we were limited."

"Understood."

"Can't we find the records of who worked there and who donated money to them?"

"We haven't found anything yet. Being private it could take a court order to make that happen. On the other hand, the grad students were from the university, worked mostly for free and had limited access."

"Sure, but they know names that I wouldn't."

"I'll text Jones about that." He picked up the phone and started to write out the message.

"Labs. I remember them talking about multiple labs." She tried to remember, but everything was faint and foggy. She'd also spent a lot of years trying to avoid thinking about the nightmare of her time there.

"As kids, didn't you joke around, play jokes on the staff or try to prank them. Surely there are tidbits that you remember that were personal."

She shrugged, understanding why he needed to know but also realizing he had no idea how painful what he was asking was. Pushing her chair back, she stood up and carried her coffee over to the table. "I'll think about it, maybe jot down a few notes and see what I can pull out of my brain." As if by magic, a blank pad of paper showed up in front of her on the coffee table. She laughed. "Right."

He walked toward the bed.

"What are you going to do?"

"Find you some clothes," he said in a dark voice and walked away from her.

She glanced down and realized the front of her robe had fallen open. She flushed and tugged the edges of the terry-cloth together. To hide her embarrassment and cleavage, she snatched up the pen and paper and curled up in the corner of the couch.

The paper stared back at her, as blank as her mind, but her heart pounded against her chest. She wasn't scared. Or alarmed, so what the hell was going on? She closed her eyes and leaned back.

Instantly, she was thrown back into a memory. Another notepad on the table, a pen beside it. And orders to do something. But what.

She hated this blackness in her mind. But there was someone talking to her. Back then.

Write it down.

All of it.

Tell me how you are doing this.

Every last detail.

The orders flew at her at an alarming pace and the tone darkened. Deepened. She placed the notepad down and stared at it. How did she do what she was doing? He seemed to think anyone could do this if she gave them the instructions.

Her current mindset tried to probe the memory for details. Looking for something to grasp onto.

"You aren't so special," he snarled. "Anyone can do this."

"Then do it," she snapped. "Just do it. Why do you need me?"

"I don't need you but I own you so you will help me or else."

"Or else what?" she screamed.

The slap had been hard, clean, and made her brains shake. She'd heard ringing in her ears for days.

The interview had been terminated at that point as she'd had to be carried back to her room. Her face had swelled up and she'd been afraid he'd broken her cheekbone. But he'd given her the weapon she needed against him and his probing.

The next time he'd asked her how she did it, she had her answer for him. "What difference does it make, you'll never be able to do it." She'd deliberately made her tone weary and calm.

He'd responded in kind. "And why is that?"

"Because to do what I do takes control."

She'd avoided a second blow then but only because she'd ducked. He was so angry he'd left her alone in the observation room for days. Like that was a punishment. Her bedroom was always isolated and locked down, but in the observation room she could watch the nurse flirt with the orderly, the men talking to Wilhelm. The fights.

Fights?

She directed her mind back to that scene. She'd often run to sit with her back along the wall under the window and listen. She could hear better there. And if she stretched her legs out then they could see her too and left her alone.

To hear.

DEAN WATCHED HER sit on the couch lost in something. She held the notepad to her chest. He felt like an ass for mentioning her state of undress. Especially when he only wanted to tear the damn robe completely off of her. What the hell was wrong with him? She was under his protection. She needed him and she'd been taken advantage of all her life. He wasn't going to be one of them.

He was going to be the good guy.

And maybe she'd not look at him as someone to walk away from when this was all over. He'd had plenty of time to ponder what he was doing with her in his life.

Trying to take his mind off her, he started searches for her parents, for other family members in the hopes they all weren't assholes.

He'd also done his best to track down as many of the employees of the lab. He'd called the parent company, but they told him nothing.

From the lab, the best leads were the grad students, but they'd only been able to track the last two of those. Surely there were dozens of others throughout the years. If there were more labs…now that was something to ask the parent company.

On impulse he picked up the phone and called the last woman he'd spoken to. "My apologies, this is Detective Walker again. I forgot to ask you about the number of labs connected to Wilhelm's work."

"There was the one we spoke about. It was connected to a different lab early on, but those two headed in different directions," she said hesitantly. "Hmm. Workman. Dr. Workman is running the other lab."

Dean nodded. The name meant nothing to him. "So none of the patients from the one lab was moved to the other?"

"Patients? No, there were no patients at all," she exclaimed. "Wilhelm was doing research on rats. Only on rats."

Dean stared out at the city sprawled below. "Rats? Are you sure," he said in a low tone. "My understanding is there were patients there. Living at Wilhelm's lab."

"No, no. You must be mistaken," she said in a harried voice. "We aren't involved in any human testing. Only animals." She cleared her throat and lowered her voice, "Now if you'll excuse me, I need to get back to work." And she hung up.

Her actions were the biggest indicator of something wrong yet.

But how could he get concrete proof? He also had the technicians who'd worked there. Even if they were the only two left, they were eyewitnesses. The company might have tried to bury the fact that their scientist had been doing illegal testing, but it wasn't going to stay buried. He'd make sure the company paid for their involvement in what they'd done to Tia.

He checked his email again, looking for something from Jones. He didn't want to text yet again, but it was hard not to constantly check in for updates. There was an email.

The subject line – an exchange.

The sender's name was a series of numbers and letters and as his stomach sank, he realized this was going to be bad.

He hated to but clicked the email to open in the pane below.

And there was a child, black and bruised and unconscious lying on a small cot. No windows to the room, no light to the space. Tears were long dried on the child's face. Dean strangled back a gasp, desperately trying to keep Tia out of this. Marshaling his thoughts, his fists clenched and wishing for a target, he tried to neutralize the anger by studying the photo carefully.

It was old was the first thing he noticed.

The child was maybe ten.

Could be slightly older.

He'd been beaten. Nothing else gave quite the same look to flesh and blood as damage caused by another person.

He couldn't tell if the child was male or female. But it had suffered.

In a horrible way.

Glancing over at Tia, he closed the image down and went back to the email. But there was nothing else there except the wording in the subject line. And no matter which way he looked at it, the message gave no more details. He immediately forwarded it to Jones and then as an afterthought, he forwarded it to Stefan.

His phone rang almost immediately. He glanced at Tia and walked out of the room so she wouldn't overhear the conversation.

"Jesus. What the hell are you mixed up in, Dean?"

"No idea," he said, his voice heavy, hating to think they had a child murder case here.

"You don't recognize the boy?"

"Is it a boy?" Dean shook his head. "And no I don't.

"I don't either. With that angle on his face, facial recognition won't be a help either."

"I was hoping there'd be some way to identify him."

"I'll send it to the lab. You know the captain is going to want to see you. Both of you. This changes everything."

He knew that, but he didn't think Tia was ready for such a visit. And he knew the captain wouldn't take no for an answer.

CHAPTER 34

WOULD HE TELL her what was going on? Or try to keep it to himself. She'd watched the shock on his face turn to horror then fear before morphing into rage. It had been the rage that worried her. Only in his case it was controlled. Calm. Clenched fists and locked down jaw. If he looked at her she knew she'd see hardened steel in his eyes. As he stared at his laptop, she couldn't imagine what might have set him off, but something did.

Then he'd picked up the phone and left. Now he was back at his laptop. She stood up quietly and walked to the back of the room and came up behind him quietly just as he clicked on an email and brought up an image.

She gasped.

He spun around, saw her, then snapped back to close down the email. Then his hand slowed. "Do you know that boy?"

"It's no boy," she whispered. "That's Billy."

"What? I thought you said Billy was a boy?"

She looked down at him. "No, she preferred to be treated as a boy, and she always called herself a he – so we did too."

"And this image?"

She shook her head, hating to think about when it was taken. "It looks like one of the rooms at the lab, but I don't know for sure."

"Did you ever see her like this?"

Again she shook her head. "No, not like this. But…" she tried to cast her mind back… "It's hard to place her because of her aging issue."

Dean stared at her again. "What aging issue?"

"She never seemed to age. She always looked like a ten year old girl."

"Jesus. I can't imagine."

He stared at the image on his computer. "Take a closer look. Can you see if this might be an old image of her? Supposedly she's deceased, remember."

She pulled up the chair she'd been sitting in earlier, shoving the food cart out of the way, and sat down for a closer look. She studied the room first. "The walls are similar in that they are plain and appear to be smooth without a pattern. The bed she's on is similar. It's metal, smooth rounded corners. The floor… She tried to see the floor in the image.

Dean made a couple of clicks and enlarged it. She leaned in a little. "The floor is linoleum looking squares and could also be from the same lab. Then again if there were two labs they could both have been outfitted at the same time and in the same way."

He nodded. "The bedding?"

"Now that is a bit different. The lab was always warm and we only ever had a sheet."

"No blankets?"

The shock in his voice made her laugh. "Like I said it was always warm in there so no, no blankets. But…" she tapped the screen. "It appears she might have one."

"Or it's a hoody or sweater."

They stared at the image, closely trying to figure out if the rumpled material under her head was either of their suggestions.

Then her eyes caught on the one new thing that was definite. "Well there's that," she said, her voice dropping as tears clogged her throat. "The chains were definitely new."

He caught his breath back and leaned in. "I didn't see them before," he admitted.

"Neither did I. They are slightly hidden."

"Not enough." He pushed his chair back and walked to the big bay window. "You never had chains?" He waited.

"No. Never chains."

She watched the relief take the starch out of his shoulder as he relaxed slightly. But she didn't think protecting him would help. And the truth was likely to come out. In a way she really wanted it to come out. "We had leather straps."

He froze. Slowly so very slowly he turned to face her. But the look on his face had her rushing to tell him. "They weren't that bad. They didn't cut into our wrists and if they did, they put a fur thing around the collar so our skin wouldn't bleed."

She didn't dare tell him that the bleeding made a mess of the sheet, which was why they protected the delicate skin. She didn't think he'd like to hear that bit.

He opened his arms and tugged her into them. Held hard against his chest, she couldn't miss the tremor that raced through his huge frame. She wrapped her arms around him and held him close. "It's okay, you know. It's over."

"I knew that, but I didn't really 'get' it until now."

His arms squeezed tighter. "You really were a prisoner, weren't you?"

She nodded. "Yes, I was. We all were." She twisted in his

arms to look back at the laptop. "I'm afraid some of us still are."

There was a convulsive movement in his arms crushing her close, his breath hot at her temple. That he cared made her all rosy inside. "I'm sorry. I'd have preferred you never found out."

"Why?"

"Because it's painful for you. For so many people, stuff like this makes them uncomfortable."

"So what if it does?" he snapped. "You lived a horrible life."

"But others don't need to suffer for it," she said with a warm smile. "It's enough that one of us did already."

"And yet..." he nodded to the laptop, "someone might still be suffering."

DEAN STARED AT the photo on the laptop. Tia was getting dressed in the bathroom with the clothes he'd brought her from the house. They had to get to the station now before the captain showed up here – and that he didn't want to have happen. This location must be kept safe. But they also needed more clothes for Tia. Jones was going to pick up some and bring them to the station.

Maybe they'd fit. Jones knew women, but even he hadn't seen her long enough to be able to judge her clothing size.

She walked out, a set look on her face. He understood. Seeing Billy's picture had affected them both. He was afraid it was going to get a whole lot worse before it got any better.

"Ready?"

She nodded. He sighed. She wasn't even close to being

ready, but it was what it was. He held out his hand, and when she placed hers inside, he tugged her close.

"We'll get through this."

"I know. Just the memories…"

"I'm sorry. We don't know that she's dead, so remember that."

"We don't know that she's alive either."

Yet given the paper work they were taking in to the office, he doubted she was. But he had to stay positive for Tia's sake. And his own.

She was too damn important for him to lose. He squeezed her hand, ignoring the questioning look she gave him. She might not know what he was thinking, but he had a handle on it. This girl was special and his grandpa raised no fool. Now that he had her straight in his head, and why it took so long he didn't know, he wasn't going to let her go.

He wanted to hold her close so she couldn't run away, and even if she did go invisible, and boy could that take some explaining to his son and mother, then he wanted to make sure he didn't lose her.

What if Stefan hadn't offered him the job at the psych ward? There'd been other guards there. What if some of them had found her as interesting as he had? He might not have made this connection – ever. His life was so much richer for having her in it. He was truly blessed.

"Are you okay?" she murmured as they waited for the elevator to arrive.

"Better than okay."

She slanted another look his way but kept quiet. He grinned, and happier than he had been in a very long time, he started to whistle.

The elevator door opened and let two men out. They got

in and took the ride down to the main floor.

Outside it had started to drizzle. They ran to Dean's truck and dove inside the cab. Laughing like teens on a first date, Dean pulled out of the parking lot and headed for his station.

"Is your captain a scary guy?"

"What can I say, but maybe?" Dean knew he should likely warn her, but the captain was the captain. Big and badass, their captain was a man with a big temper but was also a man of his word. The guys looked up to him. He was a leader they respected. But God help you if you screwed up.

"That's clear as mud," she said, laughing. "At least you didn't lie."

No point. She'd find out soon enough. And boy did she. They walked into the station about twenty minutes later to hear someone roaring in the background. Dean winced.

Then they were spotted.

"Well about damn time. Did you think this is a bloody Sunday school party? You were supposed to get your ass in here hours ago." The biggest male in the office roared toward them like a tornado on steroids. And Dean looked to be his target. "Did you see Dr. Loring like you were supposed to? He's been asking about you. As if you were avoiding him."

Dean cursed under his breath. He had missed the shrink's last appointment. "I'll call him."

"Yes, you damn well will," he roared. "We need you sound, physically and mentally."

Tia gasped and tried to hide behind Dean as the captain bore down on them.

"See, what did I tell you," Dean said. "There's nothing to worry about. He's a pussycat."

The tornado whirled to a stop just feet in front of them.

His mouth worked several times then he gave up. He stumbled backwards and swallowed hard. In a very low voice he said, "Conference room one, *now.*"

Dean raised his eyebrows but didn't say a word. He turned and, tugging Tia along with him, took her to the first of several conference rooms.

"Take a seat," Dean said, motioning to the big table in front of him.

"Okay," she whispered.

And that's when Dean understood. Tia walked carefully forward, pulled back a chair from the table and sat down. Except her body, her features, were translucent, as if more ghost than substance. Even he hadn't seen that before.

He never got a chance to say anything before his arm was yanked and he was pulled from the room, the door firmly shut behind him.

Expecting to face his furious boss, instead Dean faced a man gone white from shock.

"Please tell me I'm having a migraine and that I did not see what I thought I saw?"

"Sorry," Dean said quietly. "You absolutely did. But it's not that bad. And if you don't calm down, she won't be able to pull herself together enough to talk to you."

"I did that?" The look on his face was terrible to see.

"Anyone terrorizing her is going to do that. I don't even know all that triggers this reaction, but I can guarantee you that fear does."

The captain was a good man. Once he calmed down he took a deep breath and said, "Let's go talk to her."

"I'm getting a coffee for her."

"I'll wait," the captain said, looking at the door. "I wouldn't want to freak her out anymore."

"No, of course not," Dean muttered, adding, "Except yanking me out of there and leaving her alone isn't likely to make her very comfortable either."

"I didn't know." But he looked terrible, yet also very hesitant to enter the room. Dean remembered his initial reaction too.

"No, you didn't." Dean glanced around. "I was hoping to get through this without everyone seeing her do that."

"I'll keep them away." He turned and glared at the very curious onlookers. "Get your asses back in your seats. The show is over."

Dean poured two cups of coffee from the sideboard and came back to the observation room. The coffee from this area was generally a whole lot easier to get down than from the other side. "Can you open the door, please?"

The captain complied then followed Dean inside.

Dean set the mugs down and took a quick look around. Shit.

"Where the hell is she?" the captain roared. "She's gone."

CHAPTER 35

TIA WATCHED THE big black man like he was a viper in her midst or maybe a grizzly was a better analogy. Vipers were small and deadly, but she figured this guy would shout the world to death before he had to take a bite. Damn he was big. Dean had said big but she didn't know he meant *big*. Like holy crap he had to be close to seven feet tall. And he had the manners of a linebacker. She almost smiled. She'd never met one so maybe linebackers had no manners. The thing was, she wasn't prepared to deal with this guy, viper or grizzly.

Regardless of what Dean said.

"Tia, it's okay."

Like hell.

"Honest. His bark is worse than his bite. He's not going to hurt you." Dean turned to the captain. "Right?"

The captain glared at him. "What the hell are you up to?"

Dean ran a hand down his face. She felt sorry for him. He really had a shitty life if he had to face this guy every day. No wonder he had to take the month off. Big time.

She leaned back and closed her eyes.

"Please, Tia."

Okay, that one kind of tugged at her.

"Dean, stop joking around. It's obvious she's gone.

Where and how I don't know, but you can bet by morning I'll know. Even if I have to get some kind of security system in here."

Dean groaned. "If you'd calm down…"

"Calm down? I am calm. Otherwise you'd be out on the street on your ass right now," he roared.

Ah shit. Dean was going to get into big trouble if she didn't do something. She really didn't want to face him. But the coffee was looking mighty fine. Then again it was cop coffee – would it even be drinkable?

Not likely. But maybe…she reached across and dragged the coffee toward her. It wasn't super hot. As the other two kept up their bickering, she lifted the cup and took a drink. Nice. Much better than she'd expected. She took another sip then another. Finally, she realized the shouting had stopped.

She glanced over to find them both staring at her.

"Tia? Honey? I know this is normal for you, but for other people it's a bit of a shock."

She started. Then realized to them, her coffee cup was sitting in mid air. Dean wouldn't give a damn, but the captain pulled a chair out on his side and collapsed. The look on his face was the funniest she'd seen in a long time. With a sigh, she shifted her energy and let the edges of her form show. To hell with them. Now she should be more opaque, but that was all he deserved. Damn it.

Only the look on his face made her afraid he'd have a heart attack – like for real.

"Fine." She tried to take the disgruntled tone out of her voice but knew she hadn't succeeded when Dean tried to hide his smile.

She showed her full body and glared at him. "Happy now?"

"Yes, thank you." He sat down and calmly reached for the spare cup. "The captain, now, he might need a moment or two."

"Jesus." And this time the captain's voice was soft as a prayer. His whole demeanor had changed, shifted into a believer even if he never knew what that meant. Now he was facing a reality shift that he couldn't have ever contemplated.

"Yeah, nice to meet you. I'm Tia," she said impudently.

Dean shot her a warning look. She just raised an eyebrow back. "He yelled at me."

"I did. And I'm sorry," the captain said. To give him credit, he reached a hand across the table, still shaky but quickly trying to regain lost ground, toward her. "I'm Captain Bronsen."

"Tia Hanniger," she said with a nod, then eying his hand distrustfully she gave it a small, quick shake.

"I'm sorry I scared you earlier. In truth my wife gets on my case all the time about it. I do have a temper, but..." his eyes closed and his next words had her realizing he really did know who she was or her history at least, "I would never hurt you."

She eyed him in disbelief. "If I was forty pounds lighter, you would have knocked me over with your voice alone," she snapped.

He grinned. "But you're not forty pounds lighter and you are fine."

"Hmmph." She eyed him carefully but the thought of being lighter brought back that it had been a long time since breakfast. "How long ago did we eat?" she asked Dean.

He rolled his eyes. "It must be hours because you're hungry, right?"

She nodded. "Well, I am hungry, even if it's only been

one hour."

"I'll go grab something from a vending machine."

"Don't bother, there are dozens of donuts in the conference room," the captain said.

Tia lit up at the thought.

"I thought you needed to eat healthy," Dean muttered, narrowing his gaze at her.

"Donuts are a food group all their own," she muttered. "Anyone who doesn't think so, never ate them."

The captain snickered. "Better bring a couple and I'll have a coffee too."

Being sent out as he was, there wasn't much Dean could do, but he stopped at the doorway and looked back at both of them. "Play nice." And he shut the door.

Left alone, Tia tried to gauge the captain. As far as she could see, his energy was green and orange and had some red flares still sitting inside and poking at him, part of the temper issue, she was sure. She decided to bring it up. As she opened her mouth, she caught sight of small images floating around him. Football, oh look she had him pegged correctly. She saw pictures of a beautiful woman and two boys climbing all over him. He really was a family man. With a temper.

"If you'd let some of that go, you wouldn't be so quick to fly off the handle you know?" She kept her voice low, her tone neutral. The wrong tone and people tended to get really irritated.

The captain asked in confusion, "What? Let what go?"

"That you didn't get your chance to lead your team to victory at twenty-five. That's when you blew your knee out permanently, isn't it? And the team went downhill from there. You stood on the sidelines and screamed at them to get it right but because they needed you on the field, it wasn't the same anymore." She waited a half beat and added in a very gentle voice, "Was it?"

He stared at her in shock. There was barely any color on his face which being a mix of milk and dark chocolate looked very odd. But his red flares were lighting up again.

"It wasn't your fault. It was an accident. You can't keep that anger inside."

She leaned back to see what he'd do with that. Likely ignore her. That's what most people did. Not that she spoke to many like this over the years. But those in Land's Edge had lots of issues. Some wanted to know and others…not so much. After all, who wanted someone else to poke and pry into their lives? No one.

And certainly not this huge guy. "You've got power and prestige, a beautiful wife and two sons. You've been to anger management and marriage counseling and still you can't let go of the anger. That championship was yours. You can feel it. Taste it. And if you hadn't had that damn accident you'd have made it. But…" she waited and watched, getting an idea as the truth hit her. "You blame the other guy. The one who tackled you to the ground and the fight that ensued. You were never the same again."

He was past staring. His eyes had gotten huge but the red flares were still sitting spiking. Not erupting, and for that she was grateful, but too close for comfort. "It was a game. He paid a high price too."

At that the captain jerked in surprise, and she nodded. "There's no way an injury like that happens to just one. For all you know he's worse off than you. And it wasn't even the championship game, so he didn't get that win either. You both wanted it. You were both aggressive – too aggressive.

That's another problem here. You feel guilty. As if you were responsible for the whole team losing. If he hadn't pounded you back, but also if you had taken a different play, it would have all turned out another way. And you insisted on that play, didn't you?"

"I was so sure I could do it," he said in a voice barely above a whisper. "So damn sure."

"And you did make it," she responded gently. "But you didn't think long term. Big picture."

He nodded. "That was the coach's big phrase. It's not about winning the game, it's about taking home the trophy."

"And he was right." She watched and waited. Not everyone wanted to see hard truths. Good for him to listen and not take a strip off her.

The door opened to let Dean inside, a plate of donuts balanced on top of a cup of coffee. "I almost got mugged," he muttered. "You have no idea how my life was in jeopardy out there."

He sent a questioning glance to Tia then back at the captain. "Here's your coffee, sir."

The captain nodded but didn't say anything. Instead, he drew circles on the table with his finger as if by doing so he could change history or at least go back in time and have another chance.

Tia understood. She would do the same thing if she could. She smiled at Dean and beamed at the plate. "Captain, do you want a donut?"

"No, I've had a couple already."

He motioned to her to go ahead.

"Dean?" She glanced over at him to see him grinning suspiciously.

"Go ahead, Tia, all three are for you."

She grinned and bit into the first one. "Awesome," she mumbled. And sat back in peace and joy. Food.

DEAN WATCHED HER enjoyment. Such a simple thing. He wanted to go and get her another half dozen donuts if it would make her that happy. He couldn't imagine the things she'd missed growing up. Maybe she'd had a chance to enjoy many fun foods before she joined Wilhelm, but he doubted she'd had much opportunity.

She scarfed the first one and picked up the second and took a bite. He was trying to give the captain some time. He didn't know what had happened to the big man while he'd been gone, but something obviously had changed him. He wasn't scared, neither was he angry. He looked thoughtful. Weary almost. It worried Dean. This was not normal.

"Captain?"

The man started. And looked over at Dean. He shook his head. "I'm fine. Just a little lost."

"I know how you feel," Dean muttered, shooting Tia a suspicious look. "I can say that my life hasn't been the same since Tia fell into it."

The captain shook his head. "She's a good woman. You are a lucky man."

Dean shot his captain a surprised look then realized he'd called Tia honey, and neither of them had exactly hid their feelings for each other. "I am," he said and waited as Tia polished off the second donut. She eyed the third one but sat back waiting. She turned her attention to the men.

"So, why am I here?"

The captain spoke up. "Questions. Regarding Billy and the others."

Right. She leaned forward. "What do you want to know?"

"Everything." And with that they got started. By the time the captain had asked her a dozen questions, he'd filled a notepad several pages thick and several other people had come to join them. Tia was on her third cup of coffee and looked to be fading quickly.

Finally, Dean put a stop to the barrage of information firing back and forth. "She needs a break."

"She does," Tia agreed, her voice wan and thin. "Right now would be good." She dropped her head and rested her forehead on her crossed arms.

The captain held up his hand. Instantly the noise eased back. "Let's leave her alone for a few moments."

He stood up and ushered the others out of the room. He looked over at Dean. Dean shook his head. "I'll stay here with her."

The captain nodded and walked out, closing the door gently behind him.

CHAPTER 36

"I'M FINE," SHE mumbled from inside her folded arms. "Just tired."

"With good reason," he said gently. "Take it easy. We have a few moments alone. Close your eyes and sleep if you can."

"Can't."

"Why not?"

"Don't know."

But she wouldn't lift her head. She felt odd. Disconnected. Loose ends floated in her mind and that made no sense. She was here and doing something constructive. It's what she wanted to do. What she wanted to have happen. Only no one was talking about Simone. No one was talking about her dead partner. They were all talking about dead kids. She didn't want to talk dead kids. They were dead and gone and she wasn't. She'd survived. Why the hell would she want to take a closer look at that scenario? She wouldn't. She didn't. She wasn't suicidal.

But she did want this all to stop.

"Make what stop?"

She lifted her head and stared at him. "Sorry, I didn't mean to say that out loud."

He shrugged. "No problem. But that's still no answer."

She stared at him. "I want it all to stop. I want a normal

life. When I can get up in the morning and go to bed in the same bed at night, knowing it's okay."

"Okay?"

"Yes, knowing it's okay. That I won't be hauled out screaming from bed in the middle of the night for the next barrage of tests Wilhelm dreamed up. Knowing I will get three meals a day each and every day. Knowing I can walk the streets if I want and not have to run because they might have found me. It's not a nice way to live. I never met many street people or hooked up with the underground. I was too nervous. Many reached out to me but they scared me. They might have been part of his network. And then they'd find me like they had the first time. For the last couple of years I was living in a small town with less than a thousand people. Within a day of arriving everyone knew who I was and that I had no clothes or money and was in trouble. But not one of them terrified me. As one old guy went out of his way to say, "We're all here for a reason. Don't worry about it, just let the trouble go away and let life be."

"That's an odd saying."

She nodded. "I finally realized they'd all ended up in that part of the world because, like me, they were on the run and had run out of luck. They were going to stop and make a stand. That's how the town was born. By those on the move – for whatever reason – and they came to the end of the road. That became the town."

"Nice." He grinned at the thought. "A whole town of you guys."

"No, not like me." She shook her head. "But a whole town that accepted me. That was worth its weight in gold. I rented the back room over a restaurant and worked below. I didn't have any job skills, people skills or life skills but I was learning." She took a deep breath and tried to wrap up her thoughts that had started this. "But it never became normal. There was always the sense that someone was going to come after me. That someone was always watching me."

"And there might have been someone. But that doesn't mean it was evil. It could have been Stefan."

She leaned back in her hair. "Why would he? He didn't know me then?"

"I wouldn't count on that." Dean studied the table in front of him. "Look, my history with Stefan is different. He saved my boy and for that I will do anything for him. Anything. Yet, I also know he is very connected to others like him. Like you."

She nodded. "I know."

"He also keeps in touch with upcoming psychics. Young ones who haven't developed. Ones in trouble. Some from all around the world. And he knows a lot as to who is out there and what they are all doing in terms of their abilities."

She desperately liked the idea of a big brother looking over her from afar.

"He comes from heart. You know that."

She nodded and drew an aimless design on the table in front of her. "I *want* to know that."

"Then believe in it. If he did know and didn't help then there was a reason for it. You have to learn to trust and to do that you have to start somewhere. Let it be with him."

"I trust you."

He smiled. "Do you?"

She nodded.

"Nice. I'm very happy to hear that." He reached across and clasped her hands in his. "And I trust you."

She grinned and some of the rigidness eased out of her shoulders. "That's nice. I'd never hurt you. Or anyone." The smile wiped off her face. "Except I'd hurt *them*."

That wiped the smile off his face. "You have to stand in line."

A yawn escaped. "You know real food would be good. Those donuts have long worn off. And I thought there was a clothing store on the way here. Do you think we can stop on the way home?"

"No stopping required. I have a bag of clothes for you. You can try them on at the hotel."

At the word hotel, her inside deflated. "Right. We're at the hotel. Not home."

"Do you have a home?" he asked her gently. "Can you go back to the town you stayed at for years?"

She shook her head. "No. I left there. I had stayed at Simone's overnight but then set out to meet Stefan, and the rest is history." Closing her eyes she dropped her head on her forearms again. God, she had no place to go. No job, no place to sleep and no food. She hated this. After years of instability, it seemed a far-fetched dream now to have a regular life again, but she really wanted one.

"I have to find a job," she muttered.

"Where?"

"Anywhere." She snorted but with her head still flat it sounded more like a sneeze. "In my situation it really doesn't matter. The world revolves around money and I don't have much."

"Do you have a bank account?"

She shook her head. "No one in Land's Edge did either."

"Cash system?"

"And barter system."

"Sometimes that works better."

"Yeah, Codger used to drive the truck and he'd pick up the supplies and deliver them to everyone. He'd get his meals at the restaurant and sleep in Betty's B&B. It worked," she said.

"But you won't go back?"

"No, that time of my life is over. I stayed long enough to heal, to get stronger. They actually told me it was time for me to move on. That I couldn't keep hiding there. They wanted something else for me."

She raised her head. "Instead, this is all so much worse." Except for having Dean in her life.

"Well, no running away this time. You're welcome to stay with me as long as you need."

"Ha, you have a son and a mother staying there."

"Mom has her own house close by. It's just Jeremy and me. And you're welcome there with us." His tone of voice was firm, no hesitation, and his chocolate eyes were warm and caring.

"Thank you. That helps. But you don't have yet another room so it's hardly convenient to sleep on your couch long term. Still, it's a nice gesture."

"It's more than nice, it's real. We'll figure it out. Now, are you ready to leave?"

She reared back. "What? We can leave? I would have left a long time ago." She pushed her chair back. "Let's go."

He stood up and waited until she walked around the table toward him. "You're okay this time? You won't go invisible?"

She took a quick assessment. "No, I feel fine."

"Good. I have to grab a few things from my desk. Then we'll grab some dinner." He opened the door and they walked out. This end of the hallway was still quiet and calm. The other end was noisy and full of people. As they neared the crowded aisles, she whispered, "Is it always like this?"

"Hell, it's often way worse." He led the way to the far

end and pulled up at a desk that appeared to have been used more as a table than anything. "Hey guys, like what the hell?"

"Ha, if you don't show up for work then this table's got to be used for something. So garbage it is. Now it's your garbage."

Everyone laughed.

Dean shook his head and sat down. He opened a couple of drawers, looking for something specific.

Tia stood awkwardly at the side, trying to ignore the stares. After a few moments she asked, "Can we leave soon?"

He stood up again. "Yeah, let's go."

"Right." He reached out for her hand. "Let's go." He walked her back to the entrance, but something was bothering him. She leaned in. "What's wrong?"

"My computer, my desk, everything is different." He groaned. "Damn it. It took me a long time to set that up just the way I like it." He stopped. "There's Jones." He high-fived his buddy. "Hey, I wondered where the hell you were today."

"Getting clothes, remember?" Jones laughed. "The things I do for a paycheck. Remember what that is like?"

"Sure do and anxious to get back to it." He motioned to Tia. "I'm taking her back but was hoping to catch up on anything new you might have found out?"

"Dean, we all want to know that." The captain barreled toward them. "Nice of you to show up finally. Banker hours and all."

Jones shook his head. "I know I was due in earlier but got stuck checking in with a weasel. Apparently the patients were moved out of the one lab and taken by ambulance to another lab."

"We know that already." Dean frowned down at him. "I

hope you didn't pay your weasel much for that."

"He also saw the orderlies who worked at the lab do the driving."

"That's quite possible. Hell, the lab probably owned the ambulances."

"True, except the lab was trying to empty the place in one day. Actually…" he paused for dramatic effect. "They did it in the middle of the night."

"What? They moved everyone under the cover of night?"

"None of this makes any sense," Tia said in bewilderment.

"It will. We just don't know all the information yet." The captain stood behind them, frowning. "Dean, take her back. We have a meeting in about ten minutes on the case. If you want to come back for that, then hurry up."

Tia hated that idea, but Dean straightened up in excitement. "Or I could just wait here," she said quietly. "Then you won't miss the meeting…" *and I won't be left alone*, but she didn't add that. That was her problem. She'd love to lie down at the hotel and maybe nap but it wouldn't be so easy knowing they were here discussing her. Then again, she couldn't do anything about it.

DEAN WAS TORN. He really wanted to be part of the meeting.

But she was exhausted and needed a solid meal and some downtime.

"I'll take her back," Jones said. "And come right back."

"I hate to ask that of you…" But he really wanted to. He needed to be a part of this. He glanced over at Tia and she was smiling at him.

"It's fine," she said. "You won't be longer than an hour

or two will you?"

Dean shook his head. "No, not likely."

"So I'll go lock myself in and have a bath, order some room service, and if you aren't there by the time it comes, then I'll eat yours too!" She grinned as everyone laughed.

"Yeah, but see they all think you are joking and I know you aren't."

Jones grinned. "Come on. I'll drop you off. Make sure you're all locked in until he gets in."

She reached over and kissed Dean impulsively. In his ear, she whispered, "Enjoy."

Feeling the color wash up his neck and the cheering going on around him, he grabbed her tight and said, "Remember, we talked about this. If you're going to do a job, do it right." And he planted a kiss on her warm lips meant to sear her to the core. The cheers rose to a crescendo around them as he held her close. Finally, he broke the kiss and leaned back to look down at her bemused face.

"Now that's a goodbye kiss."

And he watched her walk out the door. Two men slapped him on the shoulders. "Damn that time off did you a world of good!"

He laughed. "You got that right."

"So, Dean, is she like yours, or available," came a call from the other side of the room.

He turned and glared. "Hands off, all of you. She's spoken for."

"Ah, but is she taken?" One of them laughed suggestively, sending the room into more catcalls. Dean was happy she wasn't there to hear the guys.

He grinned as the jokes kept on coming. Some from the women detectives. Damn it was good to be back.

CHAPTER 37

OUTSIDE THE SKY had cleared. It was late afternoon as far as she could tell. But noisy. They were downtown, not that she knew anything about the city layout, but the streets were packed and vehicles flew by in organized madness.

"I'm parked over this way." Jones led her to a mid-sized car, not a cop car for which she was grateful. Inside she buckled up and waited for him to start the car, tired and feeling more exhausted as each minute passed. She didn't understand why now, but maybe it was just knowing she was getting to go home – or what passed for home in her world. Still, it was a very comfortable shelter to stay in until she knew what the next step was.

Jones drove quietly and competently and in total silence. She appreciated that.

At the hotel, he pulled up to the side street and parked. "Come on, I'll get you up to your room."

She stumbled on her way out. Damn she was tired. He grabbed her arm and helped her across the street. She led the way to the elevators and they moved up in silence. At the top, she fumbled for her keys. They were here somewhere then remembered it was a card system. She pulled that out and walked to the door.

Inside, everything was now clean and a freshly made bed

was so appealing. "You know, maybe I'll skip that bath and go straight to bed. I can't believe how tired I am."

"Do whatever you want." He shrugged. "Dean will be here in an hour or so." He turned and studied the surroundings. "Nice digs." He walked around and did a quick search, checking the closets and looking in the bathroom and under the bed.

"Yeah, a friend of a friend or something like that owns the place."

When he was done and apparently it was all clear, she smiled at him. "Thanks for checking everywhere. And for bringing me back. Enjoy your meeting."

He rolled his eyes. "Yeah sure." But his grin was bright and crooked. "I'll see you later." He turned and walked back to the door. She waved at him as he left. Nice guy. Too bad she was already hooked to Dean or she might have been interested. But as it stood now, Dean was the one man, the only man in her world. And it felt right. It felt good.

All other men paled in comparison.

As he pushed the button to the elevator, she closed and locked the door behind him. She could enjoy stepping into Dean's world and picking up a few of his friends to call her own. She'd made friends in Land's Edge – but none she'd kept after leaving.

Walking back inside, she tossed her bag and the bag of clothes Jones had bought for her on the chair. She'd take a look at them after a nap. She lay down on the bed and closed her eyes. She just needed to rest for a moment.

Memories, disjointed thoughts, flew in and out of her subconscious. Stefan had said something about new pathways. And new skills and abilities like the telepathy. She didn't understand how that worked, but there was no doubt that something did. The colors in her mind were a scorching red for some reason and in the back were muted colors. Oranges and yellows. Nothing white or black, just this weird color. She yawned. Okay, this was silly, but she was actually going to sleep.

She woke up with a start some time later. She bolted upright and looked around, her breath catching in the back of her throat.

The room was dark. The smell rank.

What the hell?

Where was she?

She fumbled for the light, only it wasn't there.

She was not in the hotel.

Or in Dean's house.

She threw her legs over the side of the bed and tried to stand up, only to realize she couldn't. She looked down to see her hand chained to the bed. She shrieked in panic.

Her stomach instantly emptied.

Her mind screamed. Help, damn it someone, *help*.

But no sound came out. She collapsed on the bed and knew no more.

HE'D STAYED TOO long. Dean knew it. She was waiting for him, and he knew what it felt like when no one showed up. It was a pain in the ass. He reached for his phone but realized she didn't have one. Or did she? What the hell? How long had he known her, yet he didn't know if she had a phone or not.

He was angry at himself for not having considered such a simple thing. They could have just gotten her a disposable phone for the moment. Something for her to use.

Instead, he was cut off. He dialed the hotel and asked for his room.

There was no answer.

Of course not. She could be still in the bath or sleeping. Damn it.

He rushed to the truck and hopped in. He was still buckling up the seatbelt as he peeled out of the parking lot. He couldn't get that horrible sensation that something was wrong out of his head.

He parked the truck and ran into the hotel. There was a crowd waiting at the elevator. He took the stairs two at a time. At his floor he pulled open the door to the hallway and walked the next few yards. If everything was fine, he didn't want to scare her. If they weren't fine…well he was going to smash something and damn fast.

Key card in hand, he approached the door. Quickly unlocking it, he stepped inside and stopped at the doorway. The bed was empty.

The bathroom door was open and the damn room was empty. Cold. "Tia?" he called out in faint hope. He already knew inside.

But there was no answer. She was gone.

STEFAN STOOD IN his studio, his paintbrush in hand, staring in shock at the canvas in front of him. Celina, the love of his life walked in, took one look at him and rushed over. She put her arms around him, uncaring about the wet paint on his smock. "Stefan, another one?"

He nodded, so exhausted he could hardly speak. But his eyes were glued to the canvas and the woman's hand in chains. The image had been completely overlaid on top of the painting he'd been working on underneath. Instead of reaching for a clean canvas he'd literally painted on top of the one below.

"That's the first time you've done that, isn't it?" she asked beside him. She always knew. The other half of his heart and mind. She always knew when something shifted, changed in his world. And this was a change.

A big change.

Then he knew. Shit. "It's because it's that important. The vision. It's that new. Current"

"As in it's happening now?"

"Right now." He walked to the sideboard, his hand trembling as he picked up the phone and called Dean.

"I know. I just came back to the hotel to find her missing. She'd only been alone an hour. Maybe not even," Dean said in a strained voice.

Stefan listened to his explanation, his own heart in his throat. Tia had been through so much already. She didn't need more of this. How strong was she? Could she handle another session with those assholes? Stefan had tracked her down years ago, hearing her cries, finding her signature, hiding her when the others came, then helping her escape. After that, he'd let her go, let her be all those years ago as she worked to rebuild her life. But he'd kept an eye on her, waiting for her to come to terms with her life. Then she'd contacted him. And everything had come back into focus.

"She's chained to a bed," Stefan said gently. "She's alive."

"Can you talk to her? Tell her we're looking for her. See if there is anything she can tell us."

"I can't," he said. "Something's stopping me from getting to her."

"Drugs?"

"No. Steel."

Silence, then Dean exploded. "What the hell? How is that possible?"

"Someone who knows how to stop anyone from tracking her. And the others."

"Steel? You can't track through steel?"

"Or other heavy thick layers of metal. So she's in an old metal building, likely reinforced, a bunker or something similar. She's also alone from what I can see in the picture."

"Picture?"

"Yeah." Stefan groaned, hating the explanations. "I painted a picture. It's her scarred hand chained to the bed." His voice dropped in fatigue. "I can't see anything else. Just the bed frame, the same as the one in the picture with Billy."

"Anything else?"

"No." But he hesitated.

"What aren't you saying?"

"I think she's unconscious." He took a deep breath. "I'm afraid she's hurt."

CHAPTER 38

TIA STARED AS her nightmares came true. This was Billy's room, or at least a copy of the room she'd seen in the image.

This was seriously bad news.

Stefan. Could she contact him? She closed her eyes and called out to him. *Stefan…can you hear me?* But there was no answer.

"Why?" She called out again. And again. "What do you want?" By the time she finally fell silent inside, a film of sweat had risen on her arm. She was also burning through her energy. Fatigue pulled at her. What was going on? Besides the fact that she was a captive – a prisoner – again. She was so tired. Had she been given something? Drugged? Or something much worse. She didn't feel any different. But there was something…

She just didn't know what.

Leaning back on the bed, she tried to collect her thoughts and still the blind panic inside. She had to stay calm. Stay cool. And above all think, think, damn it.

This was not going to be her future. She had Dean. She had Stefan.

But she couldn't forget someone had her.

Groaning, she closed her eyes. In her mind was more brilliant color. More waves of something. Was it alive?

"Hello? Is someone there?"

What the hell was she doing? How could anyone be there? But damn if the waves didn't move, undulate in a raw fashion. But only so far. As if they were tethered or restricted in some way. She didn't understand but it was important. If they could come to her, could she go to them?

She slid forward in her mind, trying to access the other energies. She was sure they were people. She'd seen something like that with Stefan. Energy undulating around him but it wasn't really him. It was as if he led a huge pack of psychics. She needed to access the same pathway. Same vibration? Same level? She had no idea but they were visible.

And if she could see them, surely she could access them.

With ripples of frustration racking her system, she lay down and closed off the outside influences. Loving the clarity of her mind's eye and more – loving the joy of connecting with others like her. She should be terrified this time, terrified of the others and what they'd planned to do with her, but knowing she wasn't alone, knowing there were others around to help her – priceless.

But it was still up to her to help herself. Somehow.

Then she heard voices. Shit. What was she going to do? Nothing. She couldn't do anything.

She'd pretend to still be sleeping. Groggy.

The door opened.

She managed to still her reaction, breathe slowly, naturally.

"She shouldn't still be sleeping," came a harsh voice. "Wake her up."

Footsteps approached.

Just before they arrived at her side, she mumbled and frowned, shifting on the bed.

"Oh good, she's waking up."

"I don't care. Wake her up faster."

A slap slammed across her face.

She groaned.

No need to fake that.

A second slap hit her full on. She cried out and whimpered.

She opened her eyes and stared up at the man grinning down at her. It was the man from the McDonald's restaurant. The man who'd kidnapped Jeremy.

Jesus. "What…"

She shook her head. The ringing pounded through her head. "What am I doing here? And who are you?"

"You know who I am. The question is – do you know who he is?" Her head was yanked hard to face the man in the doorway. Billy, only dressed more feminine than her older masculine style. She sat up in shock. Billy? "Oh my God. They said you were dead."

"I'm not and neither are you, but you will wish you were soon. I went through hell because of you."

Tia shook her head and winced. "Why?" she cried. "I didn't do anything to you."

"No, but you were the chosen one," Billy spat out. "The one we all had to try and beat."

"What are you talking about?" Tia cried. "I was a prisoner, the same as you were."

"No. You were the privileged prisoner. The rest of us were performing seals, trying to be like you."

Tia's brain struggled to grasp the concept. She'd been the favorite? How could that be when there was nothing nice or favorite about that existence at all? "No," she whispered. "My life was horrible."

"And regardless of how horrible, it was still way better than the life we had."

Tia could only stare at the young girl who didn't look a day older than when she'd seen her a decade ago. "I don't understand. Wilhelm was always trying to make me develop new abilities."

"Sure. New ones. We didn't have ones he liked, so we were trying to get any abilities. From DNA, to blood infusions, to chemicals, and even shock treatments."

"But I went through all that too."

Billy nodded, but her childish face was twisted with hatred. "Sure you did. But who do you think was the recipient of your blood. They took it out of you and injected us with it."

"Why would they do that?" Tia couldn't comprehend how she had not known Billy had hated her. Had the others?

"To try and give us some of your abilities."

"That makes no sense." She shook her head. Too bad she couldn't shake off their words. "I was given injections too."

Billy stopped. "You were?"

"Yes. I was," she cried out. "I was probably given your blood."

Billy glared at her. "Not likely. You got the preferential treatment unlike the others."

"What preferential treatment? Don't you understand? We were all prisoners. We all had a horrible life."

"But you weren't moved to the new facility though, were you? No, you were removed from the whole program then. You were freed." She snorted. "They talked about leaving you for the last trip, only you never came. And we realized you'd been lying and that you were free."

"No." Tia couldn't let her keep believing this. "I escaped. I actually thought I'd been left behind. I woke up to a completely empty building. The door was unlocked and I wasn't chained at the time, but there was no one left inside the building. I don't know why? Maybe they planned to come back for me – maybe they thought they'd locked me in and I was finally going to die for lack of food and water, but there was no one – and I mean no one left in the building when I managed to get out."

Billy stared at her, so much hatred and anger on her face. "I don't believe you," she said. "You're lying. You have to be."

"Why do I have to be?" Tia said in bewilderment. How had she not known this girl hated her like this? When had it started? Why had it started?

"He taught you to hate me," she said sadly. "For that I'm sorry. I had no idea."

"He didn't. You did."

Tia didn't understand. "I didn't do anything," she cried.

"No, except be you. They'd do anything to have one of us be able to disappear like you did. They loved to show us how they could make you do things."

"And that should have told you how badly I was treated," she said, her gaze finally noting the madness inside. Billy had tipped over the edge. "I'm so sorry. We were in this together. I was never better than you."

"No, you weren't. You aren't. It did take me a while to see it though. The boss isn't here right now, but he will be soon. If you thought I was dead…" Billy grinned. "At least he likes me the way I am."

Tia didn't know what to say. Once she'd escaped, she'd worried that Billy would be a perfect foil for a child predator.

She'd not be on the wrong side of the law by age and the predator would always have a child to have sex with. What a horrible thought.

"What do you want with me," she said, interjecting a flatness, a dullness to her tone.

"Payback."

With that Billy laughed and turned, leaving Tia alone with the guy from McDonald's. The guy who kidnapped Jeremy.

She studied him. He looked like he was all too willing to smack her up alongside side her head again. For some perverse reason, she wanted to push him. "Were you here too? A prisoner with Billy and me?"

"No, as you well know. Or was I someone else you couldn't be bothered remembering, princess." He snickered. "Of course I was the one who broke into your house. What kind of defense system was that? Shit that hurt when I ran into it."

She stared at him. He'd been the intruder? It was too much. Her mind revolved around to his earlier comment. Princess? Jesus. Did everyone hate her? Now that she could see him up close, she wondered if he was a tech from the lab and had worked with Wilhelm. "Did you kill the doctor?"

She hadn't meant to say that, but it slipped out before she could call the words back.

"No, Kyle did."

She froze. "Kyle?" Surely not. He'd seemed like a lovely teenager. He'd been late to the program and...what? Frowning, she realized she couldn't put a face to him. In fact, she didn't remember anything about him. At least not enough to know something.

"Of course you don't remember him either, do you?" He

snorted. "Figures. Well, Kyle was sweet on Billy and after one particularly bad session Kyle lost it and the doctor just happened to be there. Kyle choked the life out of him. Of course Kyle had to be put down at that point."

"What?" she exclaimed in horror. "Kyle wasn't a rabid dog."

"No, but neither could we trust him anymore."

"You worked for Wilhelm though. How did you get onto Billy's side?"

He snorted. "You really don't get it do you. There were no sides. Once Wilhelm was dead, the place went ape shit and the prisoners tried to take over the lab. At least for a few days. Then the new boss found out and he came in with gas and put us all down. He didn't know who was staff and who was a patient at that point, so we were all taken and made prisoners in his other lab until he could sort us out. Once I convinced him who I was…and he finally recognized me, then I moved up the hierarchy. And of course so did Billy." He shrugged. "I know Billy hates you. I'm part of the reason as I helped Wilhelm spread the rumors of how you were treated so they *would* hate you. It made them try harder."

She slumped back. "God, how could this be?"

"They all figured you'd been given special treatment or released," he admitted. "Honestly, I had no idea what happened to you. We were all taken out but no one could find you. Figured you'd found a way to escape. Of course no one knew, so rumors were rampant that you'd been released."

"I wasn't on anyone else's side," she said wearily. "I was struggling to survive, the same as the rest of you. Always alone. Never included and always abused."

"Once Wilhelm died, everything changed." He waved

his arm around. "There will be no special treatment here. Billy has had it in for you since the beginning. So it doesn't matter if you're one of us or not. You'll get a heap more pain if you try to fight. The boss will be here soon. Then you'll see."

"See what?"

"See what you're really up against."

And he walked out.

DEAN STOOD IN the middle of the conference room he'd been in earlier. A team was at the hotel room and the video cameras were currently being checked. So far nothing had led them to finding Tia or the lab she was likely being held in. Stefan had brought his painting to the station, then had walked out.

So far Stefan's painting was the best clue they had to go on. The first time he'd seen it, his stomach had fallen to his toes in fear. How the hell had Stefan managed to make a hand look so lifelike and be so easily identifiable? Then again it was the scars. And he'd spent a lot of time kissing those exact scars.

He couldn't imagine the other images Stefan could paint and he didn't want to. This was painful enough.

"Are you sure there's nothing there to identify her location," he'd asked Stefan before he left. "Surely a window scene, something that would say anything."

"No," had been his only answer.

"Here are the morgue pictures on the other kids who died." Jones walked in and dropped the file on the table. "At least for the seven we could confirm."

"And the others?" Dean asked.

"No reports or no pictures on the reports."

And Dean had to be content with that. It sucked, but there it was.

He'd also called the department shrink. It wasn't that the shrink would believe any of this, but he could have valuable insights to this case.

He strode over to the table and sat down, pulling the images toward him. Dead men, children really, looked back at him. He turned off his emotional reaction and sucked in his breath. He had to find something in these images. There was nothing here to help.

The first image was cold and clear. The boy's throat had been cut. There was no mistaking cause of death there. Except the slash also bisected a half dozen other scars. More attempts on his life? Had the boy tried to commit suicide? He looked for the coroner's reports but they weren't here.

The captain walked in. "Well…" he roared. "Who's got something for me?"

Dean shook his head and didn't lift his gaze off the second photo. There was something about that one that got to him. For all the similarities to the first one, it was still…different. Of course, different boy. Different age. Different scars. But also similar scars. How the hell did anyone get cuts like that on the neck and not die?

The one boy had obviously died. This second image was another dead child but older, skinnier. A huge Adam's apple. The picture was a profile and that big bob in his throat stood out strongly. And of course there were scars along the temple, weird ones almost like burn marks and there were similar ones at the hair line. This boy had gone through hell.

He lifted his gaze, trying to remember if he'd noticed similar scars on Tia. In a way yes, but also no. Hers were different. Tia's had healed better. This kid had bumpy scars. Something akin to keloidal scarring. It made his injuries look worse.

His heart aching for what he'd gone through, Dean quickly went through the other images, looking for similarities and looking for differences.

There were some of both. Most had scars of some kind but no visible injury that caused deaths. The drugs likely were the cause. Also autopsies hadn't been done in most cases. Well documented medical illness had explained some. Did they have a serial killer in the midst, a budding one? Trying out his thing? Learning a style? Checking out different techniques? Was such a thing possible? Was it one of the doctors? One of the staff? One of the patients? Lord knew he was rooting for it to be one of the patients. At least someone was trying to fight back.

Most likely the damn doctor had killed those kids with his damn experiments.

He tossed the pictures down. The captain grabbed them up.

And if it wasn't the doctor, the problem with the killer being a patient was he was killing other patients.

Dean's mind worried on the problem.

What kind of mind would do that?

The answer was easy. A broken one.

Shit.

Tia was in big trouble.

CHAPTER 39

T IA LAY BACK down and worked on settling her senses. She should be able to go invisible here, but it wouldn't make a damn bit of difference if she couldn't get free. She'd use up her energy at an alarming rate.

That she couldn't have. She needed to conserve as much as she could.

There'd been no other visitors since Billy and Torrence, her guard. And Tia was still trying to figure out how that worked. In that image Billy had looked dead. Of course, she could have been faking it. Actually, she could have been close to death when the picture was taken, then recovered.

They'd all been there at one time or another.

How they could have believed Tia had received different treatment she had no idea. She'd met them all at one time or another, and they'd all been friendly, or as friendly as anyone could be in those circumstances. Had the doctor and staff pitted the patients against each other?

For what reason? To see them fight each other? She pondered the mental reasoning for such a thing. Or they might have used her as a prize or the prime being and pitted the others against each other to get them to try harder. Maybe they offered a better location, better treatment to the winners. What was the punishment for the losers? She hated to think about it.

There were distant noises in the background. Like shots fired. She froze. Guns?

Voices raised and shouts could be heard. She sat up. A rescue? Or was she once again going to be left behind. No one knew she was here. Damn.

She'd have to get out on her own again. She'd been so scared the last time…it had been hard to stay calm enough to function.

But this time was different.

Could she even get free?

And if so, how? She stared down at the handcuff. Except it wasn't quite a handcuff. It was like a chain with a loop over it. She studied it carefully then tried to open it. But it wouldn't budge. She tried to make her hand as small as possible so she could slip out of it, but that wasn't happening either. It was old but maybe that's why it was holding. The old stuff seemed stronger. She got off the bed and took a look at the way it was attached to the old metal bed frame. It appeared to be looped through a leg. So how did the legs come off? Several frustrating minutes later, and she realized that the damn frame was bolted together.

And she wasn't going to be able to do anything about it.

She was stuck. Shit.

With no window and the door too far away for her to reach, she was limited to the length of the damn chain. Anger built. She'd sworn she'd never get back into this situation again and yet here she was.

She glared down at the chains. If only she could slide her hand through the damn thing. What was the point of being invisible if she wasn't really invisible? Because of course she wasn't invisible, she was just wrapped up in the same energy around her. She *pretended* to be invisible. She was more of a camouflage system.

Being a hundred percent invisible had been one of the things Wilhelm had tried to force her to achieve. Her thoughts turned inward remembering the pain, the beatings, the horrific punishments until he'd finally realized she couldn't do that. He'd always believed she was holding back on him, and she had been. But now it was a different story.

What were her limits?

She stared at her arm, trying to decipher exactly what she did. She took on the energy of the material behind and around her. Cloaking or cloning the energy beside her so she blended in. Literally blended in. She could almost feel the bed beneath her. The single sheet beneath her. The material of her pants through her skin. As if they were one. Really one in heart and soul. But it wasn't like she could become invisible. She'd always been as solid as could be. Even when she didn't appear to be there. She was there. And if someone hit her, they would still feel her. That's why she'd never really understood anything good about what she could do. It would be better if she could really disappear. Then she could blend with the walls. Become the walls and actually walk through the walls. But that was fiction.

Then she stopped. Was it? Stefan did some crazy ass stuff, and according to the rumors, his closest friends could do some wild things as well. Billy's issue might be physical, a genetic deformity, but at least it was special. Unique. And maybe it was something she could change but chose not to. Maybe she'd never wanted to grow up. The doctor might not have understood the true nature of what she did, because after all, she really didn't either, but it was surely something that she could change and adapt.

Hadn't Stefan said something similar? Now that she'd

opened up the pathways, there were going to be changes to her own skills. She'd grow in ways they wouldn't be able to predict. Well this would be a good time for some accelerated growth.

She stood up and glared at the door. She'd love to walk right through the damn thing. She took a few steps forward, feeling empowered in a way she hadn't felt before. She kept on walking. The damn chain would stop her soon but in the meantime this – whatever this was – made her feel good. Powerful.

She loved it.

At the door she peered through the small window but couldn't see anything. She wished she could see through to the hallway. And instantly she was there. She was in the hallway.

The chain hadn't stopped her. She flattened against the closest wall in shock. Her breath locked into her chest. What the hell just happened? She sensed the panic shaking her control and one thing she knew was that control was everything. Without it, nothing worked. With it, everything was possible. She didn't understand how or why, but she knew it was true.

She managed a shallow breath, her gaze darting from one side to the other.

She was now out in the hallway with no one the wiser. And how that could be, she had no idea. Or had she left her body behind?

Needing to know, she glanced back into the window and peered at her bed. It was empty.

For some reason she wondered if she'd left her body and was walking around without it – as she had on Dr. Maddy's Floor. Instead, it seemed like she was really here. In person.

Jesus.

Taking a deep breath she walked down the hall, not completely convinced that she'd escaped intact, but she was willing to take the gift and run with it. There were stairs up ahead. She ran over to them, hoping for a window.

She stretched out a hand to open the door and her hand went right through it.

Instantly she pulled back. And took several gasping breaths for air. Oh Jesus. Sweet Jesus. Had she just done what she'd done? How?

By willing it? Because she needed it? Had someone helped her? Had someone shown her the way? No, there was no one here. She almost laughed. Then wanted to cry. She was losing it. Afraid it wouldn't happen the next time and afraid it would, she reached out a shaky hand again.

It went straight through.

Oh Lord.

Noises sounded around the corner, saying she wasn't going to be alone for long. She took a deep breath, closed her eyes and stepped forward. Hoping it was safe, she opened her eyes and gasped. She was partly inside and partly outside of the wall. She turned to look behind her. Her butt was sticking out of the wall. Inside her body stood tall and strong but as she leaned forward, her body stretched forward out of the wall. With her heart pounding, she stepped through to the other side.

Just as someone walked down the hall. She really wanted to see who it was and where they were going, but she had no idea if they could see her or not. And seeing her was one thing, but seeing her half in and half out of the wall – now that was something else again.

Crazy.

She waited until the voices moved past her then she took a big risk and stuck her head through the wall, feeling the different sensation as the solid wall changed in density as if the molecules shifted and made room for her. There was no force involved. No caring that she was in their space. No, it was as if all the energy around was ready and happy to share. She'd never seen or heard of anything like it.

Turning her head, she watched two men walk the hallway. Dressed in jeans and wearing dreadlocks, they actually didn't look to be more than a couple of harmless guys. That they were here changed that impression completely. She couldn't see their faces as they walked away from her, but it was easy to see that they walked easily, talking casually, not worried about her in the least.

Damn. She'd like them to be worried. In fact, she'd like them to be terrified. She was tired of everyone seeing her as a princess figure with no skills or abilities worth honing and no skills to defend herself. She'd learned a lot more than just cooking at Land's Edge. In fact, two cooks had taken great interest in her self-defense education.

She hurried to the stairwell side of the hallway, then she raced down the next flight of stairs. And stopped. Was there a faster way? Could she? She closed her eyes and willed herself through the floor to the level below. Was that possible? She opened her eyes, watching as her body morphed into the bright glowing energy of the floor below, her body accepting the energy as some of her own. She slowly slid down. Slid into the floor and down to the one below.

Holy Christ. The prayer slid through her mind as she watched her feet land and her hands high above her head slid the last bit out. She was on the landing below. She'd missed a complete set of stairs. Not quickly, but it was...so cool.

Who knew?

No one. That was the thing. No one knew what she could do. She'd spent all those years trying to deny Wilhelm any and all of her abilities and hadn't even thought she had much in terms of those. She'd gone out of her way to make sure she didn't develop more abilities just so he wouldn't know. And now look at her. She was here with at least one more – hell, now this was way more than one. First she was invisible and second she could walk through walls.

Ha.

Take that Wilhelm. And just because she could, she dropped down to the floor below the same way. And the floor below that. She had no idea where the hell she was, but it had to be the main floor soon.

A door opened in front of her and two men raced toward her.

Shit. There was nowhere to hide. She closed her eyes, praying they couldn't see her.

A gust of wind spun her around.

She opened her eyes to see the men had blasted through her, not even knowing she was there.

They'd walked right though and hadn't known.

She laughed silently.

Damn this was good.

Now to get the hell out.

She walked through the main floor and tried to sort out where the closest exit would be. She knew her energy levels couldn't keep this up. She felt energized right now but could sense the short-term nature of it.

She raced down the hallway, trying to look in the windows of the various rooms as she passed. But it was hard to see anything. She couldn't hear much either.

Why was that?

As she wondered there was an odd click in her head. There was a rumble as if a big wall of wax was shifting inside and suddenly there was sound and lots of it. She winced as noise screamed through her mind. Bending over to catch her breath against the pain, she mentally turned the volume in her mind down to a reasonable level and let the noises filter in. The largest sound was her own heartbeat. Well that could tone down. It wasn't like she needed to know she was alive. A few minutes ago she might have wondered, but not now.

Other sounds filtered in. Conversations.

"She's gone."

"Like hell."

"She's playing possum. Remember she always did that until someone went into the room. Then she snuck out. Make sure no one goes in there."

"Too late."

Shit.

Racing footsteps, screaming and more yelling. She shuddered. It was all too much to take in. With the tones muted again, it was easier to hear the other sounds going on around her. Something shuffled in the wall. Oh no. Spiders. She so didn't want to hear spiders walking or mice snuffling through the space around her. And as much as she loved animals, there was something icky about spiders.

Another sound caught her attention.

It was a series of long clicks and dashes. She couldn't make it out. Then it clicked. Someone was dialing a cell phone. She strained to hear who.

"They've lost her."

A big mumble on the other side said there was someone on the other end of the phone but it wasn't clear enough for her to make out who.

"Right." More silence. "Will do."

A louder click.

He'd closed off the phone. So someone was reporting on the others. Interesting and so typical. One playing off the other. Someone always looking to move up in life and preferably on someone else's ladder.

She just wanted to get the hell out.

"Lock down the doors. She's not getting out of here."

Instantly there was a series of loud clicks and clangs. Shit, she'd waited too long. She raced forward to the large metal front doors, but they were slamming shut. She could make it…she could…and…they closed in front of her.

Unable to stop in time, she slammed into them…and came to a nose jarring stop.

She couldn't pass.

Why couldn't she pass through them?

Panicked, freedom so close, she tried to walk through the wall beside the door and realized that wasn't going to work either. Shit. She raced back out to the hallway. There had to be an exterior wall here that wasn't reinforced steel. *Please* she cried, *let me out.*

And with that she could sense her energy draining. Once it drained, she'd become visible.

Tears of panic and exhaustion slammed into her, draining her energy levels faster and faster.

She didn't know where to go. What to do.

Dean, she screamed as loud as she could in her head, *where are you?*

DEAN SAT AT the table, command central now as several

laptops lined up on either side of him. Everyone was searching the home company's land assets. If they'd owned the one lab, they were hoping they'd also owned the second. They needed addresses. Places to search for Tia. Phone calls weren't being returned. And no one was at the office at this hour. The captain was trying to get someone from the company's Board of Directors to talk to him. Someone else was working on getting a warrant. Dean had no idea how that was going.

He was just working on the premise that they needed a large private space and something Stefan had said – that whole bunker concept. At least steel construction. Were they trying to keep people like Stefan out, or did they have people like Stefan they were trying to keep in?

The police had narrowed the search to two old bunkers in the south part of town. Two teams had been dispatched. He'd been forced to stay here and wait. And keep searching. It occurred to him that some steel fabricating businesses might be made of steel too. There was no way to tell from here. But he might know someone who would know.

He called up an old friend. A soccer buddy who worked for the city. "Hey, Bunsen, odd question but do you know of any buildings in the city made of iron or steel?"

His buddy snorted. "What, from the early 1920s or something? There could be some shacks around but not likely much in the way of a sizeable building. Why?"

"Just looking for a building with those criteria."

"There was an old cannery made of steel but not sure if it's still standing. Along the river. It was part of the old heritage site that everyone was arguing about. Talked about turning it into a restaurant but that fell through. It was partly cohabbed as a bed and breakfast or student dorms or something, but the city shut it down as they didn't put in all the windows required and until that happened it was a no go. That wasn't the only issue."

"Any idea what the address is?" Dean was already doing a search and at the same time Bunsen brought up the name of the road, he had it on his screen. "Got it. Thanks. If you think of any others, give me a call, please."

"Hey, is this an official call? Like should I be sitting here and trying to come up with more places because someone is in trouble or do you have a happy financier looking for places to make a buck and he has a fetish for steel."

Dean laughed. The first real one in hours. "It's official. And several people could be in deep trouble."

"Damn. I hate it when you say stuff like that. Okay, I'll grab a beer and see if more come to mind."

"Thanks. I'll let you know how this turns out."

"You'd better."

Dean closed down his phone to see several other officers waiting for him expectantly. "The old cannery," he said. "It was partly outfitted with dorm rooms and restaurant."

The place erupted in a flurry of activity.

He desperately wanted to be a part of this but knew the captain wouldn't let him anywhere near it. He hadn't been cleared for duty and it didn't matter what he said. It wasn't going to happen.

Needing a breath of air, he stood up and a scream ripped through his mind. His knees buckled and he hit the floor.

Tia. Screaming. For him.

The scream built inside his head. He couldn't stop it. He couldn't stand it. She was crying for help and he couldn't help her.

Stefan, help!

And he fell the rest of the way to the floor.

Men raced to his side and checked him over. He knew his gaze was glassy and wild, knew he couldn't respond to their slaps on his shoulders or smacks to his cheeks. This was something else entirely.

But Tia…

Stefan's voice slammed into him.

Dean, hold strong. Grab a hold of her voice and keep it close to your heart. She needs you. She's reached out for you. You can do this.

Do what? He asked in a faint whisper, not sure Stefan could hear him. *What can I do, I can't move.*

You don't need to. You need to hold onto her. She's failing. She's losing energy and as soon as she does, she'll become unconscious. She'll also be visible to those she's hiding from.

Can't you help her?

I can't because I'm not able to track her past the barrier. But you can. She can. Now there is a connection. Feed it. See yourself sending her energy. Charging her so she stays invisible. Stays hidden. Maybe then I can get to her.

Dean groaned.

Do. Not. Let. Go.

Dean shuddered. *The guys are going to call an ambulance. Have me taken away. You have to stop them.*

I will. You hang onto her.

And Stefan left his mind, leaving him all alone in the weird space. He knew he was still in his body, in his conference room, in the damn station, but here there were no walls, floor, chairs or even ceilings. God, he'd love his laptop – if for no other reason than to record this. No one would believe him.

Not true.

Tia would.

He closed his eyes and followed Stefan's instructions. *Tia. I'm here. Hold strong. You can do this. It's all right. People are coming. We are on the way. Stay strong. If you need energy, take mine. Do what you need to do to stay hidden. Don't let them get you.*

He kept the mantra going over and over again. He lost count of the number of times he repeated a variation of those words. And each time it was more personal. *Sweetheart. I want to hold you again. Have you in my arms, be in my life. Come back to me. Please. I don't want to lose you. Stay strong. Keep using my energy.*

You can do this.

Suddenly, in the faint tiny back end of his heart, he heard her call out, *Dean, is that you?*

STEFAN FOLLOWED DEAN'S energy signature to Tia's. Thinning out his own energy he raced down inside of her signature to the source. Very quickly he found her inside a closet curled up in a tight ball; her energy was low and flaring in small doses. She was already showing some camouflage loss. He poured energy into her system, shoring up her defenses.

He needed her out of there. And fast. His movement was limited to her energy signature, and luckily she appeared to have been travelling through the building for a while. But the doors were locked down and if there were any windows they'd been sealed up. He raced back through her path checking for new information that could help them. There was nothing he could see.

He wandered back into the room where she was hiding.

It was an office of some sort. And where there was an office, there was paperwork. Maybe something helpful. Keeping energy funneling toward Tia and knowing time was of an essence, he strode through the building, looking for something, anything, that would give them a location. It could be the cannery, but there was no time to be wrong.

There were papers on the front desk. He couldn't move them but there was something there. Colleton Labs. Immediately he connected to the office and Dean's group. He didn't know if the name meant anything or if they could track the place, but that's what he could see. Then he searched for more. There had to be an address here. Surely. The lab's name was on the header. Then something more was written below, but it was covered up. He couldn't move the papers. Hating the limitation of the experience and wishing he could move what he needed he stood at the back of the room as a woman walked in. He waited. She sat down at a desk and picked up the phone, at the same time she clicked on the keyboard that brought the monitors back to life. He slipped over to stand behind her. He wanted to hear the phone call and see what she was looking up.

She checked her email before bringing up a webpage. She surfed, looking for orange and chicken dishes. Really? Stefan wanted to pound the desk in frustration. She needed to show him something useful.

She spun around and looked directly at him. He froze then she turned back to the monitor and checked the emails again. He leaned closer. There were several business ones and a few private. She clicked on a couple of them. He caught something about paperwork needing to be filed. Then she closed it down with a murmured "shit."

The next one, she groaned and closed it too.

Is this how all offices functioned? He needed answers. Not this.

He turned back to the closet and deliberately built a wall to keep the closet from being something in her view. Tia needed time. Dean needed time. And the rest of the team needed time.

He'd do his best to give it to them.

He turned back to the nurse and waited while she stood up and walked over to the counter. *Move the paper* he whispered. *Move the papers. Spread them out.*

She slowly lifted a hand and moved the papers, spread them out on the counter. Yes. He walked closer. Holton Street. It was on the same street as the cannery. Good. Now to make sure this was the correct building. He heard a sound from the closet.

The nurse spun around. She tilted her head and stared at the closet. She took one step closer. Then another.

Shit.

She'd heard Tia.

CHAPTER 40

TIA WAS AWASH in sensations. Overwhelmed in emotions. Hers. Dean's. And even Stefan's. Their thoughts. Their feelings. Their fear. Their panic. Her terror. She was dying. She knew it. She didn't know why. Or how but she was.

Or something inside of her was dying.

She didn't know how to explain, but she wasn't the same inside anymore. She was larger. Bigger. Open. She had no boundaries. She was everywhere. Belonged to everyone. Was everyone.

Lost in the experience, she lay in wonder as energy flowed through her. Around her. Inside her. What the hell was this?

And then she didn't care.

Because it was her. She was the one. She existed. As everyone. All at once. She just…was.

Tia, I'm here.

Dean was here. Nice.

Then Stefan's voice rolled through her. *Stay quiet. There are people looking for you.*

They won't find me, she whispered. *I'm here. I'm everywhere but they can't see me. They can't hear me. They aren't me.*

Tia, you don't sound…normal, Dean said, his voice high

pitched with worry.

I was never normal. I never will be normal. Normal is not who or what I am.

You are normal, Stefan said with a quiet humor. *You just haven't met the others that are the same normal.*

Others are normal like me, she said, her tone full of wonder. Full of joy. *Here they are all so sad. They are all so mad. There is no joy in their hearts.*

Her voice deepened. *They are full of hate. Why? Why for me? I did nothing to them. Or for them.* Now her voice dropped. *I should. I should do for them. I was remiss.*

She moved and both Dean and Stefan shouted at her to lie still. She lay back down. *I am quiet. But I've been too quiet. That needs to change. I've been a mouse in a huge forest, afraid the owls were going to hunt me down. I should have been the owl as he floated freely through the sky. I am he. He is me.*

Dean's voice echoed in the background. *Stefan, is she okay?*

She's fine, Stefan said with a sigh. *She's high. Likely for the first time in her life.*

What? Dean roared.

Tia gasped. *Use your inside voice. We can't let the owls know we are here.*

I thought you wanted to be an owl, Dean said in confusion. *If that's the case we are the owls and we already know we're here. Stefan…an explanation please.*

The first time and possibly a few other times yet to come when she opens the blockages and the energy lines in the system start to flow it can be like she's high on drugs. But really she's high on life – on her first real experience of her connection to all things. To her, right now, she's connected to everything in the world. She is the world. She's lost in the past and the present and sometimes for some people they can catch glimpses of the future. She is at this moment in time connected to everything.

Including us?

Especially us. We are feeding her energy, keeping her defenses up while he hunts for her. As such she is running your energy and mine through her chakras and she sees more of you and me than she's ever seen before. She will know things after this. She will understand things. You won't know how but she'll feel like you feel. Depending on the relationship, if you can make a go of it, you will be closer than any couple you've ever seen before.

Shouldn't she have a partner who is psychic?

There was a thread of self doubt in his voice that had Tia crying out, *No, you are perfect for me. You are psychic to me. You just are.*

And you are high on life, he said in gentle amusement. *So who is going to listen to you?*

You will, she whispered in a broken tone. *You loved your wife. You gave her everything. Your heart, your soul and everything in between. In return she gave you your son. And she left. You had nothing else. She didn't give your heart back. You didn't reclaim your soul. They are still out there wandering around lost.*

Jesus, Stefan, will she remember any of this later.

She might remember all of it. She might remember none of it.

Tia gave a happy sigh. *And I do remember it. I also remember other things. You said you loved me as I slept. You said you wanted me in your life. Because I was already in your heart. I hear you. I hear things. Lovely things. Thank you for those lovely things.*

Dean's silence was breathtaking. Tia laughed in delight. *I do love you. You are so very special. It's all right you know. To know you as I do.*

Is it? He said dryly.

Her voice pealed with joy. *Yes! Right now I can do any-thing. Would you like to know me the same way?*

What I'd love most is to have you live a long life at my side. Take yourself out of this closet and come back to my house with me. Just survive, baby, please. Survive for me. I need you.

You need me? She smiled, the sweetest joy in her heart climbing into her voice. She laughed and laughed. She'd do both. He just wouldn't know it yet.

Please, baby, things are getting ugly outside. You need to leave.

Okay, I can do that.

She stood up and walked through the door. She walked through the office and past where the woman was sitting, now surfing the web, multiple screens in front of her. She should be doing her job but not even this woman could ruin the sheer love running through her heart. Tia walked past, laughing as the computer died instantly. The woman cried in distress as the printer went off line and the lights flickered and died.

Tia didn't stop. She wasn't going to die. She was finally going to live.

She walked through the doorway, down the hall and right up to the front door.

Then she walked right through to the sunshine outside.

Damn, she's good, Dean said, following her energy trail.

She threw her arms out wide. *I am good.* She could feel him continue to feed her energy even as she watched several cop cars screaming into the large gravel lot outside the front door. *So are you, Dean, so are you.*

The cops raced out of their vehicles and ran for the

building. They ran past her, but they never saw her. Even the captain had come. She could see him opening his car door.

She approached him. Loving life.

She was in them. In fact, she was everywhere. She was moving outward into the world. Outward into the universe. She was everywhere.

And just like that, as if a plug was disconnected, she collapsed.

At the captain's feet.

DEAN SNAPPED BACK from his chair, his head bursting in agony.

Stefan? What happened?

There was no answer.

Dean struggled to move.

Only the room was tilting as if in slow motion and there was nothing he could do to stop it. He couldn't wrap his mind around the spinning – until the floor jumped up to meet him. He lay on the linoleum staring at the ceiling. What the hell had happened?

Tia?

He tried to scramble to his feet only to find his body was moving in slow motion and a pain like he'd never experienced before radiated from his chest.

"Shit," he cried, but somehow instead of the roar he was feeling, it came out more as a whimper. His body burned and pulsed in an erratic fashion. This must be a reaction from his connection to Tia. Something had happened to Tia.

Stefan, he cried out in his mind, *Help Tia.*

I am. We're on it.

She's fallen right at the captain's feet. He's racing her to the hospital.

Thank God. Dean groaned. *I think someone shot her. How do I disconnect. I swear I can feel everything she's feeling.*

You are. Welcome to the world of energy. Particularly with those you love.

I don't like it, Dean whispered. *It sucks. Big time.*

Stefan's laughter rolled through his head.

Why aren't you affected?

I'm not sure, Stefan said. *But as I'm free to move, I can help Tia. We're still struggling to figure out what happened.*

They should be at the hospital now.

No, they aren't. They are on the way, but it will be ten minutes at least. The captain has a jacket pressed against her wound. The bleeding doesn't appear to be stopping. Stefan's voice deepened. *I'm going to see if I can grab her some more help.*

Dr. Maddy, Dean whispered. *Call Dr. Maddy.*

I'm trying. She's already at the hospital working on a child.

Grab her. Tia needs her. She's been through too much. She needs to have some time without pain. Without fear.

We're working on it. Don't disconnect from her in case she still needs you.

Dean laughed but it came out more as a groan. *You don't understand, I couldn't disconnect if I tried.*

You might have to, Stefan warned. *Connected like this, if she dies, so do you.*

It's all right, Dean said softly. *If she dies I will die inside anyway. I'd rather go with her than live life without her.*

Don't talk like that, Stefan snapped. *I know how you feel but this is dangerous. And a dangerous time for her. If she gets wind there might be something wrong then she might not fight herself.*

She must live, Dean cried.

Exactly. Stefan's voice thinned. *They are coming into the ER now.*

Oh thank God, Dean whispered. *I'm struggling to stay conscious here. Not sure how this works. I really want to just close my eyes and sleep, but I need to know she's going to be okay.*

He could feel himself sliding down the long tunnel to oblivion. Tia was there. He could sense her. Feel her. It was…magnificent. She was he. And he was she. He couldn't imagine living without that pulse inside of himself that was her heart beating. It was too important. To special. She had to survive.

If she was too weak to fight then he'd have to pick up the fight for her.

STEFAN RACED THROUGH the ethers.

Maddy?

Yes, she answered in surprise. *What's up?*

Tia is coming into the ER. She's in bad shape. Looks to be bleeding from a chest wound.

A gunshot? Maddy was already running and with her long legs and marathon experience she could sprint.

I don't know. Stefan could see through her eyes in a limited way as she raced through the halls.

What do you know? she asked sharply, heading for the stairwell and taking the stairs two at a time.

Even in heels. A part of his mind watched her all out sprint in amazement. How the hell could she do that?

Forget my running style. Talk to me Stefan, she ordered. *Can you see who is doing the intake?*

Sabrina someone.

Good, she knows me. Tell her I'm on the way.

Ah, yeah, her mind is a closed book, how the hell can I tell her anything. And how is it that she's the one doing the intake? Her mind is closed because she is another unaware psychic. Closing off is her way of handling the appeals from all those on the other levels. She couldn't handle listening to their cries for help. But she instinctively knows who can be helped and who can help.

And if she doesn't call you…

Then she might not think I'm the person for the job, but don't forget I'm not here much. I come in on special cases only.

I think this is a special case, Stefan said dryly.

But the world doesn't operate that way, Maddy said, bursting through the double doors on the main floor. *You know that. If we owned the universe then we could make things line up and happen the way they were meant to organically. In the meantime…*

"Oh, Dr. Maddy, there you are. I was just about to call you. We just had an unusual case come in. A police captain is very emphatic that the woman get the best care."

Stefan watched Dr. Maddy stride across to where the captain hovered over Tia's blood soaked body.

Jesus, Stefan.

I know. I can't see much because she seemed to have let everyone in at the same time she spread herself out. I'm blinded by the barrage of energy.

Dr. Maddy did a quick check then stood up and stared at the prone woman.

Stefan?

The captain stood at Dr. Maddy's side. Stefan was trying to keep track of too much. His own energy was splintering off.

What, Maddy.

This isn't blood.

What?

She's dying, but this isn't her blood. She's not the one in-jured. In fact, she's fine. But she's connected to someone else dying.

Shit.

Stefan slammed into his body and was up and running out the car door in seconds. He'd planned on going home but had been in need of a quick nap first so was still in the parking lot.

Damn good thing.

He ran into the main working area. Such was the nature of the craziness that no one noticed.

"Where's Dean," he shouted.

No one stopped. No one even looked at him.

He whistled, long and sharp.

Silence as dozens of eyes turned his way.

"Where's Dean?" he yelled for a second time. "He's hurt."

Several men turned to look at him, puzzlement on their faces. "How do you know if you don't even know where he is?"

A man down at the far end got up off his chair and yelled, "He's in the conference room."

Stefan was halfway there before the man had a chance to finish talking.

He shoved the door open.

The room was empty.

Shit.

"Where is he?" He ran around the side of the huge table.

There he was.

"He's here. Call an ambulance."

Although given the quantity of blood pooling under his body, it might already be too late.

CHAPTER 41

TIA SWAM IN the sea of loveliness. It was beautiful here. Peaceful.

She heard yells and shouts out and about, but they weren't talking to her. They weren't talking about her. And if they were, she didn't care. Life was good.

She rolled over, loving the multiple turns she did with little effort.

Tia!

Nope, not answering.

Tia, damn it. Listen to me.

No. She smiled and rolled over again. They didn't really need to talk to her.

Damn it, wake up Tia. You need to wake up. Someone else is dying. Someone else needs your help.

It's Dean, Dr. Maddy said.

Dean? She opened her eyes. *What about Dean?* Then the pain hit her. She screamed and arched her back, her hands clutching her chest.

Yeah, now you're here.

What happened? Tia sobbed. *My chest, oh my God, my chest.* Then she knew. *I've been shot!*

No, a woman's voice said urgently. *It's Dean who's been shot. He needs your help now.*

Dean, Tia whimpered through the ripping sensation in

her body. "Dean's hurt? Then help him," she cried out. "Dean needs help. Save him, he's dying."

How she knew that she didn't know, but she did. Tears rolled down her cheeks as she tossed and turned on the hard bed.

"Strap her down," someone said beside her.

"No!" Tia screamed. "No straps."

"Then stop fighting the pain. Or you'll fall. Lie still or we'll have to strap you down to stop you from hurting yourself."

"I'll stop," she whispered. "I'll stop but you have to help Dean."

Stefan's voice jolted through her consciousness. *Tia, you have to help him. Travel back to him. He's been helping you this whole time, but now he needs you.*

I can't, she cried out. *I can't find him.*

She searched through the pink and blue clouds that dotted her mind. Colors she'd loved a few moments ago and now they seemed to suffocate her, filling her mind with everything but Dean.

Think about him. Concentrate on him. Tell him to fight to stay alive.

Oh Jesus. Tears pouring down her cheeks, she closed her eyes and called out to the man who'd touched her like none other.

Dean, dear God, hold on. I'm coming. As soon as she thought of him, his face, vague and opaque showed clearly in her mind. But there was a distant quality to it at the same time. She shuddered and all the love she'd never had a chance to give poured from her heart. She loved this man. She finally knew she loved someone – after a barren lifetime of being unloved, she was now loved and cosseted herself.

And the man in her heart was dying. No. She wouldn't let him. She raced to his side, desperate to save him. But she was no healer. There he was in front of her, on the floor in the same conference room she'd been in earlier.

She couldn't help him. She could only beg him to fight. To stay alive until someone else was there to help him. *Dean, stay with me, please.*

He was there, in front of her. She cried out in joy. *I'm here, Dean. I'm here.*

And something slammed into her.

Stopping her progress.

"Hello, Tia."

Still shuddering from the quick shift and needing to find a way to get to Dean, she struggled to see who and what was in front of her.

John. But a different looking John than the young man who'd befriended her. Gave her the first kiss. Her bracelet — that she'd lost. Now he looked…old. Angry. Evil.

"No," she cried. "It can't be you."

"Why is that?" he asked, a maniacal look on his face. "Because I left and you never saw me again? Because what we had together was special," he mocked, making her wince. "I was Dr. Wilhelm's special student. My abilities used to make him rub his hands together in glee. I cooperated. I befriended you to try and help him. Gave you the bracelet that was supposed to affect your energy so he could do more. It's how I found you when you returned to town. I have an affinity for metals. And I've always kept an eye out for you — knowing you'd have to come back sometime.

"But you wouldn't cooperate. I even kissed you. Not bad for a green kid back then. I do prefer Billy though. A woman in a child's body. Perfect."

He laughed. That sound had drifted through her nightmares, waking her, screaming in the night, terrorizing her with threats of what he'd do to her next.

"He played all of us against each other. But you didn't know. Unlike the rest of us. We knew about you. We saw more of each other. Could share our stories. Not you. You were always isolated. You had *special* abilities." He snorted. "I'm stronger than you ever were. But I see you've finally come into your abilities. About time!" Another laugh. "I'm proud of you though. You look great – even without your body. Then I *knew* you could do this. Unlike you. You had so little faith in yourself. And in me." He laughed. "How do you think I could do this if I didn't have powerful abilities of my own? How could I take my research to the next level without my own psychic shells? I even managed to do something crazy Wilhelm could never do – got you to show your true self."

"So why did you attack Dean? He's done nothing to you," she cried.

"Ah, but he did what I needed done. He brought you to this point. I'd been trying to get you to show yourself since forever. Besides, he has his own ability to stabilize your energy. Oh yes, I heard all about it," he said in a conversational tone. "My position as the departmental shrink gave me excellent access to all kinds of cases. I could get my hands on records and emails, making it easy to send the photo. I'd hoped that would push you a little further over the edge."

She sobbed. "I don't care about me. I need to save Dean."

"Like you saved him weeks ago? It's a good thing you wore your bracelet that night. It allowed me to pull on you more than ever. I use dark energy you know," he said in a conversational tone. "Ancient energy." Then his tone changed. "But someone helped you escape. Someone powerful."

"Stefan," she whispered. "But Dean shouldn't suffer for that. I need to save him!"

"And that's only going to happen if you agree to come back to me. To do the testing I need you to do. But you have to agree to be there all the way, or else he'll die."

The thought made her sick, but there was no doubt in her mind what she had to do. "Yes," she said softly. "I will, but you have to let me help Dean."

He waved something in his hand, she couldn't see it, she didn't even know if he was there in physical levels or if he was there in spirit only.

She hoped he was in physical form, and she hoped there was someone there to shoot him dead.

Like now.

As if her thoughts created her reality, several harsh spits filled the air and Dr. John Loring did a mid-air dance, his energy flaring and sparking in multiple dimensions all at once.

She gasped in shock, then watched his body do a slow slide to the floor.

Dean, dear God she had to get to Dean. Dean, who was sitting up in his body, his physical body still on the floor.

He looked puzzled, then surprised, before sorrow washed over him.

No, she screamed and slammed into him, trying to send him to the floor again and inside his body. *Stay, please stay, I love you.*

Tia? Are you all right? You were dying, he cried out. *Are we both dead?*

No, but you are dying, unless you fight back. I'm fine, she sobbed. *Honestly I'm fine, but it's you who is in trouble.*

He gave her the sweetest smile and said, *As long as you are okay, I'm fine.*

And his eyes rolled up into his head and fell backwards.

She dove after him.

DEAN, CAN YOU hear me.

I hear you.

Good. It's time to wake up.

No. I'm tired, he muttered. *Go away.*

No, I won't go away. I don't think I can anymore. I'm here. A part of you. Forever. Tia's voice was a laugh.

He smiled. *If you're laughing, it's all good.* He nestled closer. *Then I don't need to wake up. Horrible nightmares,* he muttered. *This is much nicer.*

Slowly, as if not convinced, he opened his eyes to see her bending over him. He grinned and wrapped her in his arms and cuddled her close, closing his eyes and resting his chin on the top of her head.

Gentle laughter rippled around him. *This is lovely, but we can come back here anytime. You need to open your real eyes.*

What? He leaned back and looked down at her. *What did you say?*

Look around you.

Opening his eyes, he turned to see the world at large. And found himself in a hospital room, in a hospital bed with Tia sitting at his side.

He frowned and slammed his eyes closed to see Tia cuddling in his arms.

Uhm…what the hell just happened?

That's your inside vision and outside vision. Inside you are here with me – anytime and anyplace. Outside vision is the real world as you used to know it. Now you have a new dimension in which to operate.

Jesus.

Yeah, I've been dealing with it a little longer than you. Stefan has been trying to explain it since I found myself wearing your bullet holes to the extent that I was the one rushed to the hospital while you lay bleeding in the conference room.

And who shot me? he asked, his mind blurry on so many details.

The psychologist, Dr. Loring. Who was also John, one of the men who was in the institution with me. He had his own abilities. She sighed. *I never actually saw your shrink or I might have recognized him.*

How did he get to be a cop shrink?

Not an issue. He was already a grad student and had a clean record. He moved through the system and was actually a visiting psychologist if you remember and one you were supposed to go see to help you with your problems. She smiled. *It was his cover to find new patients. Not just police officers but cases. He had access to disturbed kids. And once you entered the picture he really wanted you.*

His mind raced over all the details still missing.

And one was big – potentially huge.

And Simone, he asked gently.

Tia smiled. *She was at the lab. He'd taken her prisoner, thinking she might be able to tell him something about me. And if not, then as a hostage to control me. Yes, he killed Brennan who'd tried to save Simone. But she's fine. Or,* Tia corrected… *She will be… Now that she's safe."*

Jesus. It was too much to take in.

And you don't need to take it all in now. A lot of people are waiting to know you're going to be okay though, as a lot of people had a hand in saving you. So do all of us a favor and come back.

Holding her hand tight in his, he opened his eyes to the room. This time, he saw Tia smiling reassuringly down at him, several doctors and a couple of nurses. And in the back was his big bluff captain, frowning.

"Hey," Dean said, in a faint voice. "I'm here."

The room erupted in cheers.

Tia's the loudest of them all.

Simon Says... Hide: Kate Morgan (Book #1)

Welcome to a new thriller series from *USA Today* Best-Selling Author Dale Mayer. Set in Vancouver, BC, the team of Detective Kate Morgan and Simon St. Laurant, an unwilling psychic, marries all the elements of Dale's work that you've come to love, plus so much more.

Detective Kate Morgan, newly promoted to the Vancouver PD Homicide Department, stands for the victims in her world. She was once a victim herself, just as her mother had been a victim, and then her brother—an unsolved missing child's case—was yet another victim. She can't stand those who take advantage of others, and the worst ones are those who prey on the hopes of desperate people to line their own pockets.

So, when she finds a connection between more than a half-dozen cold cases to a current case, where a child's life hangs in the balance, Kate would make a deal with the devil himself to find the culprit and to save the child.

Simon St. Laurant's grandmother had the Sight and had warned him that, once he used it, he could never walk away. Until now, her caution had made it easy to avoid that first step. But, when nightmares of his own past are triggered, Simon can't stand back and watch child after child be abused. Not without offering his help to those chasing the monsters.

Even if it means dealing with the cranky and critical Detective Kate Morgan …

Find Simon Says… Hide here!
To find out more visit Dale Mayer's website.
https://geni.us/DMSSHideUniversal

Author's Note

Thank you for reading Now You See Her...! If you enjoyed the book, please take a moment and leave a short review.

Dear reader,

I love to hear from readers, and you can contact me at my website: www.dalemayer.com or at my Facebook author page. To be informed of new releases and special offers, sign up for my newsletter or follow me on BookBub. And if you are interested in joining Dale Mayer's Reader Group, here is the Facebook sign up page.
http://geni.us/DaleMayerFBGroup

Cheers,
Dale Mayer

Shattered

Book 9 of Psychic Visions Series

T HE BLOOD …

It wouldn't slow.

It wouldn't stop.

It dripped down her arm, her hands. Droplets falling from her fingertips.

Only she felt no pain …

Except when she moved.

Hannah managed to take one step, then another. Her weight came down hard, her legs wooden. Her ankles stiff, unbending lumber blocks.

The motion jarring.

More blood flowed.

It dripped in a slow and steady stream onto the gravel beneath her feet. She was taking a big risk of being hit by a car, stumbling unseen in the dark on this narrow road, with no real shoulders, but she felt it was the only way.

Hannah watched the drips in macabre fascination. Where was it coming from?

Her head pounded. Her body throbbed. And her legs? Well, they'd been screaming for miles.

She had no idea where she was, how she got here, or why she would be walking along this lonely stretch of highway. Yet she knew she had to continue. It was important. She just didn't know why. And, of course, it was dark—black. The moon argued with the clouds above, giving her brief moments of luminescence. A heavy dampness clung to her nose.

A couple vehicles had passed her. But no one had stopped to help.

Why?

Surely she was visible? She carefully took another step and then one more. Someone would help her eventually. Right? She had to keep moving forward. She knew there was no going back. There was no other choice.

Keep walking. You're almost there, a soft male voice inside her head directed her.

"Where am I going?" She sobbed to the empty night.

Somewhere safe. I can help you.

Who spoke to her?

What if it was *him*? The man she'd been running from. At least she thought it had been a man. Or what if another person found her and didn't help her? She could become a victim again.

Those horrible images. Fights. Fire. Screams. All intermixed with sex scenes. Like that made any sense.

She gave a short, harsh laugh. She had no idea whether she'd been a victim or a victimizer. But it felt like she'd been beaten to shit and left to die. Her body injured. Her mind vulnerable. Weak. She frowned, trying to figure out the disjointed thoughts in her head. Her memories were fragmented, refusing to flow as they should. Was she okay? Had she been in an accident? Attacked?

Nothing felt normal or right. Nothing felt familiar, as if she was in someone else's nightmare.

A strange set of thoughts ran through her mind, telling her she was supposed to do something. Were they her thoughts? How could they be?

Two separate people were arguing inside her head. Someone pushing her to do something. Someone calling her away. Someone who could foretell the future?

Or was Hannah just arguing with herself, considering all angles, no matter how weird?

And then she was trying to stop other thoughts. *He* wanted to remove her. *He* wanted to hurt someone she loved. *He*'d tried to hurt him earlier today.

No, someone else had tried.

And failed, she thought.

But everything was mixed up. The thoughts were coated in fear and spiked with anger. And the words? Foreign, as if they weren't hers. Flashes of a young girl. Then an older one. A knife. Screams. All disjointed. Nothing made any sense. Confused and worried, she turned to stare at the trail of blood behind her, as she walked forward.

Of course she wasn't okay. She hadn't been okay for a long time.

More disconnected memories came to her mind. More foggy thoughts. Why hadn't she been okay for a long time?

Doctors flitted into her mind—in, then out again. Different men. Women. Names and titles all whispered through her mind and back again. She had no idea what or who they were. … Even worse, she had no idea why they were walking in an endless stream through her bedroom. She tried to focus, to force the tidbits into a coherent pattern, and pain slammed into her brain, bringing her to a shuddering stop. She bent over, gasping.

The pain, extreme, … yet familiar.

That worried her. No one should have to experience pain for so long that it became familiar. Was that why the stream of doctors? Had she been in several accidents? Was she suicidal? Born with a physical ailment that needed multiple surgeries?

A vehicle approached, the headlight beams flashing on her sleeve, before zipping past.

A sob escaped, as the red tail lights disappeared into the distance. They hadn't even slowed down. Still, the headlights had shown her something.

A driveway, … just ahead. The one she'd been looking for. At least part of her thought so …

She hobbled forward, desperate for someone to be home, and yet she was terrified at the same time.

What if the wrong man lived here?

And every man could be the wrong man. She couldn't remember who she was running from … or to.

A face zipped through her mind, only to fade too quickly for her to understand who or what that meant.

She kept walking.

Feeling the first few drops of rain, she wanted to cry.

When the thunder rumbled in the distance, the tears rolled down her cheeks in earnest. Could this night get any worse?

Every step to that driveway was one step closer to her goal. She felt a sense of inevitability to it.

She couldn't take her eyes off the reflector on a post

marking the start of the driveway. This was the right place.

That phrase stopped her. Right place?

Had she been looking for it?

Or now that she was injured—possibly dying—was she expecting a specific someone to help her?

Surely not. She studied her surroundings, trying to peer through the sheets of rain now beating down on her head. Nothing looked familiar.

She felt so terribly alone at that moment.

Why was she heading to the driveway? For help of course, right?

No, not right, but she didn't understand the mixed messages. Everything was jumbled in her head.

She had to keep in mind that she'd been hurt and couldn't decipher her thoughts or count on the assumptions she was making.

Yet something about this place seemed to call her. At the driveway, she slowly walked up the dirt road. It wasn't even paved. Why?

Was she so far out in the country? She couldn't see other lights to confirm dwellings were close by. Then again, she couldn't see lights on the dark shadow she'd taken to be a building.

Shit.

Her mind revolted, but her feet kept moving, the incline long and slow. Eventually she reached the large trees that surrounded the house.

It was a house. That alone made her feel better. Or maybe just her feet, as they came to a stop.

She swayed in place. The rain had eased. The moon peeked through the prison of clouds to stare out at the world below.

She realized she had to be more injured than she thought, now witnessing the increasing blood flow from wounds on her body.

She focused on her surroundings, her breathing. Nothing was normal about this place. The plants were huge, the leaves oversize. A wind … or something … whispered between the plants, but, at the same time, she sensed someone waiting, … as if she'd been expected.

But that was beyond foolish.

Right?

She shuddered.

And slowly, as if compelled, she turned to face the front door. The intricate faces carved in the wood.

She shouldn't be here. She should be running as far and as fast in the opposite direction as she could go.

Instead, her feet stepped closer to that door.

She took a deep breath, her struggle to stay upright waning. She wouldn't make it back down this driveway. She might not even make it to the entrance. But she managed one more step.

A light flashed on overhead, covering her in a soft white, as she stood in the center of the glow.

She closed her eyes.

And waited for whatever fate was about to hit her with.

NO. NOT THERE. Don't go there. You don't understand. That's not what I wanted. Not what I intended.

Why did you go there?

You were supposed to keep driving.

Away to safety.

This man will hurt you.

You must hurt him before then.
Attack, then run away.
All men are killers.
All men are bad.
All men will hurt you.
Run, child, run.

Oh, it's his *house. Wow. Okay, that was smart. I already tried to kill this one once. Maybe you can succeed, where I failed.*

AS DAYS WENT, this had been one of the worst—and wasn't over yet. Stefan had been working with several patients at the hospital. All newly admitted, desperately in need of help. *His* kind of help. And Trevor's help. Then Dr. Trevor Johnson had been the one who'd called Stefan in.

One of the patients—a subdued slight man—had attacked without warning and had caught both Stefan and Trevor off guard. The patient hadn't shown any violent behavior up until then. Possibly a multiple personality disorder. Yet it had erupted from one second to the next and had sideswiped both men. Stefan knew to back off and to rebalance before attempting more work, but the trigger had startled other patients, and it took everything Stefan had to control the situation.

Plus, he and Trevor had had to go to the children's ward to see several patients. He'd gotten his center of balance back before arriving there. The energy of that ward demanded that Stefan be in the right place mentally, before he could enter.

He'd found one little girl more distant, colder than ever. So sad. They'd been making such great progress with Anita.

Something was wrong inside. He was sure it was a possession issue. Maddy had been making progress—but not enough—and the child was fading before their eyes. Yet Anita had had a violent outburst today as well. Completely out of the blue, she'd lashed out at Stefan with her plastic knife and fork. It had been a mere scratch, but still … Depressed at the continuous lack of progress and afraid they were in danger of losing Anita, Stefan had come home in a rare mood.

Not wanting to taint Celina with his negativity and frustration, he'd gone directly to his art studio. But his beloved Celina always understood his moods and needs and brought her harp to play quietly beside him.

Hours later, his tensions and frustrations eased as he worked. He studied the painting in front of him and shook his head. "This one is garbage."

Celina gently reached out to him. "If it eased your demons, it's never a waste."

He laughed. "True enough." He threw down the paintbrush, wondering what insight this mess was to give him with the requisite multiple headaches. He saw some headscarved old woman but, over that, were slashes of red and black. He narrowed his gaze, his mind twisting and turning on the possibilities. Mayb—

A cry for help reached him on the ethers. The same person who'd called the last time. He'd been sending responses but hadn't received an answer yet.

An insight, one sitting outside the reach of his consciousness, finally broke into his brain, just as someone pounded on Stefan's front door. Someone believing he was hurting her? … Who was it?

Abruptly he was dragged from one reality to another.

And this one was so much worse.

HANNAH STOOD AT the front door of the stranger's house. Some*thing* pushed her to stay. Some*one* else told her to run. She wavered on her feet. Then the door opened.

Slowly, carefully.

"Hannah?"

If he knew her name, she knew her worst fears had come true. She feared to look at him. She closed her eyes. Her feet, the betrayers, hadn't understood and had led her to the worst place possible.

She opened her eyes and stared at the beautiful man in front of her.

"No," she whispered. "It's not possible."

"What's not possible?" asked the man standing in front of her, his voice so soft and caring that she wanted to cry. "What's wrong?"

She shook her head, as he gently grabbed her arm and tugged her closer.

"You're dead," she stated, her voice choking up. "I know you are. You have to be," she cried out, as the last of her strength drained from her toes. It was over. Whatever fight she'd been involved in, whatever struggle she'd been working toward? She'd lost. She didn't even know why.

"Why do I have to be dead?" he asked, leading her through the front door and beyond.

She stared at him, trying to sort through the muddle in her head, but couldn't. Only one thing was clear. "You have to be because I stabbed you."

And she collapsed into his arms.

The man she knew deep inside—with as much certainty as she had ever felt in her life—she'd tried to kill once already. A man she would try to kill again, if she had the chance.

But she didn't. And wouldn't. She couldn't.

He'd won after all.

Book 9 is available now!

https://geni.us/dmshattered

About the Author

Dale Mayer is a *USA Today* best-selling author, best known for her SEALs military romances, her Psychic Visions series, and her Lovely Lethal Garden cozy series. Her contemporary romances are raw and full of passion and emotion (Broken But … Mending, Hathaway House series). Her thrillers will keep you guessing (Kate Morgan, By Death series), and her romantic comedies will keep you giggling (*It's a Dog's Life*, a stand-alone novella; and the Broken Protocols series, starring Charming Marvin, the cat).

Dale honors the stories that come to her—and some of them are crazy, break all the rules and cross multiple genres!

To go with her fiction, she also writes nonfiction in many different fields, with books available on résumé writing, companion gardening, and the US mortgage system. All her books are available in print and ebook format.

Connect with Dale Mayer Online

Dale's Website – www.dalemayer.com
Twitter – @DaleMayer
Facebook Page – geni.us/DaleMayerFBFanPage
Facebook Group – geni.us/DaleMayerFBGroup
BookBub – geni.us/DaleMayerBookbub
Instagram – geni.us/DaleMayerInstagram
Goodreads – geni.us/DaleMayerGoodreads
Newsletter – geni.us/DaleNews

Also by Dale Mayer

Published Adult Books:

Shadow Recon
Magnus, Book 1
Rogan, Book 2
Egan, Book 3
Barret, Book 4

Bullard's Battle
Ryland's Reach, Book 1
Cain's Cross, Book 2
Eton's Escape, Book 3
Garret's Gambit, Book 4
Kano's Keep, Book 5
Fallon's Flaw, Book 6
Quinn's Quest, Book 7
Bullard's Beauty, Book 8
Bullard's Best, Book 9
Bullard's Battle, Books 1–2
Bullard's Battle, Books 3–4
Bullard's Battle, Books 5–6
Bullard's Battle, Books 7–8

Terkel's Team

Damon's Deal, Book 1

Wade's War, Book 2

Gage's Goal, Book 3

Calum's Contact, Book 4

Rick's Road, Book 5

Scott's Summit, Book 6

Brody's Beast, Book 7

Terkel's Twist, Book 8

Terkel's Triumph, Book 9

Terk's Guardians

Radar, Book 1

Kate Morgan

Simon Says… Hide, Book 1

Simon Says… Jump, Book 2

Simon Says… Ride, Book 3

Simon Says… Scream, Book 4

Simon Says… Run, Book 5

Simon Says… Walk, Book 6

Simon Says… Forgive, Book 7

Hathaway House

Aaron, Book 1

Brock, Book 2

Cole, Book 3

Denton, Book 4

Elliot, Book 5

The K9 Files

Rowan, Book 10

Caleb, Book 11

Kurt, Book 12

Tucker, Book 13

Harley, Book 14

Kyron, Book 15

Jenner, Book 16

Rhys, Book 17

Landon, Book 18

Harper, Book 19

Kascius, Book 20

Declan, Book 21

The K9 Files, Books 1–2

The K9 Files, Books 3–4

The K9 Files, Books 5–6

The K9 Files, Books 7–8

The K9 Files, Books 9–10

The K9 Files, Books 11–12

Lovely Lethal Gardens

Arsenic in the Azaleas, Book 1

Bones in the Begonias, Book 2

Corpse in the Carnations, Book 3

Daggers in the Dahlias, Book 4

Evidence in the Echinacea, Book 5

Footprints in the Ferns, Book 6

Gun in the Gardenias, Book 7

Handcuffs in the Heather, Book 8

Ice Pick in the Ivy, Book 9

Jewels in the Juniper, Book 10

Killer in the Kiwis, Book 11

Lifeless in the Lilies, Book 12

Murder in the Marigolds, Book 13

Nabbed in the Nasturtiums, Book 14

Offed in the Orchids, Book 15

Poison in the Pansies, Book 16

Quarry in the Quince, Book 17

Revenge in the Roses, Book 18

Silenced in the Sunflowers, Book 19

Toes up in the Tulips, Book 20

Uzi in the Urn, Book 21

Victim in the Violets, Book 22

Lovely Lethal Gardens, Books 1–2

Lovely Lethal Gardens, Books 3–4

Lovely Lethal Gardens, Books 5–6

Lovely Lethal Gardens, Books 7–8

Lovely Lethal Gardens, Books 9–10

Psychic Visions Series

Tuesday's Child

Hide 'n Go Seek

Maddy's Floor

Garden of Sorrow

Knock Knock…

Rare Find

Eyes to the Soul

Now You See Her

Shattered

Into the Abyss

Seeds of Malice

Eye of the Falcon

Itsy-Bitsy Spider

Unmasked

Deep Beneath

From the Ashes

Stroke of Death

Ice Maiden

Snap, Crackle…

What If…

Talking Bones

String of Tears

Inked Forever

Insanity

Psychic Visions Books 1–3

Psychic Visions Books 4–6

Psychic Visions Books 7–9

By Death Series

Touched by Death

Haunted by Death

Chilled by Death

By Death Books 1–3

Broken Protocols – Romantic Comedy Series

Cat's Meow

Cat's Pajamas

Cat's Cradle

Cat's Claus

Broken Protocols 1-4

Broken and... Mending

Skin

Scars

Scales (of Justice)

Broken but... Mending 1-3

Glory

Genesis

Tori

Celeste

Glory Trilogy

Biker Blues

Morgan: Biker Blues, Volume 1

Cash: Biker Blues, Volume 2

SEALs of Honor

Mason: SEALs of Honor, Book 1

Hawk: SEALs of Honor, Book 2

Dane: SEALs of Honor, Book 3

Swede: SEALs of Honor, Book 4

Shadow: SEALs of Honor, Book 5

Cooper: SEALs of Honor, Book 6

Markus: SEALs of Honor, Book 7

Evan: SEALs of Honor, Book 8

Mason's Wish: SEALs of Honor, Book 9

Chase: SEALs of Honor, Book 10

Heroes for Hire

Levi's Legend: Heroes for Hire, Book 1

Stone's Surrender: Heroes for Hire, Book 2

Merk's Mistake: Heroes for Hire, Book 3

Rhodes's Reward: Heroes for Hire, Book 4

Flynn's Firecracker: Heroes for Hire, Book 5

Logan's Light: Heroes for Hire, Book 6

Harrison's Heart: Heroes for Hire, Book 7

Saul's Sweetheart: Heroes for Hire, Book 8

Dakota's Delight: Heroes for Hire, Book 9

Tyson's Treasure: Heroes for Hire, Book 10

Jace's Jewel: Heroes for Hire, Book 11

Rory's Rose: Heroes for Hire, Book 12

Brandon's Bliss: Heroes for Hire, Book 13

Liam's Lily: Heroes for Hire, Book 14

North's Nikki: Heroes for Hire, Book 15

Anders's Angel: Heroes for Hire, Book 16

Reyes's Raina: Heroes for Hire, Book 17

Dezi's Diamond: Heroes for Hire, Book 18

Vince's Vixen: Heroes for Hire, Book 19

Ice's Icing: Heroes for Hire, Book 20

Johan's Joy: Heroes for Hire, Book 21

Galen's Gemma: Heroes for Hire, Book 22

Zack's Zest: Heroes for Hire, Book 23

Bonaparte's Belle: Heroes for Hire, Book 24

Noah's Nemesis: Heroes for Hire, Book 25

Tomas's Trials: Heroes for Hire, Book 26

Carson's Choice: Heroes for Hire, Book 27

Asher, Book 5

Ryker, Book 6

Miles, Book 7

Nico, Book 8

Keane, Book 9

Lennox, Book 10

Gavin, Book 11

Shane, Book 12

Diesel, Book 13

Jerricho, Book 14

Killian, Book 15

Hatch, Book 16

Corbin, Book 17

Aiden, Book 18

The Mavericks, Books 1–2

The Mavericks, Books 3–4

The Mavericks, Books 5–6

The Mavericks, Books 7–8

The Mavericks, Books 9–10

The Mavericks, Books 11–12

Standalone Novellas

It's a Dog's Life

Riana's Revenge

Second Chances

Published Young Adult Books:

Family Blood Ties Series

Vampire in Denial

Vampire in Distress

Vampire in Design

Vampire in Deceit

Vampire in Defiance

Vampire in Conflict

Vampire in Chaos

Vampire in Crisis

Vampire in Control

Vampire in Charge

Family Blood Ties Set 1–3

Family Blood Ties Set 1–5

Family Blood Ties Set 4–6

Family Blood Ties Set 7–9

Sian's Solution, A Family Blood Ties Series Prequel Novelette

Design series

Dangerous Designs

Deadly Designs

Darkest Designs

Design Series Trilogy

Standalone

In Cassie's Corner

Gem Stone (a Gemma Stone Mystery)

Published Non-Fiction Books:

Career Essentials

Career Essentials: The Résumé

Career Essentials: The Cover Letter

Career Essentials: The Interview

Career Essentials: 3 in 1

www.ingramcontent.com/pod-product-compliance
Lightning Source LLC
Chambersburg PA
CBHW072009190726
48293CB00001B/209